Sand Devil

Michael Bornstein

Sand Devil

The Toby Press, *London & Connecticut*

First published in 2001 by
The Toby Press *Ltd, London*
www.tobypress.com

The right of Michael Bornstein to be identified as the author of this work has been
asserted by him in accordance with the Copyright, Designs & Patents Act 1988

ISBN 1 902881 37 0
A CIP catalogue record for this title is available from the British Library

Designed by Fresh Produce, London

Typeset in Garamond by
Rowland Phototypesetting Ltd., Bury St Edmunds

Printed and bound in Great Britain by
St Edmundsbury Press Ltd., Bury St Edmunds

for Sally

The Negev desert, occupying the southern half of the country, is an arid, windswept region sparsely populated by Bedouin tribes and cities settled by recent immigrants to the country. Though there are a few sites of historical and environmental interest, the visitor is advised to travel lightly, with plenty of water, due to the harsh conditions.

Hart and Pilgrim's Guide to the Holy Land

Behold, a great wind will arise from the wilderness and sweep toward the daughter of my people. A wind not to reap or to winnow, but a wind stronger than my enemies. And I will judge them.

Jeremiah, 4:11

Contents

Sand Devil

*B*ehold, a whirlwind arises from the wilderness!

My father reads aloud from the Bible. Every night after sundown for many hours, long after the moon is high and the children have fallen asleep.

A hot wind of the high hills, comes not to fan nor to clean. A wind too strong for this shall come to Me.

He holds the book up to the kerosene lamp, to the yellow light swaying. Shadows like spirits dance across the canvas, through his reddish mane, in his eyes, flaming blue.

His chariots are like the whirlwind, his horses are swifter than eagles.

My mother watches him without blinking. One of the children is sleeping on her arm, another on her lap. Both snore. My father pauses to scowl. Nothing interrupts the voice of the Lord. Hurriedly, she shakes them awake and sets them in their chairs. The Bible again finds its light; my father roars:

The land shall be left desolate, and the people banished. A lion watcheth over them; any which wander out shall be devoured.

He roars but I do not listen. My ears are outside the tent. In the night with its bleating sheep and the wind growling in caves. My eyes follow through the canvas flaps, past the pens and porcelain tub overflowing with moonlight. From here I can see across the valley with its dunes and wadis, all the way to the Firing Zone. An empty place dotted with craters, where the Israeli army practices its wars. The Firing Zone is tonight alive with artillery—cluster bombs and phosphorus. I know each shell by its fire, Iblis taught me. He teaches me many things, mad, stinking Iblis, things not found in the Bible. My father hates him and beats me whenever I go. But still I go—I want to now. To help Iblis collect the metal and to hear his tales of lions.

Thus sayeth the Lord of hosts: the land is perished and laid waste like a wilderness. None shall pass through it alive.

The chair leaps from under me and my skull fills with pain. The tent grows dark as his head hides the lamp. My father stands above me with his giant fist, ready to strike again. But I am too quick. On hands and knees I scramble between the cots and awaken my brothers. They cry, snatched from their sleep, and my mother tries to hush them. I crawl behind her but she does not move, not for me but not for him either and a path to the night is open.

I dash out as his knuckles slam the air behind me. "The Lord is near to all who listen"—his voice chases me through the flaps—"To all who hear Him in truth!"

I run to the last of my breath, until his voice is swallowed by wind. The glow of the lantern fades before the lights of the Firing Zone. Dazzling bursts, silent as stars, their sound borne off by the coming winter. Already the air is chilled; I shiver in my jacket. But it is warmer out here, wrapped in darkness, than in the fire of my father's eyes.

I move to the edge of the ridge, beyond the camp that the government has given us. The sheep belong to them, too, to men who live far away up north. In their dark suits and glasses, they are evil men, my father says, damned to Hell. May the Lord forgive their trespasses.

Ewes and lambs whimper in their pens—I can hear them, and see the flock like foam in the valley below, huddling. The air is sharp with dung and with another smell, very sweet. It is the smell of fear. Maybe it's the bombs flashing in the distance or the howl of the wind in caves; sheep are so easily frightened. Or maybe they are afraid of me.

I bend to pick up a stone and feel the pain in my skull. A frightful drum, by morning it'll be throbbing. But the beating's lighter than many I have received, less painful. He's getting slow, my father, and I am getting fast. Faster with each season, spinning out of his reach. And my mother looks on with her empty face—happy or sad, I cannot tell. Only Iblis knows the answer. Limping around in his rags, along with Has-No-Name his three-legged dog, watching the world through a glass eye stolen, he says, from an Austrian duchess. Iblis knows and tomorrow I'll find him. Out there, in the smoking craters of the Firing Zone.

I wander for hours outside the camp. Long after the lamp dies out and the Bible is laid to rest. My mother's sigh, the cries of my brothers are mixed with the whimper of sheep and the only snores are my father's. I am no longer cold. Nursed by night, embraced by wind—these are my real parents. Now, toward dawn, I can feel them stirring. Around and inside me as I turn. Around and around on the ridge above the valley, hissing and kicking up dust. Until the sun, like a mangy stray, sticks it's horns over the horizon. And turning, taking aim, I pelt it with my stone.

6   Often to pass the time I throw stones at the sheep that have strayed from the herd. They crack sharply, the stones, smacking on hide or bone. Smooth and flat, like the stone David used to kill Goliath. Then, with the giant's own sword, he cut off Goliath's head. I am very good with stones. I can sit all day, throwing, and never once have had to chase a stray. Iblis says that many years ago, before time, the giants used these stones. Cupped them in hands like leather pouches and whipped them with the sling of their arms. They threw and hit, and then, on hands and knees, like lions they ate their kill. To eat like that is to live forever, Iblis says.

The days pass slowly, similar as sheep. Mornings, I feed the lambs in their pens and after lunch drive the flock to pasture. There I stay until dusk with stones in my hand to keep the rams from straying. Then, with howls and roars, I drive them home. The sheep slip through the chute like grains of sand, marking time. Dinner is hard bread and soup and on holidays a slice of mutton. Always we eat in silence, except for Grace. And after dark, the Bible. By the lantern my father reads far into the night. Prophets, Psalms, Deuteronomy—the King James version, for he cannot read Hebrew. Nor can I, but I can speak it. I learned it from the government people, just as Iblis taught me his tongue. I practice it, silently, while my father recites, his voice trembling with terror.

Each day, each week, has its rituals, all according to Scripture. Saturdays, after Vespers, the cleansing. My mother bent over the porcelain tub with her sleeves rolled up, scrubbing our necks with a coarse bar of soap. She scrubs until a mane of suds hangs from her hands, and the flesh on our bones is raw. A holy act, she must not be gentle. The children try not to weep. My father watches from afar, waiting to give the signal. At a nod of his head, we are lifted onto the sand, naked and shivering but made to stand straight before him. Above us he holds a knife. Olive wood handle, its blade as sharp as the wind. Weekdays he hides it beneath the tub, and on nights such as these, takes it out and cleans it. In one big hand my father clutches the knife while the other grabs our hair. With a single stroke he crops it off, clean down to the scalp.

Sunday is the Christian Sabbath, no work do we do. Time for prayer and thanksgiving, from morning to late afternoon when one by one my brothers come forth and

7

confess their week of sins. There are holidays, too. Pentecost and Atonement and others with names I cannot remember. It is then that my father, dressed all in white, takes a ram from the flock. He drags it to the edge of the ridge and binds it to the porcelain tub which, when turned upside down, serves as our family altar. Much of his prayer is lost in the wind but I can hear the animal breathing. Bleating as the knife with the olive wood handle rises above its neck then suddenly descends. Through the fleece it cuts, through flesh which parts like water. And my brothers and I, also in white, together chant *Thy will be done. Hallelujah*, we sing, as the carcass jerks and spews its blood, sowing our sins on the desert.

Time passes quietly, secretly, like a lion at night. My brothers, born in this camp, cannot feel it, and my mother, even if she does, says nothing. Only I, with memories of another place, of steamy streets and sirens, see the seasons turn. See my body changing, every day with new hairs and strange smells; my voice is growing deeper. Soon there will come a night when I will no longer let my mother wash me. My hair shall not be cut. The valley, the caves, the smoky haze over the Firing Zone—everything stays the same, but not me. In the throb of my skull, in the smoothness of stones, I can sense the giant stirring.

A pillar of dust towers high above the valley. Slowly, lazily the tower turns, but my heart beats fast. Long before the jeep comes into view, I jump up and down on the edge of the ridge and wave at Yoni.

A big yellow jeep with a canvas cover. Rattling with hooks and cans, the engine growling. I jump and wave but a long time passes before the honking starts. Yoni is slow to notice. With his jeep, his sunglasses and pistol, Yoni is a stranger to the desert. Yet he is like the Samaritan I've heard about in Scripture, an infidel, but good. He brings us feed for the sheep and food for the table, used clothing from the world which knows not the truth. But Yoni's truth is different—of water-pumps and politics, the truths of radio and women. Like Iblis with his wisdom of spirits, Yoni in his world is just as wise. And like Iblis, Yoni is my friend.

The jeep honks as it reaches the base of the ridge. Only I no longer wave. One of our games, I pick up a stone and toss it at the hood. It smacks on the metal and glances off the glass. The honking stops. A head of long black curls pops out of the window, a head with sunglasses and a cigarette.

"You're crazy, Bubi," Yoni hollers. "There're prisons for people like you."

The canvas door swings open, Yoni climbs out. Shorts and hiking boots, with hairy legs between.

"*Mah inyanim?*" Yoni asks in Hebrew—"What's up?" Though I speak the language, I do not answer.

Yoni's eyes, charcoal black, squint through his glasses.

"I got some goodies for you this time," he says, and hops to the rear of the jeep. "Let's see, whole grain rice, flour, beans." One by one he pulls out the sacks and lays them on the ground. "Sorghum, corn meal and, for my special guy . . ." He tosses me a can.

9

Peaches in Heavy Syrup, it says. I turn the can around and around, as if it were something very old and strange. Hands on his hips, Yoni frowns. "I don't know much Bible, but I'm willing to bet there's something in there about a 'thank you.'"

This, too, is part of the game—my silence—until Yoni shakes his head and reaches into the jeep. Returns with a chocolate bar which I catch with one hand and stuff in my jacket pocket. "You're hopeless, Bubi," he laughs.

Yoni charges up the ridge. Huge strides, arms swinging; Yoni never walks. He wears a watch too big for his wrist and, in a leather holster strapped to his waist, a freshly-oiled pistol. He stands next to me, a grin dividing his face. A funny face with a long nose and a pointy chin which he tries to hide behind his stubble. His smell is funny, too. Tobacco and sweat and a perfume for shaving—sweet, like frightened sheep.

"Don't go eating that stuff all at once." He slaps the bulge in my jacket. "Rot your teeth." He leans over and peers at my mouth. "You got to brush your teeth, Bubi. *They* did, Abraham, Isaac and Jacob. Just ask your father." Into the grin Yoni sticks a cigarette.

At last I speak: "Give me one."

"You're too young to smoke."

"I'm almost fifteen. I think."

"Yeah, well think again."

I grab for the packet but he jerks it away. Jerks it away then looks over his shoulder, at the camp, making sure my father is nowhere in sight. Yoni puts a cigarette between my lips and lights it. "You'll be the ruin of me yet, Bubi," he says.

Smoking, Yoni and I sit down on the ridge. He rests on his knees and lifts his face to the last of the autumn sun. "So what's new around here?" he asks again. "No doctors or social workers? I tell you, Bubi, the government's getting bored. Once upon a time you guys were the big attraction."

He talks but I hardly listen. My mind is on the cigarette, growing shorter as it fills me up. The hot smoke whirls inside me.

"I'm supposed to bring someone around next week. Some university person. You let me know if he gets in your hair." Yoni ruffles the stubs on my scalp. The cigarette's finished, but I want more.

"Let me see your pistol."

"Not again . . ."

"I want to hold it."

Yoni gives in easily. He likes showing off his pistol. He draws it from the holster, bold-like, as if it were a sword. He removes the magazine and checks the lock before laying it on my thigh. Black and shiny, heavier than it looks, even without the bullets, it snuggles into my palm. A perfect fit, our powers mixing.

"Berretta, nine millimeter, fully automatic," I recite, just as Yoni taught me.

"And how many rounds?"

"Eight."

Yoni clicks his tongue. "Seven."

"Seven," I repeat. "And what if you miss?"

"You don't, not in my old unit. If you can't hit with seven you've got no business shooting."

My fingers crawl around the handle, they tickle the trigger's lip. It feels like another part of me growing. This way and that I turn it, exploring its touch and color. Yoni smiles. He likes to see me learn. But then we hear it. Sand scraping and the thud of feet. The smile disappears. Quickly he glances behind him. "Give me that," Yoni hisses, and snatches the gun. Loads and shoves it back into the holster just in time. Behind us, my father makes his way to the tent. He plods across the sand, shoulders back, chin up, as if he were leading a host. In the sunlight his hair looks redder, his thorny face a flame. My father, a bush that will not burn.

My father does not like strangers, even Yoni. Especially Yoni, for he knows what goes on between us. Hikers, soldiers, he chases them all away, sometimes with his knife, but with Yoni he has no choice. Without him, he knows, we'd starve. My father raises a hand, halfway. A greeting for Yoni and a warning to me. Yoni stands and salutes. "'Morning, sir," he calls out in English, "How is the work of the Lord today?" But my father just ignores him. He plods on, suddenly stooped, to the sanctuary of our tent.

"You must not tease him," I say.

"Aw, he can take it. He's a grown man."

"He doesn't like to be teased."

"Not like you, eh, Bubi."

Once again, Yoni ruffles my scalp, only this time he touches the bruise. I flinch.

"Sorry." Yoni looks worried. "Another bad night, huh."

I rub the spot with my fingers. "It's nothing. I'm getting too fast for him."

"Not fast enough. You got to watch yourself, Bubi."

"And you—who watches you?"

Yoni laughs. "Got to move, Bubi. Be back next week—what do you say to apricots? And don't you worry about that university person. I can take care of him."

What person I want to ask, but Yoni has rushed to his jeep. I plunge down the ridge after him, but the engine's already growling.

Yoni shouts: "And remember, brush those teeth. You don't want to end up like Iblis."

Yoni steps on the gas, and the jeep speeds away. Back on the ridge, I follow the pillar of dust. I watch as it shrinks and finally disappears at the end of the trail. The jeep turns onto the highway, heading north, for the world which knows not wind.

Like a hand held out for mercy, the valley stretches before me. Veined with wadis and blistered with dunes. An ancient hand, older than Adam's. Yet mercy it never receives. Soon the rains will come, and the floods, slashing ravines and skinning the dust down to bedrock. Then, fiercest of all, the winds. Gritty pillars which shred the sand and eat it raw. Sucking and spitting. Sand devils, Iblis calls them, mighty spirits of hunger. Wondrous to watch, they can tear a man into pieces.

I set out before dawn, before my father awakens. He'll beat me for this later, I know, but I don't care. It's worth it, a morning with Iblis. Though his smell is sickening and his dog's a pest, Iblis has much to teach me. And I learn, listening to his tales as we search the Firing Zone for fins and jackets and shrapnel. Bombs are merciful, Iblis says, like God. They replenish the earth with metal.

I follow a wadi, heading south. The sun rises to the side of me and ahead, the smoky haze of the Firing Zone. Alone, I imagine myself a giant. Hunting in a time long ago, before the Bible even, before the seventh day. When the moon and the sun were gods and the clouds and the stars were their children. A big man, bigger than my father, who needs no clothes or tents or weekly supplies from the government. With nothing but a stone in my fist. Heavier than a pistol— deadlier, when smashed into bone. Once I actually tried it. After twilight, when no one could see, when the flock was safe in its pens. I crept up on it, a ewe, weak with disease and left outside to die. I took a stone, took aim and threw. A single shot, straight to the belly. The fleece, the flesh, parted—a Red Sea—and the innards gushed onto the sand. And there the animal lay, on its back with its legs spread wide, waiting to be eaten.

This is the way giants ate, Iblis swears, in the long dark nights before fire. On hands and knees before the kill, their faces bright with blood. Eating until the carcass was as hollow as a husk and the sand around it stained. Nothing—not gold, no woman—could ever equal the beauty, says Iblis. By morning their bellies would be filled to bursting but their hunger had only become worse. And so they'd start again the day-long hunt, the night-long feast, over and over throughout the fruitful summer.

Winters, though, the animals would vanish. A hard time in the desert, a dangerous time. With floods that can crush a boulder and grind a wadi through bedrock. Wind that spins the sand so fast it can suck the flesh from your bones. Wind and water, like knives and stones, can kill a man, can cut his head off. Even the giants were frightened. So in winter they took to caves. I can see them still, the caves, in the cliff far to the east. Jagged holes barely big enough for sheep—all except for one, dark and evil, a yawning home for giants. There, in the long cold months, they used their stones to paint. To etch the walls with pictures of their prey—ibex and gazelle—and, in the deepest part, the likeness of a lion. Terrible jaws, its mane the color of old blood. A spirit more powerful than the moon and the sun. For giants, the lion was God, Iblis says and as always, I believe him.

When the wadi turns to the west, I climb its bank and find the trail. Here, the dust has been packed by the wheels of Yoni's jeep, but soon this, too, will be cleansed. Winter etches its pictures into the valley—new routes, new wadis which I will learn to run. Come spring, I will be bigger yet, a giant. Living my life with pride and anger, needing no one—not Yoni, not my father—eating on my hands and my knees. Of that day I dream as I walk, as the air grows smoky and craters pockmark the sand. Already I can see him, Iblis, his crooked shadow, and hear Has-No-Name's yap. Faster than ever, I have reached the Firing Zone.

"Kayf halak, ya Iblis!"
"Kayf al-hal, ya Mahbub."

So we greet one another, Iblis and I, in Arabic. Together we exchange salutes. A scout for the Great General years ago in the war against the Turks, Iblis still thinks of himself a soldier. Though bent, he can still snap to attention and whip up his hand—two fingers and a stump. He is missing many parts. An ear, a heel, and half his nose. And then, of course, the eye. A small price to pay, he says, for honor.

I follow Iblis around the Firing Zone. Down rows of craters like cups in an egg carton, each one coated with coal. He drags one leg behind him, and behind that, his dog. Has-No-Name, a smelly old mutt that he found in the Zone, one morning after an all-night barrage. Has-No-Name—*Ma-Fish-Ismo*—also has no hind limb. Iblis found it and bandaged its wound, and now the dog follows him everywhere, yapping and hopping on three paws. Barking endlessly at me.

Iblis's rags flutter in the breeze. Tatters of uniforms, dresses, a flag of some long-vanished country. In shreds they dangle from his pole-like body, like a tent in the dead of winter. Down wind, they can make me choke. But I don't mind—not the smell, the barking or the ghostly eye. I have much to learn from Iblis.

"*Ya Mahbub*," or so he always calls me, "My Dear Boy, *Ithakir*"—"Remember, the greatest riches are not in banks or factories, but right here in the sand." He kneels down, slowly and with a groan, before an olive-green tube. Lifts it gently with his two and a half fingers and brings it to the glass of his eye. "Bangalore Torpedo," he announces, then squints inside, "with pin." He stuffs the tube into the sack which he wears tied to his hip, and softly mutters his thanks: "*Al-hamdu lilah.*" Praise be the Lord. "It will bring us a shekel at least."

A good business, Iblis never tires of telling me, a blessing. Bombs and missiles fall from heaven, like manna. Mornings after a big maneuver he can collect as much as fifty shekels' worth of scrap. Enough to live like Maliku, the mythical king of Yemen. But some bombs are not quite scrap. There's life in some yet, Iblis warns, and powder in their veins. Disturb their sleep and they'll tear your hide. They'll eat your flesh and lick your blood. Hurts? Oh no, says Iblis, being eaten is like a dream. Like paradise. Go ask the lion.

I do not understand. "But there are no more lions."
"No?"
"The Bedouin shot them all."
"There are lions that even the Bedouin can't shoot."
"I've never found any tracks."
"*Al-hamdu lilah*, nor has it found yours." Iblis scoops

17

up some 30 cal. jackets; a thousand can buy a chicken. "Listen at night, *Mahbub*, you can hear its roar in the cave."

"That's just the wind, even I know that."

"The wind, my anus. It's the *jinn* of the lion. The spirit." Iblis glares in anger. He fixes me with his glass eye, the one he stole from that Austrian duchess, a passenger on the Pasha's train, killed by a British bullet. Iblis makes his oath: "As the rain turns to floods and sand into devils, the lion has become that spirit."

In the old days, Iblis tells me, the days before time when giants roamed the valley, they hunted the lion. Hunted and prayed to it both; their food was also their God. A terrible god which could only be trapped in the back of caves, and killed with the best-thrown stones. Then, if they lived, the giants would cut off the animal's head. They'd place it in a sack, and dance wildly back to camp. And there it would stay, a prize for their women, and for themselves, an idol.

But soon the ibex disappeared, and then the gazelle. Now it was the lion's turn to hunt. It caught the giants and ate them one by one until none was left alive. You could still see the bones—Iblis swore he had—in the caves high up the face of the cliff.

Through the Firing Zone, I trail behind Iblis. Smoke rises from the craters and curls around our legs. Has-No-Name nips at my calves. Today is a good day, plenty of 155s and cluster bombs. Jets and artillery are as good as gold, Iblis says, but infantry is slim pickings. Worst, though, are the engineers. They leave Bangalore Torpedoes scattered over the sand, and beneath it, buried, their mines. They're plastic mostly, those mines, and worthless, but stepped on, they'll bite off more than they can swallow. Iblis knows; he lost his hand to one, and other parts too, though he keeps those hidden by rags. If bombs come from *Allah* than mines are Satan's, he explains. They snatch men's heels and suck them under. They watch our every step.

"Yoni says you should stay away from the Firing Zone. He says one day you're going to get blown to bits."

Iblis spits yellow. "*Kus Uchto,*" he says—His sister's private parts. "Your friend thinks he's so smart. I tell you, there are a lot more brains in this dog."

Has-No-Name whimpers and barks.

"He knows a lot of things," I protest. "About jeeps and engines. He teaches me."

"Is that so? And what does he teach you about spirits?"

"Yoni doesn't believe in spirits."

"And lions?"

"I told you, he says they've all been killed."

Iblis turns to me. His face is thinner than a skull, his skin like dusty canvas. "*Ahbal*"—he's a fool—"your friend. He wouldn't know a mine if he stepped on it."

Later, to celebrate his finds, Iblis brews some coffee. He makes a fire of gathered twigs and grinds the beans with stones, sings a funny song that has no words or even a melody, while Has-No-Name howls along. Then, with his two good fingers, he pinches the grounds into a jerry can, pouring sugar from a pouch on his belt. Equal measures of

19

each; numbers are important for Iblis. Like my father—forty days and forty nights, forty years in the desert. The ram's blood must be sprinkled seven times and seven times must the coffee boil before Iblis will agree to drink it.

"Beware of those who call you friend," Iblis says as he pours the coffee into ration cans. "They bring you strangers from cities up north, government people, achhh." He sips and spits it onto the sand, according to his tradition. "People who will eat you—not like lions with their jaws, but with their tongues. It's as different as heaven and hell."

The coffee is gritty and tastes of gas, but the feeling is warm in my hands. I take the can of peaches from my pocket and place it on the sand before him. Iblis looks at it suspiciously, as he always does. He says nothing, only snorts. Then he finds the rusty opener in his belt and jerks it around the rim. He drinks in loud gulps, the syrup running through the lines in his face. The two fingers scoop up half the fruit, out of the can and straight to his mouth, before offering the rest to me. They're sweet, the peaches, and soft enough for him to chew. Iblis smiles at me orange.

"Stay away from people like Yoni. From all people, as soon as you are old enough to be alone." Just like Yoni, Iblis likes to teach. "But first you must lie with a woman."

I stare into my coffee and blush.

Iblis laughs: "Let your friend tell you. Him with balls the size of goat pellets. I'd show you myself . . ." He points at his lap, at the knot of shredded rags. "But some things you must learn on your own, *Mahbub*, like the difference between a torpedo and a mine."

I look at his heel, his hand and his nose. In the glass of his eye I can see myself, trembling.

Iblis laughs, really laughs. His mouth is as wide as a cave, and the breath inside it roars. It echoes in the craters and runs through the wadis. Clear across the valley, I imagine, to the camp where my father is rising.

Sneaking out is one thing, slipping back in another. It's easy at night when the children's sighs and my father's snoring hide the sounds of my steps. Or when he goes across the tent to my mother, tripping over my brothers' legs, and knocking his head on the lamp. Her cot creaks and his nostrils snort. Creak, snort, creak, snort—like the engine of Yoni's jeep. He's giving her another son, a noisy business. The perfect time to make my escape. But in the daytime when the children are playing in the dust, with my father fixing fences and my mother doing chores, it's hard to get past unnoticed.

I approach from the east with the sun behind me. Keeping low, walking on the softest sand. It works. I reach the bottom of the ridge, right below the camp. My father must be in the tent, with the children, reading Psalms. The place is empty except for the sheep. Except for the tub, and bowing over it, my mother.

But she does not see me. Her eyes are somewhere else. Staring past the laundry and across the valley, far beyond the Firing Zone. Eyes as empty, as barren as the desert. In her large brown hands—once soft, now cracked—she kneads the pants and T-shirts. She knows it's hopeless,

21

trying to get out the dust. Our clothes, like our skin, are stained with it, a kind of sorry gray. Her skin, too, though there is still a ghost of pink in her cheeks and in the jagged line above her chin, just below her lips. A scar: whenever the children get sick or my father hits me, it's there that she sinks her teeth.

She wrings the laundry viciously as she would the neck of a chicken. Though she rarely seems to eat, she's fat, my mother. Rolls of flesh on her arms and neck; her bosom like a dune which grows with every season. A loose gray smock and gray hair pinned back, suds on her forehead where she wipes her wrists. She's very quiet. Except for an Amen or a Hallelujah, I never hear her voice. But there's noise inside her, I know. Shouts and cries and laughter. I remember.

Long ago, in the land where we lived before coming here, in America, I ran to her. Down a steamy street alive with cars and buses. Strange music and smoky smells and the hiss of water spraying across the pavement. I was lost and frightened, but then I saw her. In a purple dress that rose above her knees when she knelt with her arms open wide to receive me. Her arms were thin and her knees were pink, and her lips, painted, even pinker. And her dark hair flowed over her shoulders and around a neck as long, I thought, as a swan's. I saw her, outside, in front of a house. Dirty steps led up to a door that was dark. Dark windows, too, with curtains behind the grime. I hated that house, but still I ran. Barefoot on the hot sidewalk, tears tumbling off of my nose. Ran until I was close enough to leap straight into those arms which then wrapped around me and held me to a bosom still firm. And I put my head across her shoulder, and my cheek against her neck. Her skin was cool, like clean sheets, her hair a warm blanket. I could smell the pinkness of her lips. But I couldn't help looking up at the house with its dark windows. At the curtains which parted behind the grime. He was watching us, even then. The big man with the long red face and anger in his eyes. She couldn't see him but I did, and I dug my face deeper into her neck. I cried and cried as I've never cried since, and heard my name—my real name—uttered. "There, there," she said again. "Mommy's got you."

"I see you, sinner," my father snarls, standing above me on the ridge. His hand comes down heavy, this time too fast. It catches the side of my head and sends me rolling down the ridge. "Sinner. *Damned* sinner," he comes at me with knuckles like stone, so that all I can do is curl into a ball and try to scramble away. There's blood in my nose and dust in my mouth and I can hear the children screaming. And between the blows I catch sight of my mother, still strangling the family wash. Her stare is the same, so distant and lost. But beneath her lip, her teeth have sunk into skin.

The wind grows stronger, darker, as winter comes. The sand seems to huddle for safety. I watch the pillar of dust rising as the jeep turns off the highway. Leaves the big trucks with their loads of stone, and the cars stuffed with families, all heading north for the city. I have never seen a city, not since I was a kid anyway. But that was in a different place, far away in America where we lived before this. And all I can remember are the steamy streets and water hissing from sidewalks and my mother on the steps in a purple dress, a bottle on her hip, laughing beneath grimy windows.

Yoni takes his time. He follows the trail which winds in front of the Firing Zone before turning toward our camp. I throw some stones and dream of lions, and half the morning seems to pass before the jeep finally arrives. I stay squatting just to irk him. And from there I see it for the very first time: Yoni is not alone.

He does not stir, Yoni. He sits with a puzzled face, staring into the wheel as if it were a mirror. But the door on the other side opens. I cannot make out who it is, only the tip of a floppy army hat bouncing over the canvas. I stand up on tiptoes, but all I see are some strands of hair, camel-colored, an ear and, behind it, a pencil.

Yoni looks at me, then back at the wheel. He shakes his head and mutters. Just then the person comes round the back of the jeep. A person in army-like clothes, but too small to be a soldier. A boy I think: Yoni has brought me a friend. I will show him the Firing Zone and teach him to throw stones, I imagine, and my father will beat us both. But this is no boy, no friend. Just then, from under the hat, it falls, a sandy braid of hair.

Hurrying to the back of the jeep, Yoni tries to pull out a duffel bag. But the person with the braid won't let him. The person shoves him aside and a voice says, "I can manage, thank you." The *thank you*, though, sounds more like a curse, and Yoni just stands there with that same puzzled face, hands on the belt of his pistol. The duffel bag is very heavy, I can tell, but I am too afraid to help. I cannot move, not even to catch the can of apricots which Yoni throws at my feet.

The person lugs the duffel bag up the side of the ridge, puffing. Lets it drop with a grunt, and wipes an arm under the hat, pushing up the brim. The face is like no face I have ever seen before. Soft skin as white as goat's milk with freckles afloat in it, like sand. Roundish nose and swollen lips as if someone—Yoni?—had beaten them. But the brows are black and bushy, the eyes greener than cactus after rain.

"Hallelujah," she huffs, and I almost say Amen. I am as puzzled as Yoni, with no pistol to clutch, only the rims of my pockets.

"*Shalom*," she says. "You must be . . ." She wants me to tell her my name, but I can't decide which name to give her. But she does not wait, though, and speaks on: "You must be the shepherd. I've heard a lot about you." She holds out a hand as soft and warm as her voice. Softer and warmer than anything I've touched since that time, long ago, in the city. The shake is hard, though. She squeezes my fingers like udders.

"Bubi, meet Revital." Yoni is grinning. Behind the sunglasses he is brave.

"It's a difficult name, I know," she says, "but you'll get used to it."

25

"Bubi here's the oldest son. The rest are just babies."

Revital smirks. There's something she doesn't like about Yoni.

Yoni picks up the apricots, and stuffs them in my jacket pocket. A bar of chocolate follows. "Bubi's big on canned fruit," he explains to her, "a real sweet tooth."

Her smirk becomes a frown. "It's hardly good for him."

"And you should see him throw a stone. An ace, he never misses."

Revital does not answer. She reaches into the pocket of her pants, and pulls out a little book, a notebook. She takes the pencil from behind her ear, and scribbles something short and fast. The notebook then snaps shut, cracking just like a pistol.

"Do you have anything else to do here?" she asks Yoni.

He is lighting a cigarette, puffing and making a lot of smoke that blows in her direction. She swishes it away like flies.

"Bad enough you nearly killed me in the jeep," she snaps, "but why hurt the boy?"

Yoni flicks the cigarette into the sand, and steps away from the smoke. He pushes the glasses up his long nose, but they cannot hide his confusion.

"Well, I guess I'll be going," he says to the sand. "I'll be back in a week, like always. What do you say to some plums this time, huh, Bubi?"

Plums, peaches—Iblis does not care. I nod.

"And if *you* need anything . . ."

"Yes, yes," Revital says, but she is already going through her duffel bag.

Yoni walks off, slowly, to the jeep. The engine turns and the gears groan. It limps down the trail, toward the highway and the cities of the north.

"Could you show me a place to pitch my tent?" Revital asks. "Not too close to yours, of course. I don't want to disturb your family."

Without thinking I bend to take the duffel bag. She bends too, and our faces meet. Close enough for me to see golden dots in her green eyes, and smell something sweeter than peaches and chocolate together.

Revital smiles, "Please."

The duffel bag is heavier than I imagined, but I haul it over my shoulder. Around the pens and the porcelain tub, far away from our camp. But not far enough for my father. I catch sight of him, just as I reach the top of the ridge. He is in the tent, his head sticking out, bright red and quivering, as if one of the flaps had caught fire.

27

"He hates them," my mother once told me. It was a long time ago, just after we left America for the Promised Land, as my father called it, and the desert. Before she stopped speaking, and the scar appeared on her chin. "The government people, they destroy his vision."

"Vision?"

"Something you see, but with your heart."

"Like Hezekiel's wheel?"

"Yes, yes," she ruffled the hair on my head, "Like Hezekiel's wheel."

I had lots of hair then, untouched by my father's knife, and I would talk with my mother for hours. She would talk to them, too. The people who came from the cities up north, Israelis sent by the government with their tubes and rulers, great red boxes of tools. She'd ask them many questions, as many as they asked her, only they wrote hers down word for word. My brothers were not born yet, and there was only my mother and me. Her hands were still soft then, almost, and she wasn't always scrubbing the laundry. She had time to talk, and sometimes even to laugh. They were so funny-looking those government people, in their suits and ties, their glasses smudged with dust. I had to laugh at them, too.

But my father never laughed. He never talked to them either, except when he had to, which wasn't very often. He hated them, like my mother said. Like snakes they killed the vision in his heart and left it full of venom. But they just kept on coming, every month or so, along with the supplies. They were part of the deal. The government gave us the land, the sheep and a tent, dug a well for us that gave us water, and in return we let ourselves be studied. The food we ate and how we ate it, and how the herd grew and grew with each passing season. A pact with the devil, my father called it. But these devils had no horns or tails, only clocks and weathervanes. No pitchforks, either, though one or two walked with canes. They asked me questions and ruffled my hair. A bar of chocolate was always part of my deal.

Many men came in those first years, brought by trucks which hissed and rattled across the dunes. With each one I could see my father's face growing redder and redder. Like a giant's, his shoulders slumped, and he hid in the tent all winter. But my mother stayed outside. In sun and rain, she asked the men questions about their lives in the city, about music and movies, and brought them cakes that they pretended to eat. And when the trucks came to take them away, I could see her sitting for a long time on the ridge, watching their dust in the distance.

Until one time, one man came. A doctor, I think, who poked sticks down my mouth and cones in my ears and listened to my chest through tubes. Pills, round and gray and tasting of chalk, he gave me to keep away the fever. He had other pills, too, red ones shaped like bullets, which he said were good for my mother. At the time she was very big. Her belly and her bosom were swollen; the back of her dress was torn. She could not run to greet him, but limped like a breeding ewe. He would look at her and then they would talk and talk, for hours sometimes, about what I never knew, though once I heard her laugh—my mother, laugh.

But my father did not laugh. Angrier, redder each day, he forbade her finally to take the pills, forbade the doctor to poke her. And when the poor man tried, my father came storming. He broke the sticks and crushed the tubes. He ordered my mother to the tent. Then he shouted at the doctor, words I could not understand, and threatened to strike him dead. But the doctor did not move. A little

29

man with no hair on his head, half my father's size, he stood straight before the terrible judgment.

My mother was in the tent for many days, and my father did all of the washing. He asked her questions which she would not answer, brought her cakes that she did not even pretend to eat. I heard her cry in my dreams. The doctor kept away from her, though, and spent his time with me, watching sheep. We did not talk. As if along with his tubes and cones he'd also lost his tongue. He just sat there while I hit the strays with stones. I was beginning to get real good.

Then one night I awoke to a terrible scream. A lion, I thought, killing the flock. My eyes opened to a yellow light flashing on the canvas. Shadows ran like men on fire, wrapped in bloody sheets. My father stood before the flaps with the lantern swinging, and blocked the doctor from entering. Stopped my mother, too, though she charged like a ram, head down, at his belly. Fists like stones hissed through the air. One of them smashed on the hairless head, another on a swollen bosom. One by one, they all fell away, until only my father was left, breathing hard with the lamplight rising and falling. The screaming was gone, and in its place, a quiet cry—my mother's, I think, or mine.

The next day the doctor was gone. Without waiting for the truck, without food or water, he walked the trail to the highway. And in the tent, with hardly a sound, my mother gave birth. A girl, I think, though I never saw the baby. I never found out where the doctor went or what happened to my mother's chin. Not once did she ever mention it, nor once did I dare to ask.

Yet still the people came every season, but fewer and fewer. Even though the flock grew bigger and Yoni's jeep replaced the trucks. Men arrived with maps and rods and telescopes, but no more doctors. My mother did not talk to them, no more than she did to me, and my father kept up his silence. But I can still see that look on his face, a cringe as if something had bitten him. I see it now, that cringe, as Revital sets up her tent. Revital, the first to come with little more than a notebook. The first who is not a man.

True to her word, Revital keeps her distance. For three days now she's been off alone somewhere. Cleansing herself, I imagine, getting rid of the city smells, the smoke from cars and buses. We go about our business—my father fixing the pens and my mother wringing laundry—as if she weren't there. But they know. There's this stiffness, the way he hammers a stake and the way she wipes that wrist on her forehead. The way I get just before a beating, holding myself inside.

I cannot help looking at her, though, and as often as I can, from the valley. The round nose, the thick brows, the green eyes with golden flakes like dates on desert waters. Just her face, all the rest is baggy clothes and hat. I believe Yoni liked her, even though she was mean. I wonder what Iblis would say. I throw a stone at a stray—an old and mangy ram—and hit it smack on the snout.

Then, late one afternoon, I see her. Squatting by her tent on the top of the ridge. Her back is turned to the setting sun and her floppy hat's pulled low. Swiftly, she writes in her notebook. Writes hard and fast as if someone were hitting her with stones. What can it be—the size of the flock, the shape of our camp? Like Bilaam spying for his king, *How goodly are thy tents, Oh, Jacob, thy pavilions, Oh, Israel.* Then suddenly she stops and bats her knees together. She looks out over the valley, at the caves and the Firing Zone, and her shoulders rise and fall. Biting the end of her pencil, she opens her notebook and writes and writes. She is writing still, I imagine, long after the sun goes down.

Grace, in our tent, is said in silence. Heads bent over hands folded before the dinner which is also eaten without words. My father eats with big chews, swabbing the soup with hunks of bread swooped straight to his mouth. But my mother never seems to eat at all. She is too busy keeping my brothers quiet, and stuffing their faces with food. And just as my father finishes, she is on her feet and cleaning. The cots are pushed away and the chairs placed in rows by the time he comes back with the Bible.

And it came to pass one evening that David arose from his bed and walked upon the roof of the king's house, and from the roof he saw a woman bathing, and the woman was very fair to look upon. And David sent and inquired after the woman. And one said: Is this not Bathsheva, the daughter of Eliam, the wife of Uriyah the Hittite?

My father reads with a growl in his voice. He is very angry at David. His fist beats the page as its does my skull on those nights when I do not listen. But tonight I am listening. David is my favorite.

And David sent messengers and took her, and she came in to him, and he lay with her, for she had purified herself from her uncleanliness. And later from her house she sent word to him: Behold I am with child.

My mother sits with her empty face. The words flow over her, never sinking in, like rain on bedrock. Once, though, she was like I am tonight, hanging at the end of the chair, chin in palms. But that was a long time ago, before my brothers were born. Now she seems asleep almost, except that her eyes are open.

Then David wrote to Yoav, his general, saying: set Uriyah in the front of the hottest battle, and withdraw from him, that he may be smitten and die.

33

My eyes are very open. Now and then they peep out of the tent flaps, up the ridge toward Revital's tent. A funnel-shaped tent, like a sand devil turned upside down. Nighttime she sits outside, and brews Turkish coffee on her stove. Just sits there by the tiny blue flames, dreaming. Then, very late, she enters the tent and turns on her flashlight. A brilliant glow, not old and yellow like our lantern. It paints figures on the tent walls—ibex and gazelle—which dance and crumble with the wind, dying, all at once, in darkness.

And when Yoav besieged the city he assigned Uriyah to a place where he knew the fighting was. And the men of the city went out and fought. They killed many of David's servants, among them Uriyah the Hittite.

Uriyah dead with Bathsheva on the roof, and David, hungry David, awaiting the news in his palace. The pictures fly through my mind. Outside, though, there is only blackness. The night has eaten her tent.

To his house David brought Bathsheva, and she became his wife and bore him a son.

Something is happening. A want deep down in my belly, as wide as the desert, opens. Winds and floods are ravaging, but nothing can ever fulfill it.

And it came to pass on the seventh day . . .

My father pauses, breathless with pain. The Bible in his hand is trembling.

that David's son did die.

"That's a pretty good throw."

I leap to my feet and feel my face go hot. My stone has just winged over the flock, through the branches of a dead acacia, and onto the horns of that mangy old ram.

"Must take a lot of practice."

I shrug and kick the dust. I thank the Lord my jacket has pockets in which I can hide my hands. Revital smiles and skips down the ridge to where I guard the flock.

"So this is your job, shepherd. A big responsibility, don't you think?"

The smell has followed her, as heavy as the syrup in Yoni's cans, sweeter. I do not answer; I cannot look at her.

She sits down next to me and hugs her knees, resting her chin between them.

"I mean, all these sheep—why there must be forty, fifty—and you have to keep an eye on all of them. What if one of them strays . . ."

"No!" I say, so loudly she flinches.

"No . . . what?"

"No, they do not stray. Not when I watch."

"I'm sorry." Revital pouts. "I didn't mean to insult you."

I like it when she apologizes, something she would never do to Yoni. I hope she will say more, but when I finally look up she's back at her notebook and writing.

"What do you write in there?"

"Oh, things."

"Things about me?"

"Yes, about you—the way you live. Here you are an American family, very religious, who chose to leave its easy life and come here to Israel, to the desert, and live like the patriarchs in the Bible. It's fascinating."

I lean over as much as I dare. Soft lines squiggle across the paper, like snake tracks in the sand. But I jerk away, her pencil in my face.

"Here," she says, "you can try."

I turn away. "I can't . . ."

"Go ahead."

"I can't . . ."

The pencil flies away, back to the perch of her ear. "I'm sorry."

"I can read just fine. English, as it is in the Bible . . ."

"I'm sure you can."

"And chocolate bar wrappers . . ."

There's something funny about this, though I'm not quite sure what, and Revital's laughing. But then she gets serious again, and starts to ask me questions. Questions about the flock, when I lead it to pasture and how to handle the strays. I answer and she writes fast and hard. The black brows are knotted, the lips pursed. Lips like dunes, skin as smooth as stones. I try to imagine her as she was at my age. White dress on green grass with a house and smiling parents. I see her in that dress as she throws stone after stone at me, a stray.

"You're staring at me."

My cheeks are as red as my father's. "I never . . . saw . . ."

"A notebook?"

I shake my head. "You know."

She bites the tip of her pencil. "Really now, with all those visitors?"

I turn away. I do not like to be teased.

"Well there's nothing to be afraid of. There are plenty of us"—the pencil points across the valley, to the highway heading north, "out there, just like me."

How could there be, like her? The milky cheeks, the sandy fleece, without blemish.

Revital asks, "You've never been to the city, have you?"

"Once. But that was a long time ago, before we moved to the desert."

"A long time indeed." She flips to the first page of her notebook. "Why you must have been . . ."

"Very small. But I remember."

"Remember what?"

"The street. Lots of cars and smoke and water coming out of the sidewalk."

"Sounds scary."

"Not at all." I lean close to her, so close I can count the freckles. "All those sounds and smells. I could wander around and around and really get lost. Yet somehow I always found myself back in front of the house with the big steps. My mother was always there with a big smile and a purple dress, and she'd put her hands around me . . ."

I talk on and on, more than I've talked to anyone— Iblis and Yoni—together. But then I stop. Revital is not looking at me. She is staring up the ridge, at the camp and my mother hanging the laundry . She cannot see her face or even her body—they're hidden by a sheet—but only the bottom of her skirt with the threads hanging off it and her feet dark-stained with dust.

"She must have been very young then," Revital says, but not quite to me.

"I guess."

"And very pretty."

"The dress was pretty, I remember, and she smelled good. Like you."

Revital tucks her chin to her chest, her knees rise to her forehead. She smells good, but not at all like my mother. More like the parks my mother used to take me to. A park filled with old statues and sticky grass that shone with diamonds after rainfall. Revital smells more like that grass. Her eyes are the color of statues.

"What are you *doing* here?"

Revital's head shoots up. She looks surprised, as if I had just asked for her deepest secret. "I am . . ." she starts to explain then uses a word I've never heard before.

"An . . . apologist?"

Revital giggles. "An *anthro*pologist," she says and then gets very serious. "We study different peoples, they way they live and work and pray."

"And you want to do that?"

My question makes her angry. "Of course, why else would I be here?" But then she sees she's hurt my feelings, and tries her best to repent: "I mean, I like it here and talking to you. It's just that being an anthropologist is very hard work."

"Harder than being a shepherd?"

"Depends. What do *you* want to be?"

I want to tell her about the giants, about the caves and the spirit of lions, but all I say is "hunter."

"A hunter of what?"

"Ibex, gazelle, that sort of thing."

"Sounds . . ." she makes a face. "Messy." Revital stands and slaps the notebook against a leg of her baggy pants. The braid has wound its way around her neck, and slithers down the front of her shirt. "Frankly, I like shepherding better. But you have time to think about it." She wipes her hand against the other leg and holds it out.

"You seem to have a lot of names, which one should I call you?"

I stare at her fingers, long with tiny nails, like a row of sharpened teeth. "They used to call me Bobby, which I suppose is kind of funny."

"I like funny names. Mine is."

The hand sticks out further, almost into my belly. I grip it and shake out the sounds: "Re . . . vi . . . tal."

She cheers, "Fantastic!" and her eyes are like flares over the Firing Zone.

With a little tug, Revital takes her hand back. Mine is still in the air, though, still shaking, and Revital looks slightly confused. But then, ruffling the stubs of my hair, she says, "It's been great talking with you, Bobby," and it is almost too delightful, the sound of my name in her mouth. "We'll do it again, yes? Soon?"

Like a lantern the moon sways through the flaps of the clouds. It scorches their edges; the stars fly away like sparks. There's quiet in the valley and darkness over the Firing Zone. The caves are veiled in fog. Stillness freezes everything—the pens, our tent—and hushes the bleating of the flock. It is a stillness I know, I love. The moment when muscles tighten and the teeth can be bared. The moment before the kill. A strange chill runs through the camp. Secretly creeping, toe-to-heel, in the manner of lions. But only I can hear it. I can sense the passing of time, the secret change of seasons. I alone can feel the spirit's presence. Across the desert, around the ridge, the wind is warning of winter.

Long after sundown, we march. Silently, my mother and my brothers and I in a straight line clutching our towels. We head toward the porcelain tub which gleams like a chip of the moon. It has always been here, the tub, was here when we arrived from America. A piece of junk, my mother said, but my father wanted it saved. So it became our altar for sacrifice, our cleansing place each week in the late night after Vespers.

We strip off our clothes and stand in the cold shivering. My brothers go before me, the youngest first. Swooped in the fat arms of my mother and dunked. I can hear the cries when their skin meets the icy water, and then the moans as my mother scours their scalps. The coarse bar of soap rises and falls, her hands wring their hides like laundry. Then, briskly, they are snatched up and sent scurrying to my father. He stands at a distance, a giant shadow with a knife. One by one he grips their hair so hard he almost lifts them. The knife flashes, their curls take flight in the wind. My brothers like cherubs flutter past me.

Finally it is my turn. I take off my clothes, but still hug the towel to my chin. I am too big to be scooped by my mother, and my skin is coarser than the soap. The water, black by the time I enter, laps noisily over the tub. Though I might fight her off, I let my mother wash me. And with me she is gentle. She glides the soap across my chest and around my arms, down my belly to where the hair has started to grow. I hold my head up to the bar which is coarse and gritty but pure. I climb out into the towel, and hold it around my waist. The air is cold and the water dirty but I feel warm and clean. I have no need for the knife.

The knife. I remember the knife, or one just like it, in America. In the city where we lived—Chicago, I think we called it. The knife was lying on the floor. It was nighttime and the music came gray through the grimy windows, with the honks of cars and buses. Loud noises—crashes and shouts—brought me from the bedroom. Blinking in the naked light, the first thing I saw was my father. He was seated on a chair with his face in his hands, staring at the floor. At the stain spreading darkly. My mother was there, too, though I did not see her. I only heard her crying. And looking around for her, I saw it: the knife. Splattered with red which dripped toward the stain, as if the blade itself were bleeding. Pale light swam in the stain, it danced on the steel. Then came the footsteps outside the door, and the knocks, loud knocks, and a voice commanding us to open up. My father rose, and bent to take the knife. He wiped its blade on the back of his pants, and hid it in his jacket pocket. Only then did he receive the law.

41

I have no need for the knife now, years later in the desert. Yet I go. Walking slowly with the towel around me until I reach the place where he waits. My father stares down at me and I can feel the fire in his eyes, but my eyes are looking elsewhere. They are looking up the ridge toward Revital's tent. Little blue flames are licking her kettle; the coffee is seven-times boiled. But she does not drink. She is watching, I know, watching and writing fast in her notebook. I do not want her to see me like this. Like this I must not appear on the page. But my father's big hands grab the towel and tears it away. One grips the knife and the other my hair. The strands rain onto the sand.

Later, after prayers, I sneak out of the tent. I sit on the ridge and follow the fog as it shifts across the valley. Something is alive in the Firing Zone. The night is adorned with tracer rounds, like necklaces. Flares dangle sparkling in the sky. The engineers are back—I know the signs—with their Bangalore Torpedoes, their mines. I worry about Iblis out there in the dark with nobody but Has-No-Name to guide him. I hope he has the sense to stay away from the Firing Zone, just as he keeps clear of people. Mines and people, they'll bite off more then they'll swallow.

The fire is gone from Revital's tent. Nor is there light inside. I can smell the sweetness of her sleep in the night, and feel her heavy breathing. I want to crawl up the ridge and squat beside the tent. I want to tighten my muscles and bare my teeth and take her breath within me.

But I cannot. I stay on the ridge, my towel, like dampened wings, around me. I am not yet what I must be. Not fast enough nor brave enough; the hunger is not yet in me—not yet *me*. The wind plays on my hairless scalp, on my skin scrubbed pinkish clean.

I stay a long time, almost until dawn, watching the tracers file across the sky. Flares pop and cut through the darkness, like raindrops down a grimy window.

*   *   *

I can run straight across the valley now without stopping for breath, not even once. From wadi to wadi thundering like a flood. It is not without pain. My chest burns and my eyes swim with blue; sand seems to fly up my throat. And just when I think my belly will burst, I am there at the craters. Free amid the coal and the smoke. The Firing Zone, a world of haze and silence. A world of one person who right now is nowhere to be found.

I pick my way around the craters, and look for signs of Iblis. What kind of signs I'm afraid to say—teeth, rags, slivers of glass. One never knows with mines. I, myself, am scared, recalling what they did to Iblis—how they took off half his foot and two and a half of his fingers, exploding between his legs as well. I move as Iblis taught me: one foot trailing the other, careful as a cat. My eyes search the sand for circles, like paw prints, that will show me where the mines are buried. Crater by crater, peeking in each, I make my way across the Firing Zone. And still not a hint of Iblis.

A jagged growl tears through the smoke. Has-No-Name, that scrawny mutt, hobbles toward me. He hops on his three stubby legs and yaps around both of mine. Hands in my pockets, I imagine whipping out the stone and letting it fly, smack into its brittle skull. But Iblis can't be far, I think. Between two craters made the night before, I see him. Down on his knees by a ring in the sand, digging.

"*Kus uchtah*," he curses. "*Kus emak*." Iblis digs with a sharp piece of stone, a flint which once belonged to the giants. Up and down, he saws around the ring, around the flat gray disc of plastic. The mine is not dead. It is alive, like an animal living only to kill. Iblis spits, "Engineers, they're devils, *Mahbub*. Worse than even people."

I see that Iblis has found other mines. Four or five, round and gray, like the pills I used to get from the doctor. "Don't," Iblis shouts as I bend to smell them. He holds up his two fingers and points them at the rags between his legs. "Don't, if you ever want to lie with a woman."

I back away and squat beside the craters. I watch as he sticks the fingers gently into the sand and lifts. Another gray pill rises up and sheds its sand. Iblis lays it on top of the others and wipes the dirt on his rags. Has-No-Name barks at them and through his missing leg showers them with yellow. Iblis laughs, and I laugh too. It's good to be back in the Firing Zone.

We celebrate, as always, with coffee. With the plums that drip purple syrup through the leathered lines of his face. I want to tell him about the new visitor at our camp. About the braid and the notebook and the smell stronger than smoke. I want to ask him if Revital is like all the other people, from whom I must stay away. But all I can do is to sip the coffee and frown at the taste of gas.

"*Ya Mahbub*, you are an angel." He wipes the syrup with a rag from his head and tosses a plum to the dog. "And soon you will be a man."

"I want to be a giant."

Iblis laughs. "I told you, better to be a lion."

"I want to be like the giants who hunted the lion," I say, "who trapped it in caves and cut off its head and brought it back to their women."

Iblis says, "*Inshallah*."—God willing—"But first you have to be taught." He stares at me, and I can see myself shrinking in his eye.

"You are afraid, *Mahbub*, why? Everybody has to be taught, even a giant."

"I try to be brave," I say, "I teach myself to run and throw stones. I don't need anyone."

Iblis gulps the coffee and spits it into the sand. "*Majnun*," he scowls. "Don't be crazy. The stones teach you to throw. Wadis teach you to run. The earth itself can teach you—*if* you are ready to learn."

Why is he doing this, making me feel small when at last I am getting big? I stand up, so fast the coffee spills on my thigh. It stings, but I do not cry. "I *will* be a giant."

Iblis with one of his rags tries to wipe my thigh. "Then let the lion teach you," he says.

Furious, I push the rag away. Has-No-Name looks up from the plum and snarls.

"There is no lion. I told you, the Bedouin killed it."

"The lion, yes"—his mouth is a blackened crescent— "but not its spirit."

"And where can I find this spirit?"

Iblis sits back and stares at his lap. The glass eye, though, looks up. Across the valley to the cliff, to the caves as dark as craters. "You are big but not yet wise, *Mahbubi*," he sighs. *Mahbub*, he's told me, means 'beloved.'

He says, "It's time you started to learn."

The sun is high when I follow Iblis to the last of the craters. To the deepest of them all, lined with black and

45

filled with beads—the mark of a cluster bomb. Here he lays the mines one next to the other, and covers them with coal. Then he stands back and lowers his head and speaks in a whisper—more curses, maybe, or a prayer. Has-No-Name howls at the grave and the wind howls along with him.

Later—it is already afternoon—I make my way back to our camp. I do not run, though. No longer will I let my father beat me; I have a stone to throw if he tries. I am not afraid of him now, nor of anybody. Except Revital. It's not her hands that frighten me, or even the gold in her eyes. It's something else. Something inside me which is spinning and turning, tearing to get out. The hunger: soon I will understand it. Tonight, I will start to learn.

Sunday prayers begin at dawn and continue to late in the evening. Psalms, Chronicles, stories of David with his harp and sling, of Saul the king who loved him and later wanted him dead. The wind beating against the tent flaps lulls my brothers to sleep, and even my mother's head is drooping. Only my father stays upright. He clutches the Bible and strikes it with a fist. His bristly hair lashes canvas. By dusk, it is only the two of us, and I pretend to listen. Pretend, for all the while I dream of harps and spears and David running for his life. I am still dreaming, long after moonrise, when I hear the creak of his cot. In the darkness of sighs, my father begins to snore.

Silently, I rise from my chair. Move on feet that make no noise or even, I imagine, footprints. I unhook the lantern and glide through the flaps. Through the night I escape, past the pens and the tub and down the ridge to the valley. Behind me the tent sags with sleep; I do not look back, only ahead at the cliff and its caves. In the moonlight I can pick them out, circles as round as mines, as black as craters.

The cliff is more distant than I thought. It looks close enough to touch, but the farther I run the faster it seems to flee. I am getting tired. The wadis are long and the lamp grows heavy. Wet, out of breath, I force myself on. An hour at least, until the sky thickens and the moon sets behind the clouds. But another moon rises, a great black one, surrounded by holes, like stars that died before time. The caves: home of the lion. Of the spirit, as Iblis tells it. The place where I will start to learn.

I climb. With the lamp tied to my belt and my hands groping for holes, I lift myself up the cliff. The stones are soft and break in my fingers; my feet slip and dangle. But I will not fall. Already I can see the mouth of the cave and feel the wind like a chilling breath on my shoulders. Soon I hear a strange noise, like my father's snoring, only deeper. But I am not afraid. My heart drums, and yet I feel peaceful, as if I were in a dream I dreamed long ago, just after we came to the camp. A dream in which I ran down the street toward the house with the steps and the dirty windows. Not crying but laughing. The excitement, the dream, of home.

I pull myself into the cave and brush the dirt from my hands. I turn the button on the lantern and watch the flame rise inside the glass. Shards of light shoot into darkness; shadows bleed down the walls. I walk my cat

47

walk, one foot after the other, deep into the belly of the earth.

The floor turns from dust to rock and then to something brittle. Bones, hosts of them scattered around my feet. Ribs and skulls and horns. And stones, round and hard, like the ones I throw at the strays. I pick one up, the biggest I can find, and let it weigh in my hand. Like Yoni's pistol only heavier, with one shot instead of seven, but with all the power to kill. A giant's stone, able to turn beasts into bone, and in winter, into pictures etched into walls.

They are there, too, just as Iblis said. Holding up the lantern, I see them. Gazelle and ibex and animals I cannot name. The light breathes life into them and they run again, through the wadis where the giants hunt them down. My heart is dancing a crazy dance and the hunger in my stomach growls. Wind roars wildly in my ears.

Deeper I seek, and the air grows thin and cold. The flame in the lantern flickers. The wind gets louder not softer, shrieking, and a strange smell fills my nose. Dead sheep and burnt-out craters, a rotten smell, and yet I love it. More beautiful than Revital's, than my mother's long ago, back in the city. A smell I have known all my life, living inside me, that only now arises.

The bones are gone and so are the pictures. All but one. On the wall before me a mane, dazzling as the midday sun. Serpent's eyes, teeth the size of stones, sharp stones. I stand perfectly still and listen. A roar like the wind lashes me and draws me forward. Through the mouth, through the wall. Down, down, into the very jaws of the cave.

The floor suddenly drops. No walls, no cave, but only a chute of darkness. Through the ages of rain and silence. Past the time of hunters and stones. Giants chase gazelles through the wadis. Ibex with stone-split bellies, like canned fruit, spilling out. Terrible howls, the thud of distant thunder. The howl is mine too, and the thunder. I am before it. Within it. The spirit. The timeless hunger which wants only to kill. I smell my smell and hear my breath, my heart which thrives on poison. I fall to my knees, my face to the wound. Partaking of the spirit, I let myself be eaten.

It is morning when I finally emerge. From the cliff I can see our camp far below, the pens and porcelain tub. I can see the Firing Zone and its craters smoking. The valley lies before me, bare as flesh, veined with wadis soon to flow with water. I stand as the giants must have stood, a stone in their hand and their bellies full, warmed by the memory of meat.

49

    I watch the sun scaling the face of the sky. I could catch it if I tried, I am that fast, that hungry. I clutch the stone in my pocket, so tightly it cuts my palm. But there comes no pain. Only a roar that whirls from my throat and out to the desert, far, where even my father might hear it.

Her brow is like a rush of reeds. Thick black reeds along the pool of her lids, shading them from the sun as it rises.

    I am peeping through a tear in her tent. A tear that I, myself, made with the olive wood knife, but so small that nobody else will notice. Just wide enough to let my eyes see hers. The lids of her eyes like shimmering pools, and her brows, beaded with the dew. My knees tremble. They long to bend and bring my mouth to drink.

But then, suddenly, a buzzing sound fills the tent. A fly. It lands, still buzzing, on her brow. The reeds twitch and the waters ripple. The eyes roll open, naked to blades of sunlight, blinking and bleeding green. The fly takes off and so do I, scurrying down the ridge, away from where Revital awakens.

The flock is anxious today. I have led the sheep through the wadis, deep to the east toward the cliff. The caves seem to frighten them, as if they sense what sleeps there. As if they know my secret. I will not let them tarry, though. Stone after stone flies through the air to targets of fleece and bone. For strays there is no escape. Not even for the mangy ram that bleats with each rock I throw at it, but goes on standing its ground. I eye the mound of its belly, the throat rebelliously raised. Once again, my muscles tighten; water gathers in my gums. Now it will happen, I think, but before I can move, the growl of an engine stops me. Peering over the wadi, I can see the pillar of smoke, a lazy devil, twirling from Yoni's jeep.

The jeep is there when I return with the flock, not by the camp, though, where it usually sits, but up on the ridge. And there's no sign of Yoni. A strange noise comes from Revital's tent, as strange as any I heard in the cave. I sneak up behind the jeep and listen. Laughter. The tent trembles with it. Louder and louder it grows until the flaps suddenly part and Yoni comes stumbling out. He slips and falls to one knee, groping for his glasses. He tries to stand but Revital appears behind him and shoves. Yoni falls to his hairy chest; his face is coated with sand.

Revital laughs and laughs and wraps her arms around her breast. "You, you pathetic lamb? *You?*"

Behind the mask of sand, Yoni's face is pink. His eyes are as wide as a straying ram's, struck on the horn by my stone. He snarls at me beside his jeep. "And what are you looking at?"

Revital answers for me: "A jerk, that's what." The floppy hat has fallen from her head, the braid lashes wildly around her. Yoni's still crawling, and I hold out my hand to help him.

"Get out of here, Bubi . . ."

Revital throws fistfuls of sand that rain on Yoni's head. On hands and knees he slides down the ridge to his jeep. Gripping the canvas door he pulls himself up. He wipes the dust from his face, and hides his eyes behind sunglasses. "Crazy bitch," he mutters.

Revital stands above us on the ridge. There's a hand on each hip and a frown on her mouth. Her lips are wet with laughter. "Nobody tells me what I need and what I don't," she shouts, "Least of all you."

Yoni pretends to ignore her. He shakes a cigarette from his pack and sticks it between his teeth. The match hisses sharply at Revital. He says to me, "Be careful of her, Bubi. She's a devil."

"A devil?" Revital puts a finger under her chin. "Now *that* I like."

"She'll play the big sister, then, when you're not looking . . ." Yoni smacks one fist into another. "*Pow.*"

"Look who's talking. The big man with a pistol."

"At least I know how to use it."

"Sure, to blow yourself up."

"I always wanted a sister," I say quietly, but loud enough for Yoni and Revital to hear. They grow silent, the two of them, and stare.

"Of course you do," Revital tells me, "It's only natural."

Yoni scowls at her. "You . . . you make me sick." He flicks the cigarette into the sand, and climbs back into his jeep. "Mark my word," he hollers over the engine, "two weeks out here and you'll be begging for it."

Revital laughs again, louder now, but Yoni cannot hear. The jeep is crawling away, the dust like a tail between its tires.

Revital starts back to her tent, but I stay, bending to save the cigarette. On my knees in the sand, I suck the smoke from its end.

"Don't." The cigarette is snatched from my mouth. I look up to find Revital's face close to mine. I can smell her smell and almost feel her skin's smoothness. Beneath me, my knees are shivering.

"You must not be like him, Bobby."

"Like Yoni?"

"Like Yoni or any man. Stay away from them."

"You sound like Iblis."

"Like who?"

I lower my head and shuffle in the sand. I should not have told her about Iblis. "A friend. On the other side of the valley. In the Firing Zone."

"In the Firing Zone . . ."

She smiles at me. The same smile my mother gave me at the bottom of the stairs, once, a long time ago in the city. "It's nice to have a friend out here, when you're all alone. I could use a friend too, Bobby." She takes my hand and gives it a gentle shake. "You will be my friend, won't you?"

My head moves up and down, but inside it's turning. Filled with sandy wind and a roaring sound. I bare my teeth and stretch my jaws. "Friends," I tell her.

53

She is talking to him, I cannot believe it. I rub my fists into my eyes and look again. But there he is with his knife, kneeling onto the mangy old ram and trying to saw its horns. I might have been glad—those horns had often gored—but he is not alone. She is next to him, asking questions and writing fast in her notebook. I have never seen him talk so much and without the Bible. It goes on for hours, long after the ram hobbles back to the pens. He seems to be enjoying himself. His giant hands strike the air; his face grows red like sunset. And Revital writes, hardly looking up. Never noticing my mother as she scrubs the tub—a weekly task—spotless.

It is only much later, after I drive the flock to the pens, that I find her seated on the ridge. Hatless, she has let down her hair; the braid is almost undone. She chews on one of the strands and gazes out to the east, toward the highway. Her eyes are searching for dust.

"What did he tell you?"

Startled, Revital gasps. "Oh, Bobby, you scared me!"

"My father," I ask again, "what did he tell you?"

She takes the pencil from her ear and twirls it between her fingers. "He told me . . . everything."

"About God?"

"About him. About why he came here and what he believes. He's quite a man, your father."

I shake my head and shrug my shoulders, as if she were speaking in tongues.

"He told me about life in the city, all that dirt and noise. It was a dangerous place, he said. One night a robber actually broke into your house and tried to kill you and your mother. He told me the whole story: the robber had a knife. Your father wrestled him to the floor and somehow stabbed him—your father, who wouldn't touch a hair on anybody. And then and there he decided."

I listen to this with my eyes closed. As if it were a dream and Revital its interpreter.

"He wanted a better life for his family. For you."

But the meaning is wrong, all wrong. I can't stop my head from shaking.

"No, Bobby, I'm right," Revital insists. "You should

talk to him yourself, sometime. Maybe you'd understand him better."

I come close to her—too close, her back goes stiff. "Is that how you understand things?" I point at the notebook on her lap. "You write and understand?"

Now it is her turn to shake and shrug. I reach for the notebook. She tries to pull away but I am too fast. I grab it and flip through the pages. Strange scribbles like scratches on a cave wall, scripture without spirit.

"It's that easy. You come into peoples' lives and write them down, what they eat and how they sleep. This," I wave the notebook in her face, "is my life?"

"No, Bobby, not your life . . ."

"I would like to do it to you." Again I reach, this time for the pencil which I snatch from her ear. I open to an empty page and start to scribble. "Rises late and drinks coffee. Wears a hat, then doesn't wear one. Wants to be everybody's friend." Slashes and squiggles and angry dots.

"Please, Bobby . . ."

"Writes when she cannot understand. Talks like a giant but acts like a lamb."

"Enough!"

Revital grabs the notebook from my hand. Tears the blank page and breaks the pencil. "Damn, look what you've done." She clutches the notebook tight with one hand and with the other scoops up the two pieces of pencil.

"You like him, don't you?"

"Your father is an unusual man."

"Not my father . . ." My chin points to the highway.

"Oh, *him*." Revital laughs. "I told you, he's a jerk."

"But you like him."

Her laughter stops. "Listen, Bobby, nobody tells me what I can and cannot do. All my life people were trying to do that, even now, at the university. But I've never let them and I don't intend to start. Not my professors—they said I was crazy for coming here—and not your jerky friend, either." Revital speaks to me but her words, hot and angry, are for somebody else. For Yoni. "And nobody tells me who I do and do not like."

"But you do like him, don't you?"

Revital shifts her buttocks in the dust, she turns her back to me. I gaze over her shoulders through the sandy strands. At the golden fluff on the back of her neck and swells of flesh above her bosom. There's howling in my head, in my belly. In my pocket, my fingers stroke the stone.

"After sundown, you must not be out here alone. I have seen you, drinking coffee and looking at the stars. It's dangerous."

"Which—the coffee or the stars?" Revital tries to be funny, but her voice is dry and flat. She is frightened but she will not show me. Stubborn, she holds her head high.

I whisper in her ear, "The lion."

"There is no lion, Bobby. Stop trying to frighten me."

"Who told you there is no lion—my father?"

"Yoni," she lies.

"Yoni only knows about jeeps and guns. Iblis knows about lions."

She turns now, halfway. She seems excited. "I'd like to meet this Iblis."

"No!" I shout, so suddenly it makes her jump. "Iblis will not see anybody. Especially not a woman."

"Then I don't believe in him either." Revital now stands with her arms folded. "Lions, Iblis, they're all in your imagination."

I hold my ground, hold the stone in my pocket. "Then I'll take you."

"To the Firing Zone?"

"No, to the cave."

"But I thought you said he lives . . ."

"Iblis, yes, in the Firing Zone," I smile. "Not the lion."

Revital's hands are cold at night, damp as laundry, while mine are too hot to touch. She pulls her fingers away whenever I try to take them even though she stumbles. She does not see well in the dark, nor is she fast. I have to stop and wait for her at every turn of the wadi. She wants to beg me to wait, to clutch my hand and be tugged by me, but she is too proud. Too scared. In this night of lions, Revital is a lamb.

We hear it, still far from the cave, the howl. She freezes for a moment and I can feel her muscles in the dark, straining to turn and run. Beneath her scent I can smell her sweat of fear. But I keep going. On feet of fire, I burn through the wadi toward the cliff.

We arrive well after midnight. It has taken a long time to get here, and the climb is longer still. Dangerous now that the moon has set and the rocks have turned to shadows. Revital has to grip my hand and surrender her weight to mine. She grows heavier, this woman of air, as I rise, and she trembles. Her breaths are broken and short. Once she mutters my name, but nothing can stop me. My muscles, my jaws, are set. I drag her into the mouth of the cave.

Inside, I light the lantern. She watches through the glass as the flames rise to lick at her cheeks. Her hair, her clothes are dripping wet, and her hand is clammy as I take it and lead her inside. She walks with me, her steps matching mine, until suddenly she stops. A crunching sound: the bones. By the lantern she sees them, horns and shanks, spines and skulls thick on the floor, and on the wall—pictures.

"What is this . . . ?"

"The hunt," I explain. "Drawn by the giants in winter. See how they kill with nothing but stones." I sweep the lantern across the pictures, turn them like pages in her notebook. "See them on their hands and knees, eating."

"Stop it," she pleads. Fear freezes her face.

"There is nothing like it in all the world. Iblis told me."

"Iblis?"

"To eat the flesh while it's warm and gushing. To eat as if you yourself were being eaten."

"We should go back."

I pull her, hard, into the cave. Past where the pictures end and the bones turn to dust. Soggy dust, soaked in a heavy syrup. The smell is heavy, too. I step carefully, heel-toe, heel-toe. Over bones different from those before: white, freshly-gnawed. A hoof, a thigh, ribs like pale fingers praying. Shreds of fleece and hide. And there, like a sentry blocking our path, its eyes afire with lamplight, a ram's head.

Revital screams. She tries to break loose, but my fingers won't let her. Like teeth, they sink into the pulp of her hand. "Imagine," I whisper. "The jaws moving inside you. Emptying you into another."

"Bobby, please . . ."

"Your body opened as it has never been opened. So wide it can never be closed."

She shivers. Her freckles are sparks, the gold in her eyes is molten.

"You saw the pictures—the hunters' delight." I pull her forward, deeper. "To eat and be eaten, all at once, that is the true heaven. Iblis says."

I pull but she no longer resists. Her body is as still as a carcass which I haul into the den. Into another sound now, a low and sleepy growl. Here, the smell is heaviest; wetness drapes the air. I cannot speak, can hardly breathe. Revital whimpers. The swish of lion tail on rock, mane whisking the dust. We have found it. The secret we have always known but never dared to confess. I put my arm through Revital's and hold her close beside me. Together we step, heel to toe, toward the spirit . . .

She breaks, suddenly, and runs. Footsteps echo down the cave, bones crackle. She runs blindly, stumbles into walls; she's on her hands and knees until finally she meets the night. She is out in the cool air, on the face of the cliff, but with no way down again. Rocks flee from her grasp. She slips and catches herself, slips and is caught on a thorny ledge. All this I imagine and more: Revital falling through the air and breaking on the sand below. Her blood will flow through the wadi.

"Revital!" I call after her, but the only answer is wind.

She does not die. The cave, the spirit, spares her. I follow the footprints through the wadi and all the way back to camp. Her tent is dark; not even the coffee is brewing. Yet I can feel a shudder in its flaps and hear the sand around it stirring. I squat on the ridge with the lantern on my lap. Listen through the rest of the night and long after dawn to the drone of Revital's weeping.

And it came to pass on the morrow that an evil spirit from God came upon Saul and he raved throughout the House; and David played on his harp as always. The spear was in Saul's hands and he raised it saying 'I will pin David to the wall with it!' But David turned aside and Saul was afraid of David because the spirit of the Lord was with him.

My father recites from the Bible, louder than ever, as if Revital could hear. She cannot, of course, being far away in her tent with the flaps laced tight, a wall of wind between us. It has risen, finally, the wind. The winter thunders into the valley like a herd of beasts. No hunter, not even the giants, could stop it. A storm unfolds in the southern sky, above the Firing Zone. Lightning, sharp as flint, pierces the clouds. Soon they will gush with rain.

Another night with the Book of Samuel. David hiding in the Wilderness of Zif, in his cave with the wild goats and the Holy Spirit upon him. David, his hands stained with the blood of Goliath, weighted with the prize of his head. Who better knew the power of stones?

My father's words blow like gusts, they fan the flames in my head. The same flames that once burnt in King David's heart the day that he danced naked around the Ark, around and around, so that the people thought he was crazy. One must stay away from people, Iblis says, they can never understand. The mad delight of spinning, the wildness of wind and sand.

I alone, at this late hour, am listening. The others have long gone to sleep. My mother's cheek on her own fat arm, her mouth open as if to scream but all that comes forth is a snore. Her scar, wet with drool, appears to bleed. As if the wound were still open, kept fresh by her teeth that bite it secretly during the day. My mother with her children asleep on her bosom, biting for all of them—for me, too, as if it were not too late.

My mother, my brothers, everybody is asleep, and my father is waiting for me to drop off too. He gazes into eyes which have seen him speaking to Revital. His blue eyes on my black as if to test which color, which fire, were stronger. It is a contest I will not shrink from, not tonight. Though the sky outside is lashed with lightning, and the Firing Zone with bombs—phosphorous, surely Iblis is pleased—I will look only at him. He must not leave my sight.

He is fixed. Framed by the tent flaps with a halo of hellfire. I know the signs. The dullness in the eyes, the hand that grows too heavy for the Book, and words like the wounded crawling: *How the mighty have fallen . . . Tell it not in Gat . . . publish not . . . in Ashkelon . . . Mountains of Gilboa give no dew . . . for the shield of Saul is cast away . . . Saul . . . swifter than eagles . . . stronger than a lion.*

Soon the Bible drifts to the end of his cot and his body floats down beside it. Lying on his back, throat to the night, he watches the lantern dying. He rests uneasily. From side to side my father turns and mumbles. After midnight, my mother rises and moves the children to their cots before slipping back quietly into her own. The tent is thick with dreams. The children with visions of goats' milk and my mother of steamy streets. So different from mine. Ancient, without end or beginning. Spirits and snakes, lions and devils, the sand all strewn with bones. A seamless sleep, I dream of the desert and wake to it.

But I will not sleep tonight, nor even close my eyes. They stay wide open until my father's are shut, then guide me through the flaps. Out into the wind that is arousing the sand, grain by grain, like David his men to war. Wind and sand prick my face as I move up the ridge, toward the sound of splashing water.

Water slaps the sides of the porcelain tub. I fall to my knees and peer. In the lightning I see strips of naked flesh—they gleam in the flash of cluster bombs. A shoulder, first, and then a flank glistening with suds. Like my mother, she scrubs hard to cleanse herself. Head rises to water pouring, her hair in heavy strands. Her back is to me, a back like the desert—ribs for ridges, rising dunes—through which the water flows, carving.

I watch as Revital bathes. Revealing things I have never seen, nor even imagined, a mystery as wondrous as the cave's. I wait with my breath sealed in my heart, amazed that she cannot hear its pounding. Wait for the slightest turn that will show me more. Teeth grind, muscles twitch, and the hunger grows deeper, needier, ready to feed on itself.

Then it happens. She turns but only slightly, exposing a single breast. It shimmers, an oval stone, and seems to float in the air. The skin looks as sleek as metal, and the nipple, strangely, like the eraser at the end of her pencil.

I cannot bear it any more. I must bite my arm— anything to keep from howling—and taste my own rusty blood. Eyes closed, I wish that the dream will fade. But my dreams are seamless and everywhere Revital bathes. She bathes and is suddenly startled by a sound which is not the wind's. Crossing arms over her breasts, she turns away from the tent. The flaps are still stirring, and I think: my father. He, too, has been watching. Not only Revital, but me.

I awaken to the sound of thunder. So loud it makes me think a storm has come to the desert. Sand sticks to my brow as I lift my face from the ground. I have slept here, the place from which I watched Revital. Stayed here long after she disappeared behind a towel as she ran to her tent. The tub is empty now. It stands, our altar, gray in the early morning. Above it rises a pillar of smoke, very black—not from the tub itself, I see, but from the Firing Zone in the distance. The pillar does not move—it is no jeep's or truck's—but climbs higher and higher. Then I remember: the night of engineers. The Bangalore Torpedoes, the mines. Iblis . . .

I run. Faster than an ibex or gazelle, than any hunter. Flying, my feet barely skimming the sand. Iblis. The mines. Though I have often closed my eyes, at Sunday services or Vespers, and cupped my hands, I have never truly prayed. But I pray now. To God and the spirits, to giants and lions and stones. There is so much I have yet to learn. Take a leg or another finger, I plead, but leave his teachings for me.

The pillar grows thicker as I near. I can smell the bitter smoke and hear a painful cry. A cry no man could make, not even Iblis. A yap, a snarl. *Ma-Fish-Ismo*—Has-No-Name. The dog with three legs is hobbling around the newborn crater. Deep and coated with coal, darkly smoking. The mutt for once ignores me as I approach, and look down into that terrible hole.

How the mighty have fallen in battle!

Rags and buttons, bits of white that once were bones. Burnt and smoking, but with hardly a trace of blood.

You were dear to me, your love more wonderful than the love of women.

Mines are hungry, Iblis said, they'll bite off more than

they'll swallow. A fingernail, a tooth. And gazing at me from its nest of cinders, like the egg of a crystal bird, the eye. Lapis blue as the day long ago when he stole it from the Austrian duchess. Unblinking, all-seeing. Gently I bend to pick it up, my face encased in glass.

How the mighty have fallen and the weapons of war cast away.

I turn, winding my away around the craters, until I come to the last one, coated with a cluster bomb's beads. On my knees I sweep away the coal. They are still there, just where he buried them. The mines stacked like an ancient tomb. Each with stars and numbers—a deadly curse—and a spirit that lives to kill. I count them, five, six, seven mines, though all I need is one. Then, neatly, I cover them. Into a mound I pile the coal, and mark the grave with his eye.

Has-No-Name is scampering around the crater which holds his master's remains, sniffs at them and whimpers at the smoke still rising. The dog does not see me as I sneak up behind him, heel to toe, and reach into my pocket for the stone. I hold it high above my head and rear it back, my arm tight like a sling. The muscles snap, the stone flies, hissing through the air. Onto the skull with a crack of a shooting pistol.

Has-No-Name stares at me. The shattered head swings side to side as if trying to understand. Foam flows from its mouth and blood from its ears; the legs—one, two, three—buckle. Then, like a tent in the wind, the animal tumbles. Over and down into the crater with the ashes of

Iblis. I watch as it shivers, and the carcass slowly grows still.

I do not run back to the ridge. Though my father might beat me, I take my time. Things are much clearer now. Iblis has taught me, even in death. I know now all that I need.

The stone is in my hand as I wander back to camp. It is wet and slippery but still I clutch it. So hard it cuts my palm. Blood mingles with blood, man's and animal's, thicker than syrup—sweeter—as with lashes of my tongue, I taste it.

In the dream that is not a dream my mother sings to me. She sits on the edge of my bed in America, in her purple dress and painted lips. There is a sour scent beneath the perfume—I can smell it as she leans over and sings:

If religion were a thing that money could buy
the rich would live and the poor would die

Her bosom is a floating shadow, the light from the kitchen is her halo. The only light in this house of dirty windows.

All my trials, Lord—
Soon be over

In the street below I can hear cars and music, laughter and shouts. Bells in a tower, in the truck jingling with ice cream. It is very hot in the room, and hard to breathe. My mother puts a cool towel to my forehead and dabs the skin beside my eyes. And all the while she sings:

> *The River Jordan is deep and cold*
> *It chills the body but not the soul*

A low, sweet voice, gurgly like the beer she drinks. I hope she never stops. I want her to sit by my bed forever in her purple dress, singing to me. But this is a dream from which I must awaken. In the wedge of light between bosom and armpit I can see into the kitchen. I see the empty table beneath the naked bulb, the single chair with the torn seat, and on it the person I have always called my father.

> *The River Jordan is swift and wide*
> *Milk and honey on the other side*

He sits with his face in his hands, cheeks dancing. His eyes burn the pages of the Bible. His lips move not with words but with anger. My mother's song seems to harm him, as if each word were a well-flung stone. His hair is short—rows of reddish bristles which he tries to grasp while grinding a palm into his forehead. I feel sorry, but not for him; afraid, but only for her.

> *Hush little baby don't you cry,*
> *you know your Daddy was born to die*

"Enough!" he hollers, and his fist slams onto the table. "Godlessness!"

The red lips are suddenly on my cheek, a kiss soft and warm. The bed rises as she leaves, the floor creaks with her heels. Then darkness as the door closes tight. The halo is stretched to a square around the hinges. Shadows flutter in the cracks like devils. Whispers become hisses become shouts. Something crashes, a rain of glass, and then a crack as sharp as lightning. The sound of that fist on wood, on bone. I curl in my bed, under the tent of my blanket. Peeking through the flaps at the storm outside. The room is a desert, and I am alone.

Sometime later, when all is quiet, she slips back into my dream. She rolls back the blanket and runs fingers through my waves of hair. Trembling fingers which stroke my brows and cup my cheeks. The lips are shaking, too, as they touch mine. Again I smell the beer and perfume. I taste the paint which is wetter now and sticky. A taste I have known only once in my life, after falling on the street, my nose bleeding into my mouth. I taste it and swallow and I am hungry for more. But all I get is music.

All my trials, Lord—
soon be over

I've heard that song many times since then. Under my blanket and within the tent as the wind rose from the desert. As my father grunted and her cot quickly groaned. I sang it to myself over and over as he forced her to make brothers whose names I could hardly remember, and the sister I would never forget. I heard and swore that I would someday taste that taste again.

The last lion was the greatest, Iblis told me. Bigger and faster than any lion before it, and hungrier, for all the ibex and the gazelles were gone, and the giants, too, scattered in bones. The lion crouched in the cave and watched the valley below. Nothing moved, nothing breathed, only the wind-driven sand. It might have eaten that, too, until its belly, like a sack of grain, burst at the seams. But then the lion saw something, Iblis said, something slithering in the dust. It must have looked like a snake at first, but one with fur instead of scales. But the lion did not wait; it pounced. Jaws crushing, it swallowed as fast as it could. The lion howled with pain and roared with delight as the tail became a leg and the leg a rump. Flanks and paws, kidneys and bone—round and round the lion turned, spurred by madness—spine to neck to mane. And then the mouth wound about itself and, with a last vicious bite, it vanished. The lion was no more but much, much more; dead, it would live forever. A spirit which spun in the deepest of caves, and roared with a bottomless hunger.

The flaps part for me as I sail out into the night. I float over the pens and across the sand on which my feet do not leave prints. The stone is in my pocket and beside it is the knife which I pulled from beneath the tub. Steel and rock rattle in my jacket, a sound which only I can hear.

But then another sound. From Revital's tent—a ewe's

bleating, the grunts of a mongrel dog. She is not alone. Yoni's jeep is where it was the other day, just below the ridge. There are no sacks of grain in the back, no cans of fruit or even a chocolate bar. He has not come for me. With my best cat walk I creep to the back of the tent. To the slit that I cut in it with the knife.

Revital lies naked on the dust. Like an ibex in death, she squirms. Her arms flail, her fingers claw the flesh of Yoni's shoulders. He rides on top of her. The shoulders rise and fall, his hips rear and shove. In the moonlight I can see his blade, glistening wet as again and again it plunges. Revital groans and arches her back to the thrust. Her hair is wild, coated with sand and knotted with Yoni's curls. Her mouth is a crater, her tongue flutters like smoke. Then, slowly, he slides down her belly. On his hands and knees with his head between her thighs. Eating, gorging himself on her wound. She clutches his hair, gasping in delight, just as Iblis said.

Down the ridge I swoop like a gust of wind. This is the moment and I must not stop. In the valley the flock has awakened. A fleecy cloud, it thickens with the smell of danger. All but the mangy ram. It stands apart, as always, threatening to stray. Ready to charge with its newly sawn-off horns. But my stone catches it first.

Well-thrown, hard enough to kill, the stone smacks the ram on its spine. But the animal is hardly shaken. It staggers back and forth and aims its stubby horns at my knees. Before it can move though, I leap. I dive, fast and straight, clutching the knife. One hand grabs the flank while the other points the blade and pushes it, deep, into the belly.

The ram buckles on top of me. Its head lashes this way and that; a horn finds my neck and cuts it. Yet I feel no pain, only rage. I hug the ram around the middle and roll. Stabbing, hammering, the blade sinking high to the olive wood handle. The ram thrashes at first, then shivers. It turns over, legs spread, onto the sand. The flesh parts and surrenders its innards—peaches, plums, apricots, all flowing in heavy syrup.

Now is the time. Crouching, I bend forward. The smell is terribly thick. My lips touch the flesh and shut with the taste—stale, rotten—but I still force them open. I force my face into the gash and try to bite, but all I can do is gag. I bare my teeth and stretch my jaws. A roar rolls across the valley. Warm syrup splatters my cheeks and pours down my throat. I drink and swallow as fast as I can, yet still it gushes. It coats my chest and anoints my hair. I bathe in it. The mad delightful hunger, spirit with tail and mane. There, on the sand, in the moonlight, the giant at last eats his kill.

A scream awakens the camp. My mother first and then the brothers. They stagger through the flaps, pale and confused, as if the tent were on fire. But my father is angry. He comes last, fists ready, looking for a fight. He stomps to the edge of the ridge where the others have gathered around Revital. It was her scream that woke them and now she stands with her hair wild and knotted and her baggy clothes encrusted with dust. Only the notebook seems as clean as ever, folded around half a pencil. She holds it tight in one hand, while the other points down into the valley.

My mother mutters a prayer. Her hands cover the eyes of two of her children, her hips push the others away. She steps back from the edge as if the valley were Gehenna itself, all the while biting her scar.

Revital opens her mouth for another scream, but all she can do is whimper. My father clasps her by the shoulders. "Calm yourself," he says to her, "Have faith."

Drawing himself straight, my father goes down the ridge and walks upon the valley. Two, three steps is all it takes, and already he has reached the carcass. A shell, really, skin stretched over barren ribs which close upon nothing but rot. A husk. The ram's eyes, pasty white, are wide. They look up toward the camp, at the tub, freshly-washed and glistening. They point directly at me.

My father sees what the ram cannot. That I am clean, too clean. He picks up the knife, and feels the wetness of its handle. With eyes burning—bluer, glassier than those of Iblis—he storms to me at the top of the ridge.

"You saw it."

I nod.

"And what did you do?"

I shrug and in shrugging reveal my wound.

My father tugs the collar from my neck. "And this?"

"A thorn. It caught me chasing a stray."

"Liar." My father's hand snaps up to strike. He is big, very big, but not as much as before. I have grown, too.

He does not hit me—not yet—but says, "You saw it and did nothing."

"There was nothing to do. It is too powerful."

"Not for me." He blows his chest full. "I would have torn it in two."

Now it is my turn to act confused. "Can one tear what cannot be touched?"

"Stop talking foolishness," he shouts. "With one of your stones you could've killed it."

"Killed what?"

He points down into the valley, at the hollowed-out ram. There, in the blood-soaked sand, a print. Dark as a shadow, sharp as a picture scraped into rock: a paw print.

"The lion," my father says. "One stone would have done it."

I look him in the eye. "Lion? But, Father, there are no more lions. The Bedouin killed them all."

"All but one."

"Not even one."

He takes my collar again, and pulls me toward the edge. "No? No?" His fingers fasten around the back of my neck, they find my open wound, "Then what, pray God, is this?"

I look at the print, at the carcass and the eyes frozen in horror. "No lion," I whisper, "Spirit."

Another scream. Revital has heard me. She screams through her teeth and the knuckles they bite. My father stares at her and then back at me. His fist lands on my temple, a terrible blow that would have felled me had not his other hand been clutching my neck. I try to break lose but I am caught. The jaws of his fingers tighten as the paw strikes again—my forehead and cheek. Blood flushes from my nose and into my mouth, that rusty taste, and darkness fills my skull.

My father strikes but I no longer feel the pain. No longer smell or taste, hear nothing but the children's cries and Revital's whimpering. I look up at the raw morning sky, at the sun with its rays like knives.

I wait for the blade to descend. All is silent but for the wind and the grunt of heavy breathing. But nothing happens. A moment passes, and I look again, this time in wonder. My father's hand is stayed by another, far smaller but godlike in strength. Face placid, eyes calm, my mother holds him with no sign of weakness or strain, only the blood that streams from her scar.

By sunset we are gathered around the tub. Dressed in white, as we are commanded, barefoot in the cold sand. My mother and the children. Only Revital stands apart, in the shadows. She still wears her baggy clothes, though they hang on her like wet laundry, and carries the notebook in which she no longer writes. She watches with eyes whose green has turned a muddy brown; the golden flakes are stains of yellow. Her pupils shift back and forth, fast, as once her pencil darted.

We wait in silence. Nobody moves, nobody whispers, not even the children. Only the animal, a ram with hobbled hooves, bleats and rocks in the sand. The tub has been scrubbed and turned upside down. Its flat bottom gleams gray in the last of the light. Behind us, suddenly, the tent rustles. The flaps snap and part for my father. He, too, is dressed in white, a long robe with no crease or seam. He moves among us but gazes straight ahead, at the tub and the hobbled ram. He stands before them with his back erect, his eyes gazing up at the heavens. At the horizon and the clouds, at the faint ghost of moon—he takes them all in with his arms out-spreading. He says a prayer which only God can hear.

The ram is lifted, no heavier than a sack, in my father's big hands. Laid on the base of the tub and held there as the knife appears. The blade has been sharpened, the handle gleams with oil. The knife rises and hovers over the ram then, lightning-like, it flashes. The animal jerks, its legs twitch in the rope. Blood speckles the seamless robe and runs over the base of the tub. Into the rusty puddle my father dips his finger. Seven times he dips and seven times he sprinkles. And with each we sing together *Hallelujah.*

Hallelujah, May His will be done. We pray, but Revital says nothing. She does not stir, even as my father scoops out the innards—two kidneys, a liver—and handfuls of fat. These will be burned as a sin offering. The head, cut off, with the legs and belly will be tossed into the valley and left for the ravens and dogs. *Amen, amen sela,* the children cry. I cry, too, so beautiful is my father's work. Amen, I say to Revital, trying to teach her. But all she does is shake her head as though to shoo a fly or awaken herself from a dream.

I say to her quietly, "This will stop it."

I step toward her but she backs away, deeper into the shadows.

"The sacrifice will fill the spirit—you must believe."

She glares at me. "Don't tell me what I must believe!" Anger gushes beneath her cheeks. "There is no lion, and no spirit, got that?"

"But Iblis said . . ."

"Iblis can rot in Hell."

Now it is I who turn away. "Iblis is dead."

To my surprise, Revital laughs. "As if he'd ever lived!"

Somebody—could it be my mother?—whispers "hush." Revital lowers her voice. "He is in your head, Bobby, just like that spirit. Inside you, there's a devil."

Late that night, by the light of sacrificial fires, the children line up for their bath. Once again the tub has been turned, and once again scrubbed. My mother serves at her altar. But I will not go—not tonight or ever again. My mother senses this and does not beckon to me to come. And my father, a blade shimmering in the distance, he knows it too. Never again will that water wash my skin nor will his knife shave my scalp. From now on my hair will grow wild over my shoulders—*Tell it in Gath, in Ashkelon*—a glorious mane.

At last, the devil comes to the desert. A pillar of wind which feeds on sand and drills down to bedrock. It churns, so strong it can tear a man in two. Not even a giant could stop it, Iblis once said. Spinning, it turns skin into shreds and bones into dust. It comes, rising from the Firing Zone and blazing across the valley. Like a madman it whirls. Like David, naked and dancing.

Searching for straying sheep, I am lost in the memory of last night. Of the flesh in my mouth and the syrup in my throat. The hunger which deepened even as I filled it. Last night two sheep, and the one before it, three. Each morning brings its carcasses, the sand stained and etched with prints. So the flock, once fat, grows thinner. And each day my father paces back and forth on the ridge, one hand clutching the Bible and the other curled in a fist, praying and cursing at once.

The devil approaches. It lashes toward the camp where my father stands, his back to the desert. He does not see it, though, and I do not warn him. But then, suddenly, it turns eastward. Toward the top of the ridge and the tent in which Revital sits.

Lately she appears only at sunset. Sits on the edge of the ridge holding her notebook, her hair lost in the wind. She looks out to the valley, waiting. For Yoni, maybe, or winter. But over the horizon the gray clouds gather and still there is no sign of the jeep. She does not know what I know: Yoni will come less often now, once every month, because of the rains. The wadis when flooded can snap the yellow jeep as easily as I did her pencil. Against water, even a pistol is useless.

The devil sweeps toward the tent. A quiet hiss is all it makes—sand slicing the air. It is tall, twice my height, and darker than a crater. Twirling, churning, it pauses before the tent as if to savor the kill. Flaps crack and canvas rattles, stakes fly from the ground. And as the tent unwinds I can see Revital with her hands on her ears, eyes closed and mouth open. Her body is frozen but her hair leaps, as if it had caught on fire.

I do not have to run—the wind sucks me inward. It drags me into the tent, the very eye of the devil. I stretch out to hold her but a force tears us apart. Armed with sand, it cuts my lips and cheeks; my fingers bend like twigs. Yet I reach her, catching first a tatter of her shirt, one shoulder and then another, and pulling her toward me, holding her, as the devil closes around us.

Piece by piece the devil rips the clothes from our backs. It eats them along with the sand. We are nearly naked, laughing and screaming as we turn. For a dazzling moment we are alone. No camp, no valley, the desert as distant as the memory of that city long ago. Around and around, like a lion with its tail in its mouth, we slowly disappear.

Then, just as swiftly as it came, the devil departs. Leaves us panting in a circle of rags. Revital blinks the dust from her eyes and glares at me with horror. She sees my nakedness and, sensing her own, hugs some canvas to her breasts. She backs away and I follow, wanting only to ask if she is all right, though I know she will not answer. She backs away but something has changed. On its wheel of wind the desert has reshaped her. Remade her, a hungry being, in my own image.

Outside the remains of her tent my father gasps. He

has rushed to save her from the devil, from me. Soon he is joined by my mother and then the children. All of them standing there without a word, wondering at the miracle before them. A pair of giants alone in their crater, together in their cave. The winter sky gathers grayly; the wind whispers of storms. And from the heavens, the pages of a notebook come fluttering, anointing our heads like rain.

Great sheets of rain as thick as canvas fall. The sheep huddle together, while we hide inside our tent. The rain beats against the flaps and seeps between the stakes. The lantern dances drunkenly. On one side of the tent my father prays and on the other my mother hugs her children. But it does no good. God is angry, the Bible tells us—the spirits are mad, said Iblis. The ground trembles beneath us; boulders fall from the cliffs and burst into sand. Seven days and seven nights it will last, an awful chastisement. And in the end, our sins will be swept away.

79

I sit in a corner by myself, waiting. The cots are stacked with sacks of flour, so there is only the wet ground on which to crouch. No matter; the wait, I know, will not be long. Already on the first night she comes. Almost falling into the tent with her feet and hair full of mud. She shivers terribly—her clothes are in tatters—and her skin has been washed of its color. My mother rushes to wrap a blanket around her and tries to steer her to my corner. But Revital pulls out of her grip, with her last bit of strength, hurrying to the other side of the tent, as far from me as possible.

We wait like that for nights and days—the darkness

outside will not reveal the difference. Silent, unmoving, except when a bolt of lightning crashes above and makes us jump. The children cry and my mother holds them tight beneath her blanket. But my father does not jump, does not cry. With his hand to the lamp he reads aloud from the Bible:

A fire has kindled my anger, and shall burn the nether-most parts of the earth. They shall be sucked empty by hunger and devoured by burning heat. The teeth of beasts shall be set upon them . . .

Revital listens and nods her head. Once or twice I hear her whisper Amen. Amen, I say, though my mind is elsewhere. I am busy completing the plan. On the walls of my mind the pictures surface. Older than time yet bright as blood, the entire story from beginning to end. He will come, I tell myself, tomorrow or the next day, any minute now, my deliverance.

And so the hours pass. Breakfast and dinner my mother makes bread on a low flame. Flat and gritty, it warms our hands and fills our bellies. But the wet and the cold are piercing. My brothers cough, my mother moans in her sleep. My father reads on but in a voice which only he can hear, and the Bible sags in his hand. Revital listens, though, and says her Amens. Sickly Hallelujahs arise from her corner. With eyes that never close, never move, I watch her but she will not look at me. Instead, she gazes through the flaps, through the gray veils of rain which hide the valley. She, too, is waiting. Like me, she knows that he will come.

Then, one morning—or is it night?—the rumble starts. Faint, at first, no more than a whisper. The children hear it one by one and lift their feverish heads. My mother and father blink in the dark, but only Revital rises. She leaps to her feet and runs out into the storm. I cannot stop her—must not, for all this is in the plan. The rumble becomes a growl and then a roar. The sound of tires groping for sand, the gears painfully grinding. Revital slips and falls, gets to her feet and stumbles again down the side of the ridge. Into the mud on her hands and knees with the sheep swarming around her. She might be drowned or crushed but the flock quickly parts—not for her, but for the jeep which arrives just in time to save her.

Once yellow, the jeep is now coated in black, its wheels as big as boulders. Yoni is different, too. Without his sunglasses his eyes are small, squinting like a snake's in the rain. His clothes are soaked and spattered with mud, and he looks less like one who has come to save us than one who needs saving himself. Still, he helps Revital to stand, then crawls up the slippery ridge.

"Is everybody all right?"

The children, my mother and father just gaze at him. With blankets over their heads they look like a tribe of Bedouin, a nation of priests. Yoni asks again, speaking to my father. But he can only look away. Not for this, not for Yoni and his muddy jeep, has he prayed all these years. He says nothing, but my mother comes forward and nods.

"Good," Yoni says. "Then we have to get moving. The trail is still open but not for long. The whole valley is flooded."

Gazing over the ridge, I can see that he is right. The valley is covered in water, a shimmering shield. So the desert cleanses itself, protects itself from intruders. Soon the flood will rise and overflow the ridge, taking the tent and our entire camp with it. Yoni must move swiftly, and so must I.

"I can fit all the children in and one or two adults. But the more I take the heavier we'll be."

My mother looks at her children, at my father who sees only the flood. Already she is shepherding them toward the jeep. She lifts them, lighter than fleece, into the back, and holds out her hand to Revital.

"No," she says. "I'll wait for the next one."

Yoni pleads, "But there may not be a next one."

"No," she says again, just as I knew she would.

Then it is my mother's turn. She opens her arms and spreads her fingers to me.

I tell her, "You go. I am not afraid." Her face, soft and round, tilts to the side. Her eyes—eyes which I have not seen this close, this warm, in a very long time—fill with tears. "Go, Mother, and do not fear. This was meant to be."

And then she speaks. My mother who has not spoken to me, to me her son, for many years, since the time of the doctor. "I am so sorry, Robert. I wanted only good things for you. A good long life with happiness. I am so sorry."

She starts to bite the scar above her chin, but I touch my fingers to her lips. I tug the ends of the blanket around her face, and place my hands on her shoulders. "I am happy, Mother. Happier than you could ever imagine. And my life will be very long, don't worry. I will live forever."

From under the blanket the weeping comes, but I will not let her wait. I guide her to the side of the jeep, and help her climb inside.

"I'll be back as soon as I can," Yoni shouts over a blast of lightning. "Stay in the tent as long as possible, then get to the top of the ridge."

Yoni starts toward the jeep, but then he stops. As if he has forgotten something, as if at last he understands, he turns and looks at me with terror. Without his sunglasses, the cigarette, his face looks weak—white, like a slaughtered sheep's. Still, he tries to act tough, slapping the pistol on his side, and saluting the three of us who remain. The jeep grunts and spits, kicks forward with a wave of mud, and lunges onto the trail. From the ridge I can see my brothers huddled in the back, and my mother in the front with the blanket over her head, fluttering like an angel.

Soon the jeep is swallowed by the rain, its tracks licked clean. "We must go back into the tent," my father announces, though he is looking only at Revital. Wordlessly she follows him. Walks right past me without a glance. But I do not mind. Now, like a spirit, I can roam. The stones in my pocket and in my jacket, stuffed, a sack that I have emptied of grain.

*   *   *

Once I ran inside these wadis. Faster and faster as the seasons passed, each year crossing the valley more swiftly than the one before. But now I fly. I glide and soar, though the mud grips my feet and water rushes to drown me. The older wadis, those I knew, are gone. Erased like the lines in Revital's notebook, while new ones are scribbled in rock.

I follow a jagged gorge, turning east. Down a chute and around a bend where I am met by a wall of water. I leap to the bank and try to climb as the flood laps at my feet. I claw the pebbles which turn to sand, and dig my knees into the cracks. I rise, but not before the flood is at my chest, yanking my jacket, dragging me down. But it cannot have me. Not now, with so little time. I pull myself over the top of the bank. Wiping the mud from my eyes, I check to see that I still have my stone and my sack. Then, once again, I take flight.

The valley is already a lake. The flood is upon the face of the desert, covering all. Beneath the shallow waters, though, I can see the craters. I have reached the Firing Zone. I count them as I move—four craters, five—until I reach the very last. Until, poking through the slime, it greets me—Iblis's glassy blue eye.

I hold the eye in my hand, smooth and cold, and slip it into my pocket. Then I dig. Scooping the mud between my legs like Has-No-Name whose carcass now floats on the water. I smile with the first glint of gray. The surface slick with its secret markings, the curse on all who tread. I dig and pull, scoop and lift and then suddenly fall onto my buttocks. In my lap there rests a mine. Still alive, still hungry, ready as Iblis said to bite off more than it swallows.

The way back to the trail is tougher now. The rains are heavier and the floods run deep. The mine keeps slipping through my arms. Darkness thickens; in minutes the unseen sun will set. I do not have long. Even now I can see to the west, from the highway, how a pair of lights stop and turn, entering the valley in the direction of our camp. I scramble to a lane of liquid dust—all that remains of the trail—and fall to my hands and knees. Here the digging is harder. I scoop and gouge, scrape till my fingers are raw. Soon there is a hole big enough to bury the mine, and I do, together with Iblis's eye. Only then I head back to the camp.

I am wet and tired but there is still so much to do. Looking up to the ridge I can see our tent or what's left of it. The flaps are torn and the stakes uprooted. Nothing remains but a sagging hood, the faintest halo of lamplight. Inside, I know, Revital crouches with my father. Perhaps he is hugging her, kissing her and telling her about God and His redemption. An evil picture, I want to scrub it clean, but now is not the time. First come the sheep. A ram and four ewes, the last of the flock. I cat walk toward them on toes like paws. In a darkness as deep as hunger.

The hunger is still strong long after my belly is full. After my flesh is more animal than man, soaked more by blood than water. Then, as if by commandment, the downpour ceases. Stars arise through the clouds, the moon is resurrected. In the valley, on the trail, the headlights no longer move.

*   *   *

Yoni steps hard on the brakes. He climbs out of his jeep, and squints into the darkness. Takes two steps and rubs his eyes. Above the purr of the engine he hears a distant roar. Pinned by the pitchfork of headlights he sees the teeth and the blood-red mane. He sees but at first cannot believe. But then the roar grows louder, along with the thud of paws. Yoni reaches for his pistol.

With shaking hands he tries to aim. His finger squirms on the trigger. The pistol leaps, spitting fire. One shot, two. And still the thudding comes. Three, four, five, as fast as he can shoot, but nothing stops it. Yoni runs back to the jeep, turns and fires twice more. Seven bullets and none have hit. A pistol is useless against spirits. He dives behind the wheel and steps on the gas. The jeep jerks forward and charges.

Like a stone, it strikes to kill. And like a sheep it is eaten. The jeep explodes in a blinding flash. A blast of sound which in the camp my father will mistake for lightning. Shards of metal, of canvas and bone, whirl into the night. On the trail spits a ball of fire, a bush which burns in the downpour. Soon all that remains is a coal-black crater and a pillar of smoke. The sacrifice is finished. His will has been done. Hallelujah.

It is dawn by the time I return to the camp. The hour when, once, my father used to beat me. But there is no strength in him now. His camp has been washed away. The pens, the tent, even the tub is turned on its side, rusted. Only Revital still sits cross-legged in the mud. Sits writing hard and fast with the wrong half of a pencil, into a notebook that has long since disappeared. She is muttering something, a single word over and over. "*Tiroof*," she says, a Hebrew word with two different meanings—madness and the eating of flesh.

I wade through the mud to where my father sprawls, on his hands and knees before the carcasses. Though it might be the wind, for a moment I think I hear him weeping. But when I near him he stops and looks at me. He rises, no longer a giant but an old man stooped and gray. His face is gray, too—the fire has been doused—and the red has drained from his hair. I want to laugh, the plan is so simple, but all I do is greet him.

"Good morning, Father."

He mumbles, "It's gone, all of it."

"His will be done," I reply.

"Not His, the lion's."

I pretend I do not understand.

"It's killed the last of them."

"But Father I told you, there is no lion."

My father stiffens. "Silence!" he shouts and for a second a spark rekindles in his eyes.

"The spirit, Father," I remind him, "You believe in so many things, why not that?"

"Blasphemy. Idolatry."

I shake my head. "No, Father, the truth."

"Where did you get that?" My father points to the knife with the olive wood handle.

"Under the tub, where it always was."

"Give it to me."

I step back—I cannot make it easy—but still he comes. "Give it to me. Now!"

My father lunges at the knife. He twists my wrist until the blade falls to the mud where it is trapped beneath his feet. "Spirit," he laughs, "I'll show you what spirit."

"No, Father, you shouldn't . . ."

He turns and walks away, faster than I thought him able. I must run to keep up. He storms through the mud, sinking and slipping, all the while waving the knife above his head. I look back at Revital. She watches us but does not see, scribbles but cannot write. This, too, is good, I think. All is as planned.

He makes his way across the valley. Through the freshly-cut wadis and the sands heavy with death. I walk behind him and tell him again and again how he must not go. How he must believe in the spirit and not fight it. But the more I say, the faster he moves with the knife slicing before him.

It does not take long. Less than an hour and already we reach the base of the cliff. He does not wait, my father, but climbs. Pulls himself up the face of rock too loose to hold his body. A rain of stones falls upon my head, but still I follow. Into the bleeding light of dawn we rise, to the top of the cliff and the cave there awaiting us.

Gasping before the great black mouth, I beg him one last time. "Please," I cry, "it is stronger than you, Father."

And there he looks at me, at last. A look such as Moses gave, on the mountain before being gathered to God. His eyes see the land, the past and the future. All lies before him, but none of it is his. My father grasps the knife tight in his hand. He knows how to use it, remembers that night long ago when the robber came to kill us. But inside the cave is no ordinary robber. Its jaws hold a mouthful of knives. Yet I say nothing—it is useless. My father recites a silent blessing. Then, like a mirage, like a miracle, he is gone.

I stand at the mouth of the cave and wait for what I know will come. The echo of his footsteps, deafening at first, grow faint. Jaws of darkness close around him and swallow him whole. I count my breaths, imagine him pausing to look at the bones, at the pictures scraped into the walls. What horrors must flash through his mind, I wonder, what revelations. But they will not stop him. My plan, my will, must be done.

The waters grow still over the valley, the wind surrenders and dies. All is quiet as the moment before the storm. And then it bursts. Noises fly out of the cave, howls and roars. Sounds both man and animal, the killer and its kill. The devilish voice of hunger. Then a scream. It whirls out of the cave in a blast of rotten air. Spins past me on its path across the desert.

I wipe a hand on the back of my jacket—hard work is yet to be done—and dip it into the pocket. I hold it, feeling the weight, the power. Against spirits, knives are useless. Against giants, all one needs is a stone, and clutching it, I, too, enter the cave.

I make my way back to camp, turning as I go. Dancing around and around in a pillar of dust. I am one with the wind now, howling, roaring. To the desert I have come, a sand devil.

Knife and stone clang inside my pocket. The sack bounces against my thigh, a heavy weight, sodden. But nothing can slow my stride. With lion-like steps I head back to the ridge. To Revital who waits for me and the lives we will live forever. I will teach her, as Iblis once taught me. To hunt and to kill, to eat and be eaten. In the cave we will make our home and in the winter scrape our pictures. And with spring we shall emerge. Seasons like children will sprout from our loins, and our tribe will spread as the sands. On hands and knees we will pray to the gods and ask them to fill our hunger.

House of Bondage

A
ny afternoon, but especially Tuesdays, you can
find them in the *shuq*. Weaving through the hagglers, the
donkey carts and crates. On one hip they lug plastic wicker
baskets laden with groceries, using their bodies as ballast.
They ply the covered stalls, pausing only to squeeze a melon
or sample a grape. Deftly, they sidestep the slicks of dis-
carded gizzards. They are the daughters of Moroccan immigrants, modern working women, but still bound by their
mothers' traits—the thick black hair, the soft knowing gaze
that darkens in the presence of men. Often frail, their limbs
spindly, bent by the weight of their baskets. Yet they drag
them, like their names, traditional and jarring to the con-
temporary ear: Bruria, Mazel, or Batya.

Batya waits in the fumes of passing buses. Dust and

heat swirls on the pavement; the air is a gritty stew. With the back of a wrist she wipes her temple and herds stray hairs from her brow. The other hand coils, still clutching the basket, its plastic handles slicing into her palm.

The number four—her bus—presently arrives. Flatulent with hot metal seats and bars on the windows, it is the kind of bus no longer seen in the cities up north, in Tel Aviv or Haifa, but only here, in the boondocks of the south—rusty outside, and inside packed with workmen and housewives, Arabs and Jews, each with that identical plastic basket overflowing with food.

As always, Batya has to stand, rocking as the bus starts and jerks, stretching on the tips of her sneakers to reach the iron bar above. Heady smells envelop her, babies' cry, the radio's bleeping with news. Unpleasant but ordinary, this is part of her weekly routine. Work at the Registry, eight to four, Fridays until two; Tuesdays at the *shuq* and Saturdays—the Sabbath—at her parents' house.

It's a twenty-minute ride on the number four to her stop on the outskirts of town. From there, she walks five minutes to her building, a drab structure of chipping stucco, its balconies flagged with laundry. One side is bordered by a mangy park and the other three by sand. Here marks the farthest point of the city's sprawl; beyond it there is nothing but desert—nothing, except for the prison.

In the hallway, dank, desecrated by graffiti, Batya reaches under the broken lid of her mailbox. The contents are typical—bills for water and telephone, and her monthly treat: a fashion magazine. Grimacing, she climbs the four flights of stairs to her apartment. Her sneakers squeak and the groceries rustle—the slightest sound will alert her downstairs neighbor, Nafarstig. Gas company pensioner, curator of a rotating collection of cats, Mr. Nafarstig is always anxious to help. Whether it be carrying her basket or fixing a faucet, he's forever offering, though Batya does fine on her own. A man with one gold tooth and a priceless heart, poor old moonfaced Mr. Nafarstig, she thinks as she tiptoes past his door.

Her door has three locks, two of them added in the years since she first left home, as break-ins became a problem. She has separate keys for each. One by one the tumblers fall, soothingly clicking, until the last unleashes the door.

Wearily, she lays the keys on the stand by the telephone, and steps into the salon, as she calls it. In fact, it's little more than a foyer, sparsely furnished, with a television set and a pine wood table. An armchair, her sole indulgence, sits beneath the sill. The window above it is large, relative to the size of the room, but marred by iron grates. Installed to keep children from falling out, the grates serve a different purpose now, preventing burglars from getting in. But Batya doesn't mind. The place is solid, impervious to sand and rain, quiet except for a constant dripping sound, like a beating heart, of water.

Safely inside, exhausted, she fights the urge to drop the basket, eggs and all, and wilt into the arms of her chair. In her tiny kitchen, Batya starts to unpack. Fruits and vegetables in the refrigerator, bread and cans in the broom closet, each in its appointed place. Order is important to Batya; never once has she altered her routine.

It's then, while stacking the last of the groceries, that Batya sees it or, more accurately, senses it, for the afternoons are hazy and the desert plays tricks with her eyes. Beyond the kitchen window, across a stretch of littered sand, lies the prison. From where she stands it's no more than a blur: gates and wires, a hint of towers protruding. National Penitentiary, Southern Sector. High security, electrified fence, and widely rumored to be escape-proof. This is the vista from three of her four windows; the other looks down on the park. She can see the prison from anywhere in the apartment, except for the bathroom. And even in there she can feel it, a constant, almost comforting, presence.

She hangs the basket in the broom closet and, pinching its collar, airs out the front of her blouse. It's stained, she sees, with what first looks like grease. But no: it's blood. Blood from her hand, sliced by the basket's grips. She angles out of the kitchen, crossing the salon toward the bathroom, and the prison follows her from window to window. Winks in and out of sight like the moon in the thick of a sandstorm.

Batya pries the heel of each sneaker with the opposite toe, unzips her skirt and unclips her nape-length hair. She lifts the gold pendant—her only jewelry—from around her neck and coils it in the soap dish above the sink. The bathroom, too, is simple: plastic fixtures, whitewashed tiles. A nylon curtain half conceals the tub and, above it, a window with smoked-glass panes. It's from here, this window, that Batya can see that park: the old men in berets seemingly chained to their benches, the corralled square of sand. A jungle gym swarms with children, like caged monkeys squawking, while their elders look on.

Batya opens the sprockets of her faucet, twisting briskly. This is the source of the drip which she hears each afternoon when she enters the apartment, the drip that ticks her to sleep at night and drums her awake in the morning. The leak that defies all rings and washers, the many times that Mr. Nafarstig tried to fix it. But that was long ago, before she decided that she *liked* the leak, that subtle meter, its resilience.

She scrubs her face and neck and dabs her chest with a washcloth. Occasionally, she glimpses herself in the mirror. Hers is a plain face: flat nose, thin lips, a chin cowering beneath her mouth. Lackluster eyes that look no further than the lonesome evening ahead. Not the kind of face, she knows from her mother's ever-lengthening sighs, to catch a husband.

Back in the kitchen, Batya prepares her supper. She peels a cucumber and dices a tomato. The knife, a bread knife, is too long for the purpose, but Batya's stroke is sure. She sprinkles olive oil and *zaatar* onto the salad, beats the egg for her nightly omelet. She tries to mind the frying pan, shifting it until the butter browns. But her gaze cannot stay with the cooking. It strays inexorably toward the window.

People not from this area, from the north, think the desert always looks the same. But Batya knows how it's constantly changing. Silky cream in the first light of morning, tawny by noon, and then, as the afternoon ages, sepia, almond, bronze. It's almost lavender now, with the sun descending. Objects flattened by the glare of the day, rise and leap out at her at twilight.

So it is with the towers. They loom tall now against the sunset, masculine in form. Between them is a churning coil of wind—a sand devil, it's called, a common sight in the desert. It sucks up the dust and everything around it: stones, bottles, twigs. To get caught in one can be dangerous, even fatal, and yet she finds it fascinating, hypnotic. She watches as the wind whirls toward the prison, threads its way between the towers and infiltrates the gate. The guards, tiny men in blue uniforms, scatter.

She takes her plate, with a glass of black beer, back into the salon. Though she might sit at the table, she prefers the armchair. Overstuffed, rebelliously green, the chair is her only indulgence. Batya mounts it sideways, as is her custom, with her legs draped over an arm.

Darkness washes over the desert, the prison sinks with the sun. All that remains is a flotsam of yellow lights, of search beams sluggishly pacing. Batya feels a sense of longing, though for what she's not quite sure. Her hand drifts toward the window and opens it. If only she could touch the lights, snatch and stash them here, in her apartment, where no one would think to look. A treasure, hers to hoard and cherish. Her hand squeezes through the grates. Its fingers splay in the night only to furl suddenly and fly back to Batya's throat.

Later she returns to the armchair and leafs through

the pages of her magazine. The models seem to smirk at her, lithe *Ashkenazi* girls with their white skin and icy features, dazzling in the latest styles. There are tips on cooking and house-keeping, too, but most of all on love. Batya no longer reads them, and eventually the magazine slides off her lap and onto the floor, next to her half-eaten dinner. Only the night holds her attention, the window and those lights, a search beam dangling like a pendant.

Days pass, as indistinguishable from one another as the droplets from her faucet. It is seven years since she left her parents' home. There was a time, in those first winters with the sandstorms rapping at the panes, when the loneliness nearly smothered her. She made some friends, fellow clerks at the Registry, who joined her for lunches and films. But the conversation was always the same: husbands and wives, families and children. But then, one by one, her friends peeled off into marriage, and she wonders what went wrong. Every day women as plain as she was, or even homelier, found their mates. It mystifies her mother, too. None of her offspring was particularly attractive, but all the same they were married off and having children. Three sisters and two brothers, all younger than herself—her mother never lets her forget it.

Saturdays they are bound together in the kitchen, Batya and her mother, welded by heat and by the steam of boiling *couscous*. From the dining room comes the howl of pampered infants, of older children quarreling. Men harangue and the cutlery clatters, but Batya is grateful for the din. It helps her to ignore the questions.

"What are you doing this Thursday?" her mother asks. "Nissim said a nice young man came in to have his watch fixed. A mechanic with his own garage, but his hands were clean, Nissim said. Expensive watch, too. *C'est un bon parti.* He's supposed to pick it up on Thursday, at two."

Batya rinses a plate, so hastily that it slips out of her fingers, into the sink.

"Watch what you're doing, Bati, that's my wedding set. Here, let me do that."

Her mother butts her aside with an expansive hip. She is a big woman; her girth has grown over the years, like a tree's. Handsome now but once—so family legend has it—beautiful: high cheeks, wide mouth, those almond eyes so prized in the *Atlas*. Her children, though, look nothing like her, and Batya least of all. If her mother is a tree she is a bush—withering over time, getting gnarled. Batya shifts her weight from one foot to the other. She's wondering how she can make her escape. Either she's here, in the kitchen with her mother, or out in the dining room with her jabbering family. Her only thought is to get back to her apartment, to flop down in the armchair and gaze out of the window.

Her mother hefts her bosom and sighs. "Why don't you go out and see if anybody wants something? The men might be ready for coffee." She holds out the sugar bowl— shrewdly, Batya thinks. "Remember, three cubes for Rami Cohen."

This, of course, is a hint and a useless one as far as Batya's concerned, coming far too late. Years ago, maybe, in high school or during her army service, she and Rami Cohen might have married. He was the ideal suitor, her third cousin on her father's side, a policeman with a promising career. With his slick, black hair and swarthy complexion, his fame as a local football star, women adored him. But then Rami Cohen—people always called him by both names—quit playing soccer and put on weight, and though he reached the rank of sergeant-major, he could never advance beyond. As for their courtship—his mind was elsewhere, on his dream of shedding his uniform, the patent-leather hat and wad of parking tickets, and rising to detective. A golden shield, that's all that Rami Cohen ever wanted, and still yearns for, but the promotion doesn't come.

"If I could only solve one big crime," he'd complain to her on Monday nights long ago when they used to go out for coffee. "All I need is a break."

Batya carries the tray into the dining room, stepping over toys and cradles. Rami Cohen has taken up his usual position, at the far end of the table. With bluff gestures and gritted teeth, he regales the in-laws with tales of crime and detection, true stories from the cities up north. Though it's Sabbath, he still wears his uniform. The brassy buttons strain at their threads; chevrons, like bars, constrain him. Batya lays the cup in front of him, but he doesn't miss a syllable. Rami Cohen no longer looks at her, but merely nods, as if to a wife of many years.

Hers is a traditional family, perennially branching out but never far from the roots, gathering every Sabbath in tumult. At the table's head sits her father. Deaf to the racket, indifferent to the food, he hides beneath a shiny homburg. Batya looks like him—he is the source of her plainness— the same nose and lips, the same eyes, as dim as the chin is weak. And yet this harmless man was once a boxer, sturdy and fleet, the champion of Casablanca. Batya finds it hard to picture him with muscles, a crown where the homburg now rides. And yet at fleeting moments she pictures him bouncing bare-chested in satin trunks, flailing against the ropes which try to rein him in. Amazing, Batya thinks, how roles have a way of reversing; how a towering man like her father in his youth could, in old age, become so diminished. The King of Casablanca is now confined to this house, to the desert, by the tethers of a failing heart. Incredible, too, how her mother, the timorous bride of fourteen, has grown to twice her husband's size and is now ruling the household—and Batya's life, too, if she let her.

Bedtime comes early, never after ten. Batya lays the plate alongside the knife on the kitchen counter. Tomorrow she will wash them while the kettle boils, before heading off to work. The apartment is always spotless, except for the dust which filters through the windows. Every morning she wipes it from the sills and the furniture, yet in the evenings when she returns it is there again, a thin khaki layer. It astounds her that, with all those locks and grates, there are things that can still get in.

Shutting lights behind her, Batya leaves the kitchen and the salon. She stops in the bathroom, and retrieves her pendant from the soapdish. Only then does she enter the bedroom, the furthest reach of her home. Like the other rooms, this one, too, is spare. Family photographs on a night stand and deployed around her pillow, stuffed animals. The bedspread has a purplish hue, the same as the desert at sunset, and the lampshade is the color of sand.

Batya makes her way across the room and around the bed, to the window. There, with the last of her strength, she raises the pane. The wind rushes in. It whips her hair and scrapes her cheeks, but Batya doesn't retreat. She remains at the sill a full minute longer, lolling. With motions of her narrow hips, she sways as the wind flattens the slip on her chest and whisks her hair from her face. She imagines herself one of those models in the magazine, wistful, seductive. Golden lights glint in her eyes. In the quiet of night when she is most alone, Batya can be alluring.

Usually she puts on a cotton nightgown, but the heat of the *shuq* has drained her. Though the slip is stained, she hasn't the energy to remove it. She falls onto the bed and shimmies between the sheets. The sensation's delicious, the caress of linen and breeze. Sleep will come quickly—it never tarries. Batya has only to stare at the walls, dripping with yellow reflections, and listen to the thump of her faucet. In her mind an image forms: a downpour of gilded beads. Her eyes are vacant already by the time they finally shut.

*   *   *

Those eyes cannot see other eyes, watching her tonight as they have watched her many nights, passing from window to window. Learning her movements, her never-changing routine. Knowing her: a woman who lives alone, without visitors, without vices except for a tendency to gaze. Those eyes watch as the lights go off in her bedroom and her apartment—fourth floor, the building closest to the edge— goes dark.

Her nights are studded with dreams, often vivid, unsettling. Her mother features prominently, cast as a baker whose loaves can never turn out. A dog, reminiscent of Rami Cohen, barks viciously but never bites. Sometimes she visits the prison—tonight, for example, when she's given a guided tour. She passes the rows of cells, each of them occupied, though she cannot see the faces inside. She's fascinated but must not show it. After all, hers is a position of authority. The key that bulges from her pocket, that jabs deep into her groin, opens all the locks.

After the tour, she is ushered outside. The heat is suffocating, salted with dust. A guard dog yelps at the sun. She fights back her sweat, and despite her weariness, walks, sprightly, toward the fence. It's there that she spots it, twirling in the corner of her dream. *Sand devil, sand devil,* somebody screams, and all around her people are scrambling. But she doesn't budge. She is petrified, yes, but also enthralled. Writhing, the devil spews dust and pebbles; a scorching wind rifles her skirt. She shuts her eyes and lifts her face to the debris. It is painful, as they say, but only at first. Then, suddenly, she's inside it, trapped in the devil's eye with the world hurtling around her. Barbs and knives circle her head but none so much as scratches her—on the contrary, here she feels perfectly safe.

Batya sits up in bed. Confused, she staggers into the bathroom. Splashes water on her cheeks, which are flushed and hot to the touch. The face in the mirror looks puffy. Maybe I'm coming down with something—the flu, Batya wonders, as firmly she shuts the faucet.

It's heading back to bed that Batya hears it: a sound. At first, she thinks it's the faucet again, and continues. But so does the sound—not the hollow *plink* of water dropping, but a sharper, more insistent sound. Clicking. She freezes. The prison lights shimmer on her windows; the search beam peaks through each pane. *Click click.* It's the door, Batya realizes. Someone is trying the door. Mr. Nafarstig? Couldn't be, not at this hour. Had she locked all the locks coming home, she wonders, and if not, how could she have been so distracted?

She flies into the salon just as the latch breaks open. Batya throws her entire weight onto the door and smacks it shut. The handle rattles, once, twice. She reaches for the keys but they slip onto the floor; fumbles for them then lunges for the phone. Rami Cohen—the number she's known half her life suddenly eludes her. She struggles with the dial but then the door explodes. A wicked force rips the phone from her hand, from the wall, and grips her hard by the throat. No breath, no blood. Her chest is squeezed like a melon, her head, pressed like a grape. Lifted, she's weightless. Feeble hands tear at the iron grip, her naked feet thrash. Batya hears herself gurgle.

Into the salon she is carried, by the neck. The room grows very black. No more attempts to breathe; no need now. A limb twitches, but she can't tell which. She is drifting through the ceiling, toward freedom. *So this is what it's like!* But then she is cast onto the armchair. Raw air sears into her lungs. She chokes and coughs and tries not to cry. Behind the chair, beside the window, he hunkers.

"Quit blubbering." The voice is deep and gruff, not unlike her father's, but malicious.

She sees herself bolting through the door and screaming for Mr. Nafarstig. Instead, she gasps, "What do you want?" A dumb question, Batya knows, dangerous. But the intruder merely snorts. Squinting, she can tell that he's enormous. Thick neck, square head, shoulders hunched— like some prehistoric tool, primitive and crude.

"Take anything," she blurts out, but there's nothing in the apartment of worth. Only her life, which can't mean much, and the pendant. She clasps it tightly and curls between the arms of the chair.

"Shut up!" he commands in Hebrew—*shtucki!*—then in Arabic slang: "*Ya sharmuta,*"—you whore.

Nobody's ever talked to her like that. She is ready to be robbed, even raped, but not humiliated. The shock of it numbs her terror. Just long enough to let her look him straight on, a very large man indeed. Slightly stooped, neck sunk between the shoulder blades in the manner of cornered beasts. She sees those mammoth hands opening and closing and wonders how it was that they hadn't crushed her. She's aware of a smell, potent and repulsive—tobacco, sweat, and dirty socks. She hears his breathing, as fitful and frightened as her own.

The search beam strikes the window and shatters over the grates. The man takes cover behind the wall, but is grazed by slivers of light. They illuminate for a moment a denim shirt emblazoned with numerals, baggy pants torn at the thigh. Ravaged eyes peer venemously into hers.

"You . . ."

"Shut up!" The intruder strides toward her, hand raised mallet-like over his head. Batya cringes and tries to shield her face. "You talk when I tell you to," he hisses. "You got that, whore?" Involuntarily, she nods.

A patrol jeep transverses the desert below. Flashlights prowl the salon. The man returns to his place beside the window. He stays there for a long time—an hour or more, there's no way of knowing. Then she hears him snore, laboriously, interspersed with sighs. Batya's neck is sore and her legs are cramped, but she doesn't dare to stand. She remains in the armchair and concentrates on the images inside her mind. In black and white they flicker, like frames in a silent film: a blurry photo of herself in the morning paper and, next to it, a close-up of the corpse; a graveside tableau of her parents, mother inconsolable and father confused; portraits of Mr. Nafarstig and Rami Cohen—all those who would have helped her, had they been present. The visions leave her less afraid than bitter. Why had she, who had asked for so little, been denied so much? Where

were the other pictures—of settings for two on the kitchen
table, of the bed disarrayed by love?

The images, like the desert's haze, vaporize with the
first heat of dawn. Morning uncovers the intruder slumped
against the wall. Batya can now study him. Though not
nearly as monstrous as he appeared in the dark, he's still
enormous. Close-cropped scalp engraved with scars, pocked
cheeks, a tattered ear—a scavenger's face, frozen in headlights. Twisted by hatred, but also by pain. There is a rip
in his pants' thigh and from it spreads a viscous pool of
blood. Batya sits motionless in her armchair and listens to
the faucet. She watches as the desert blanches with light.
Another day has begun, seemingly like any other.

"Dina!"

The man startles himself awake. Disoriented, he gazes
around the room—the door, the table, the window and its
grates, and finally, at the armchair. Batya clutches her pendant. He seems disappointed at first, as if he were expecting
someone else.

"What are you looking at?" he snaps.

Batya shakes her head, but her eyes stay fixed on him.

"I said stop looking at me, whore."

The words come from deep inside her, an instinct of
sympathy or, perhaps, survival. "I think you're hurt . . ."

"When I want your opinion I'll ask for it." He stabs
a blackened finger at her face. "Until then . . ."

"I have . . ." she interrupts him suddenly, without
thinking, then murmurs, "I have to pee."

With swollen eyes he seizes her, dismisses her with a twitch of his chin. "One minute. No more."

Her legs are rubbery when she stands, but they manage to bear her into the bathroom. She considers locking the door, but in the end leaves it unlatched. It won't make a difference, she realizes, a man of his strength.

The gush of urine eases her tension. She wishes it would last an hour, to give her time to think. But soon her bladder's emptied and her mind is still a blank. Washing her hands at the sink, Batya sees herself, pale and haunted, in the mirror.

She leaves the bathroom, calmer now—more confident for having gone. Back in the salon, the man is trying to get to his feet, cursing as he shoves his back up the wall. Unable to stand on his injured leg, his power gives out. He clutches the leg and slithers down to the floor.

"I could look at it," Batya says evenly, "if you'd let me."

She advances, foot before foot, as if on a tightrope. "I'll be careful. I promise." One more step and she's above him. She pauses, savoring the advantage, then kneels beside the leg. Her fingers reach out to touch, but freeze the instant he flinches. Batya swallows hard and lifts a flap of cloth. She sees only a crust of blood, but the wound seems deep, already infected. Batya looks up into his rigid face. "I can't get at it. I'll have to cut away the material."

Having let her go this far she expects him to agree. Surely he'll stop threatening her, show gratitude. But his hand lashes out, gripping this time not her neck but the

109

pendant. Tugging it, he pulls her toward him. Her eyes are crammed with his pitted cheeks, her nose with acrid breath.

"What the fuck d'you think you're doing?" He twists the gold chain around his fist until it bores hard into her throat. "Want to play nurse with me, yeah?"

A punch on the collarbone sends her reeling onto her coccyx. Her hands fly up to her neck. She's going to be hit again and tries to crawl away, and sure enough the man lurches after her. But he's blocked by another burst of pain. He doubles over, swearing.

"Do it," he grunts. "Quick."

"I need something to cut with. Don't . . . try not to move."

She stands and falters: the bathroom—no, the kitchen. On the counter, beside the yet unwashed plate, lays the knife. She feels its weight, watches its edges flicker. Her mind careens with possibilities. Outside the desert is teeming—patrols, Bedouin trackers, dogs. They will find him, soon; how can she occupy him till they do? The best chance, she thinks, is to play along, to make it through each minute as it comes. Bearing the knife across her outstretched palms—a pacific gesture—Batya reenters the salon.

The man spies the knife and sniggers at his own predicament. Somehow he knows that she'll actually cut the pants and not, as he would in her place, his throat. He twists his leg to one side, offering it to her.

Batya slips the knife into the tear in his pants, slits upward to the top of his thigh and down to below the knee.

She separates the folds, like slats in a Venetian blind, and peeks inside. The wound is more serious than she thought, a jagged gash clear down to the muscle. He needs a doctor, but she bites her lip—he'll only call her a whore. Matter-of-factly, she says, "We'll have to wash this out."

He pretends to chew his nails: "Ay, I'm so afraid of pain." It takes a second for Batya to realize he's joking, and she doesn't like it. People might laugh at her behind her back but never to her face. It takes all her control to keep from slapping his face, erasing that grubby smile. She wants to hurt him but knows he can hurt her more.

"They're all over the place, you know," Batya informs him. "The police. They have trackers."

Again, he nibbles on his nails. "Trackers? God help me."

"And dogs."

"You don't say."

"It won't take them long."

He glowers at her, so coldly it makes her shiver. Batya takes shelter in the wound, closely inspecting its contours. The man hardly seems to notice.

"You don't get it, do you?" he says. "You've been locked up in this house too long." He lays his head against the wall and speaks to the dusty ceiling. "You think a man plans for seven years and doesn't fix every detail? You think that when he finally picks his night and makes his move he's not sure that everything—and I mean everything—is perfect?" The intruder yawns and stretches triumphantly. "I took the sewage ditch and backtracked through the wadi. Trackers, dogs, my ass."

"What about me, then?" Batya, affronted, inquires. "What happens when I don't show up for work today? Don't you think they'll suspect?" She raises the nub of her chin. "*There's* something you didn't think of . . ."

The man laughs through his nose. "Excuse me, I didn't know I had the honor. The prime minister's daughter, or is it the chief of police?" His expression darkens.

"You know as well as I do that nobody'll even notice you're missing, not for days anyhow. Fact is, lady, you're a nothing."

She *will* slap him—to hell with the consequences—once and so hard it'll break his neck. Her hand cocks back, rearing to strike. But then they freeze, the two of them, scarcely daring to breathe. Somebody is knocking at the door.

Batya can see his eyes fixing on the knife, the notion in them gelling. She shakes her head slowly and mouths the word: *Please.*

"It's me, Batya," a voice calls out from behind the locks. "Is everything all right?"

She replies—it's the only hope—before the man can silence her.

"I'm fine, Mr. Nafarstig. Really there's . . ." But then he snatches the knife, shoves her away and struggles to his feet. With the blade, he motions her toward the door.

Two more knocks. "Are you sure, Batya? See, I found . . ."

"Yes, yes, Mr. Nafarstig," she says firmly, "Now go back to your apartment."

A silence in the hall; he's still there. The wounded man staggers to the armchair and then to the table. They stand close enough to touch, she by the door and he to her side, knife raised.

The door is unlocked, and Mr. Nafarstig could easily barge in. But he's a gentleman and won't unless he's needed—an impression she mustn't give him. Batya opens the door to the width of her eye. The tip of his slippers, a sliver of his shoulder appear.

"I didn't mean to disturb you, Batya." His tone is delicate, the pitch unusually high. A child's voice, she has thought.

"You're not. You're not disturbing me, Mr. Nafarstig. And I didn't mean to snap at you. It's just . . . I'm sick."

"That flu, yes? It's going all around the city. You should take better care." He angles his face toward the door. Placid as a pond, his face, the golden tooth gleams within it.

"I will, I promise. Now please excuse me, I must get back into bed." She starts to close the door.

"But Batya . . .".

She sighs, "Yes, Mr. Nafarstig."

"Truth is I came to tell you about what I found this morning. On the stairway and here."

He points down—she can follow his finger—to a russet stain on the floor. Dried blood in a trail leading, it appears, to her apartment.

113

"It's . . . it's . . ." Above her head, the knife hovers. "Me." She puts her hand up to the gap in the door, palm outward. "That plastic basket, you know with the sharp handles. It cut me."

"For the thousandth time, Batya, let me carry your groceries. I'm not that old that I can't . . ."

"No, of course you aren't. Next time."

She again closes the door and hears his slippers slapping. But they never reach the stairs. "Oh, and Batya . . ." She swoons at the sound of her name. "You really should lock your door. Somebody escaped from the penitentiary. Last night—did you hear the news? And he's still out there somewhere. A murderer."

The word lingers in the hall as Mr. Nafarstig descends finally. Batya wants to run after him, to hide behind him for protection. But that would get the both of them killed. And so she shuts her eyes and waits for the knife to plunge, to pierce or to slash—however he does his work. Breath held, heart racing. She expects the hiss of a blade, but all she hears is a tingling sound. Her eyes open to her own set of keys dangling in front of her face.

"Do like he says, Batya," the prisoner chortles. "You're only safe inside."

At mid-morning they move into the bathroom. He sits on the toilet lid, his bad leg propped up on the tub. On her knees, Batya dabs at the wound with a washcloth. Heat penetrates the apartment; there's no escaping it. Batya pauses to wipe her brow with the heel of her hand, to push damp strands from her eyes. It is wretched work, malodorous, cleaning the pus. But worse than the sight or smell is the thought of whom she is treating. A criminal, a murderer, a man who has taken others' lives; what right has he to his?

Batya has many questions, but they come out harsh, as accusations. "You would've killed him, wouldn't you?"

"Why do you say that?"

"The way you were holding that knife. And what about what my neighbor said, Mr. Nafarstig?"

"You talk too much."

Batya wrings out the washcloth and soaks it under the tap, the water scalding. The convict's leg recoils at the touch, but otherwise he is still.

"Maybe," she says. "But I would never kill."

"No?" The man lowers his face until it levels with hers. Ugly as ever—the flared nostrils and ravaged skin— yet it has some quality—helplessness?—she cannot hate. "With half a chance you'd kill me."

Her favorite defense, Batya pretends not to hear.

"Of course you would."

She turns her head away. She's afraid again—of him, but also of the possibility that he might be right, that she, too, could be capable of murder.

The prisoner goes on: "Everybody's a killer. Old women crash their cars into bicycles. Little kids get pushed out of windows. Happens every day, just listen to the news. Not a person in the world who can't kill somebody

115

else, and if you want to survive, you got to kill 'em first."

Her eyes dart up, livid. "You'd kill old women? Children?"

"If it came down to it, them or me."

"And if it didn't?"

"Then I'd want them to think I would."

Batya swabs the wound, brusquely. "So you walk around with knives . . ."

"Knives, guns, doesn't matter. You can kill with anything. Those keys of yours, if they're used right, or that washcloth."

She produces a bottle of iodine. "This is going to burn," she says.

"Shut up already and do it."

She pours with a vengeance. The solution froths in the gash. He grunts then stifles it; his leg goes rigid. "Batya," he growls, "a name like that, your mother must've really hated you."

She chooses to ignore him. But his next words catch her off guard: "I like it."

"I never thought about it . . ."

"Old-fashioned, kind of, high class. Let me guess, Marrakesh."

"Casablanca."

The man flips a flaccid wrist, a gesture of high regard. "We're from Fez," he volunteers, "My father, the shit of the earth."

"Was he a . . . you know . . . too?"

"A criminal?" He gives a bitter snort. "Worse. He left us alone, five kids in a single room in Ramla. My mother scrubbed floors for rich *Ashkenazis* up north."

Batya starts to pour again, then stops.

"What are you waiting for?"

She tips the bottle gently, as if she were feeding a baby. "My father was a boxing champion," she says.

The man clenches his teeth: "I believe it."

Batya dries the foam around the wound. It should be bandaged, she knows, but that would mean cutting the pants off entirely. The man drapes his arm along the lip of the sink, lays his head in its crook. He's studying the leaky faucet.

"You must be hungry," Batya says as she rinses out the washcloth. "I can get you something to eat."

"Make me food," the man commands, as if it were his idea. As if he hadn't listened to a thing she'd said. His stare is reserved for the faucet. "I could fix this."

Here is the moment—Batya senses it—the juncture, a turning point. Rising, she wipes her hands on her slip and hazards a grin. "I don't think so," she says.

Slices of fruit, a dollop of jam, pita bread warmed over the stove—Batya arranges the plate. In the kitchen she can hear the shuffle of his leg as he hauls it out of the bathroom. A glass of black beer, a fork and the knife. She places them all on a tray and starts toward the salon. She starts, but pauses to glance through the window. It's afternoon and the prison is shrouded in haze; the towers seem to wither.

But patrols are still combing the desert, determined despite the heat. *I took the sewage ditch and backtracked through the wadi*, she recalls him saying, and the thought is strangely comforting. It occurs to her, though she dismisses it at once, that possibly she doesn't want him caught.

Entering the salon, Batya finds the man slumped across the table. One arm cushions his head while the other is stretched, fingers extended, as if to something beyond their reach. He appears not to notice her when she walks in, or even when she lays the tray alongside his arm. She pushes the fork across the table, until it touches his thumb. The scarred head rolls over; small black eyes size up the meal. He straightens himself, takes the fork and spears a piece of fruit. Chews it carefully, testing it, then heedlessly digs in. He makes a lot of noise, sniffing and belching, whisking the food into his mouth.

Batya watches him, pleased by his hunger. It's been years since a man last sat at this table and ate. Since the days, shortly after she left home, when Rami Cohen would come around for a four o'clock snack and make it last until dinner. She would prepare the food and serve him, just like this, and he, too, would gobble, talking all the while of the break he needed, his dream of becoming a detective. But his visits gradually dwindled, along with his chances for promotion, then finally ceased. And now there was this man—this interloper, a felon—seated in Rami Cohen's chair. Much bigger than Rami Cohen and with a hardier appetite, too. Perhaps he's more like her father—her father of thirty years ago, the champion. She remembers how, as a child, she loved to sit and watch him eat, the ferocity of it; the way his shoulders hunched over the plate, forearms working, and the clang of silver on glass. A fight for the title, to the death, with his food.

The man drags a hand across his mouth. "More," he grunts, and pushes the empty plate toward her. Batya regards it for a moment, half in wonder, half in fear. At this rate he'll finish all she has, and then what? Yet, back in the kitchen, she forgets about quantity and heaps an even larger portion. She almost forgets about the window and the desert, the prison and its patrols. She does not linger this time, but hurries with his plate to the table.

The man devours the second plateful with the same voraciousness. As if eating were a necessary task—one of those things, like theft and murder, one does to stay alive. He's oblivious to his surroundings, to the sudden growl of a jeep, a dog, just outside the window. Indifferent to her. Batya doesn't mind. With each forkful, mauled and swallowed, her satisfaction grows.

The second plate is nearly cleaned when he finally notices her. His jaw hangs in mid-chew. "You're looking at me."

Blinking, Batya confesses.

His hand flips up and down, skittishly, gesticulating, *What's up?*

"Nothing," she lies, then lowers her head. Batya whispers, "I was just trying to guess your name."

"And I'd be stupid enough to tell you."

He finishes his mouthful and starts back to the plate,

but Batya gets there first, filches a wedge of orange. "Maybe," she says and sucks the juice from her fingers. "I mean, what difference does it make?"

He purses his lips—women, such a nuisance. "Dairyman. They call me Dairyman. Okay?"

"Why Dairyman?"

"From the days when I was working in protection." He winks over a chaw of bread. "I used to milk 'em dry."

Batya laughs curtly, then peers at him. "But I want your *real* name."

Once again she's crossed a boundary. Again, he's going to curse her, or maybe smash the plate. The man impales the last piece of fruit and holds it before his teeth. "Marco," he says begrudgingly, and bites.

"Mar-*co*," she repeats. "I like that name."

"You like Batya."

"I never said I did. It's just my name. But Marco. It's very . . . down-to-earth. Manly."

Marco scratches himself, first his chest and then his temple. He scrutinizes her, tipping his head from side to side like an animal assessing a trap. Then, suddenly, the color drains from his face.

"I don't feel so good," he mutters. Again, he lays his head across his arm, and appears to fall asleep.

Batya leans toward him. This close, she can see the savagery of his scars, can smell his breath of danger. She knows it's a risk but cannot stop herself. Her finger, as her mother would say, has a mind of its own. It glides across the table and alights upon his cheek. It traces the ragged outline, the patches of bristles and pits. So ugly, she thinks, he's almost beautiful. Marco.

Batya stretches further; her breasts are pressed to the table. Her finger continues to wander. Along the jaw-line and around the knobby chin and then up to the corners of his mouth. There it touches, barely brushes, his lips. Soft and tepid, so unlike the rest of him, all that angle and stone.

Marco bursts from his chair, his hand locked around Batya's. She is dragged full across the table and she thinks, *here, here it will happen.* He starts across the salon, stumbles and pitches with Batya in tow, toward the bedroom.

Marco swats the stuffed animals from the pillow and pushes her down on the bed. Batya curls on the sheets. She's paralyzed, with fright but also anger. Anger at him as much as at herself. Tepid and soft—she really *is* stupid. And now what? Punch and kick? Resist and die? Or just let him have his way? Marco teeters over her. His complexion has gone from white to green; his mouth and eyes are screwed. His body stiffens and seems to rise before collapsing diagonally next to her. He lies motionless, so still that Batya wonders if he's awake. She tries to straighten her legs, watching him intently, when his eyes abruptly open.

"The slightest move," Marco rasps, "and I'll know it."

The afternoon simmers. The sun, approaching the prison, steadily surrenders its heat. Batya does not sleep. She watches as motes of dust, like renegade stars, filter through the window. Light creeps down the sill. She hears the jeeps and dogs, more distant now, hears the screams of children on jungle gyms and the old men cheering them

121

on. From Mr. Nafarstig's apartment wafts the tart aroma of cats. The faucet, as always, tattoos.

Marco sleeps heavily; the yoke of his shoulders rises and falls. She might slip out, rush for the door and fly down the stairs. But she might be caught, just off the bed, and throttled. Batya's miserable. She's tired and dirty, indignant and afraid. For the first time since this whole thing started—could it be, less than a day?—she cries.

Darkness comes. The wind surges up and rattles the grates. Shadows turn to search beams on the walls. At some hour—twelve, perhaps, or two—Batya falls asleep. A deathlike slumber, despite the awkward position, and the callused feet in her face. She dreams of nothing, not of sand devils, not of the prison.

122   She's shrouded in heat and dust; the crowd and its stench are choking. For the life of her she can't understand how she got back to the *shuq*. A strange cry, more like a howl than a shriek. Something fastens around her neck and mouth; a mawkish taste that might make her gag if only she could swallow. Writhing, she flings the soggy sheet from her face. The crying goes on, though, and it takes a moment before she recalls that she is not alone. She is Batya, in bed, with the prisoner.

Batya turns on the light and gasps. The sheets are streaked with blood. The wound in his leg in hemorrhaging, oozing pus and rheum. Marco stares through glassy eyes at the ceiling. "Dina," he moans as his head flops on the pillow. "*Sharmuta*."

The mattress is drenched, the air, rancid. She puts her hand to Marco's forehead; he's burning. Batya squirms out from under him and rolls onto the floor. She jabs her hands under his armpits and fastens them over his chest, lifting, though his weight must be double her own. Yet, slowly, he begins to rise, just enough so that she can balance him on her hip and help him limp to the bathroom. Marco, delirious, curses and swipes at her, but Batya drags on, through the door and around the sink to the toilet, easing him onto the seat.

The bath fills with water. How will she get him inside? She starts with the clothes, the easy part. The soiled material tears in her hands—his pants, shirt, underclothes. Naked, he seems less a monster, scrawny, in fact, pale. He reminds her of the cattle she once saw on the news, starving cattle, in Africa. The sight at once relieves and disappoints her. The genitals, the first she has seen since childhood, are dark and shrunken, like fruit left too long in the *shuq*. Wiping hair from her eyes, Batya bends to hoist him. This time, though, he seems to float. He sails over the rim and into the tub, as buoyant as a baby.

Batya rinses the sweat from his chest and thighs and daubs his brow with the washcloth. Marco stares at the tiles and shivers. The water soon turns a milky gray—God knows the last time he bathed—so she drains and refills the tub. A scalding stream pours into the wound. Marco's head lashes from side to side, grunting, swearing. His fists pound the porcelain.

Batya soaks and Batya rubs, over and over, ignoring

123

his curses, his smells. Throughout the night she remains, scouring, until the walls are striped with dawn.

"It's no good, Marco." Batya sags over the rim. "You've got to get to a doctor."

Marco tries to lift himself only to slither back into the water. His pallid face, tilted and open-mouthed, almost looks angelic.

"You could lose the leg."

"No doctor," he murmurs, "Promise me."

What can she tell him? How can she give him her word, this man, and never take it back?

"I promise," Batya says.

Another day or is it longer? Batya can hardly tell, scurrying back and forth from the bedroom to the bathroom with bowls of soiled water, and to the kitchen, for cups of julep tea. Marco slips in and out of delirium, cursing, calling out for some person named Dina whom she doesn't know but has already begun to resent. Batya tries to hush him, warning him about the neighbor downstairs and the patrols in the desert outside. Warning him—is she mad? A murderer?

And yet, unconscionable as it seems, she feels a certain contentment caring for him—a dangerous man, true, but one whose life now hangs on her. Coincidence has brought him here and fate, of the sort her mother believed in, keeps him. As for weightier questions—morality, the law—Batya prefers not to think about them. She sticks fast to her new routine. Only once, late at night, does she pause to sit in her armchair, to sling her legs over one arm and arch her head toward the window. The hunt has died down. The pack of jeeps has been replaced by a lone police car, a white Escort, the kind that Rami Cohen drives. Its bluish strobe flickers around the great yellow search lights, like a moon in search of its sun. But then a sigh comes from the bedroom. Marco says her name—for the first time, affectionately, her name. And Batya goes running.

She sleeps to the vicissitudes of his fever. Cuddling near his thigh, she dozes, though never deeply, always alert to his call. Batya wonders how much longer she can go on. Food is running out. Her strength is dwindling. Her absence would have to be noticed eventually—at the Registry or by Mr. Nafarstig or her mother. They'd try to phone and find the line was dead; find out she hadn't been at work, or even out of the house. And what was today—Wednesday? Thursday! Saturday, she's expected at her parents.

"Batya."

His clammy hand touches her temple. It makes her shiver, but she makes no attempt to remove it.

"Batya." The voice is heavy, so low it rumbles in the pit of her gut. She's frightened again, though the fear is somehow different.

"I think the fever's broke."

She raises her head, turns her cheek so that it nestles against his hand, and feels the mattress quiver. His hand follows the grain of her hair, the row of fuzz on her nape. Instinctively, her body contracts. She coils, knees close to her throat. But the hand cannot be stopped. It delves into the back of her slip and burrows around her ribs. Batya remains still; she neither helps nor hinders. Her mind, stripped by fatigue, is raw with emotions; brilliant with nerves. Her skin bristles at his touch. The hand reaches her belly, hesitates, then makes its way up, cupping, finally, her breast.

They lie like this for some time. Tonight there is no rush. The hand moves from one breast to the other. Her nipples stiffen. Like quotation marks the two bodies are curved, like parentheses and, between them, silence.

Submerged beneath the sheets, they embrace. The pent-up heat, the unwashed odors, are intoxicating. Batya strokes the length of his chest, his throat and his shoulders. So many textures—gnarled, gristly, smooth—all of them new. Then, unexpectedly, something brushes against her wrist, something hot and turgid which glides across her leg.

"Batya . . ."

Marco hugs her, so tight she can't tell her heartbeat from his. Awkward at first, careful because of his wound, they eventually find their fit. Marco is on top of her—incredibly, she can take his weight—with her feet wedged beneath his buttocks. He hunts for the gap, she serves as his guide, between the thrusting thighs. The pain between her legs is searing, tearing, sweet.

Marco heaves. A wanted man, armed and deadly, Batya's his willing victim. She feels slashed, gutted from crotch to throat, yet strangely released. The sensation's exquisite—pain or pleasure, she can't tell which, nor does she have time, for a violent spasm shoots through her groin. Batya shudders, she groans and clutches his sides. Soon,

Marco, too, is groaning. Only then, through a last cord of consciousness, does she hear her mother's warning, so useless at the time—a date with Rami Cohen—but now improbably apt. "Not inside," Batya whispers as molten waves wash across her hips.

They lie there, the two of them, linked. They listen to one another's breathing, at the wind slapping at the panes. The faucet beats: a tin cup rapping on bars. They lie until the apartment grows hot and silent and the desert sparkles with light. Only then does Batya free herself from his arms and patter barefoot to the kitchen.

She boils the water for Turkish coffee and toasts a slice of pita. Her mind is reeling. She has just made love for the first time and to whom, a convicted felon, a killer? Is she now an accomplice and if so, to what crime? What if they find him, Batya asks; what if he has to flee? Would she hide him or turn him in, save or sacrifice herself? These are the questions she asks as she stirs the coffee and spreads some jam on the bread. She feels his seed on her stomach, taut and desert-dry. She tries not to look out of the window, at the prison, but hurries with the tray to the bedroom. Marco is sitting up. He seems smaller, somehow, dwarfed by the bed, and his face is drawn.

"Look," Marco points to a fresh patch of blood on the sheets. "It's opened up, my wound."

"Not yours," Batya blushes. "Mine."

That day, whichever it is, they spend in bed. Now is the time for discovery. Meticulously, she maps his body. Jungles of hair, bony ridges, rippling tracts. She is particularly taken with his scars, like hieroglyphs etched in his skin, each telling a story that Batya is only too eager to hear. Then it is Marco's turn to wander. Batya displays herself spread-eagle on the sheet, allows him to look and touch as he pleases. It pleases her, the image of herself as foreign terrain, the knowledge that she is his first woman after seven long years alone.

"How did you manage it? Is it true what they say, you know, about men in prison?"

Marco nods. "But not me. I made a vow."

"It must have been rough . . ."

"And you, a woman, you never missed it?"

"Not love—you can't miss what you never had." She grinds an ear into his shoulder. "It was the loneliness I couldn't stand." Batya pets his cheek; she turns it until his glance meets hers. "Do you know what it's like to live all by yourself, year after year, in a tiny home?"

Eyes popping, eyebrows arched, Marco makes an incredulous face—a prelude to laughter. But it's Batya who breaks out first. "You're right, you're right," she squeals, "I *am* stupid."

They make love again, and though she's chafed, she delights in locking him inside her. She can feel the power burgeoning, a masterful sense, as Marco's seems to shrink.

The night passes in conversation. Naked in the dark, they bare their tenebrous secrets—their childhoods, the one painful and the other, painfully quiet; his frustrations taken out, hers, scrupulously hidden. They talk and the prison lights glisten through the window. They shimmer on Batya's pendant.

"This? Oh, it's something my mother gave me the day I left home. She even had it blessed." Between her thumb and forefinger, Batya clamps the golden disk; she holds it to the light.

"Look, see that—it's the Ark of the Covenant with the Dove of the Presence inside. And here, on the other side, there's writing." She flips the coin and reads: "*Remember whose mighty hand brought you out from the house of bondage.*"

Marco squints at the ceiling, as if it, too, were inscribed. "Deuteronomy, chapter eight," he cites, "verse two or three."

Batya is astonished. "How did you know that?"

"I took some classes with the prison rabbi. It gets you extra privileges, you know. Very handy, specially if you're planning an escape."

"Your mother must be very proud," she chortles.

"My mother died two years ago."

Batya doesn't know what to say. She is overwhelmed by Marco's past, the breadth of his suffering. Who was she to complain with a mother still robust and a family who loved her, more or less? What was her loneliness compared to his? Batya latches herself to his side and fastens her forehead to his shoulder. She wants to protect this man from all unhappiness, she thinks, forever. She will never let him go.

*   *   *

Another dawn. The sun glares through the grates. Marco snores loud enough to wake not only Mr. Nafarstig but the entire building—loud enough to muffle the patter of her feet on the tiles.

For the first time in days, Batya looks in the mirror. Her hair is matted and dark circles shadow her eyes. Yet the picture is not unpleasant—quite the opposite: a blithe, supple, Mediterranean face that she recognizes from early photos of her mother. She wets a finger under the dripping faucet and uses it to moisten her lips. No, she is not ugly nor even plain. In this certain light, in love, Batya is almost beautiful.

She runs a bath and immerses herself. Soaps herself, finding new textures, new curves. Suds slip between her breasts, down her belly to the grooves inside her thighs. Areas that Marco has roamed, her hands slides over them, reenacting his journey. And as she does she imagines him ripping aside the plastic curtain, tearing off his clothes, forcing his way into the tub. Into her. The walls spewed with foam. Fingers delve within her and pull her apart. Beneath his weight, under water, Batya can barely breathe. All she can do is cling to the porcelain and leave him to his crime. Her hands caress, furiously they rub, until her whimper echoes around the tiles.

Batya lies gasping in the tub. The water is still; the park outside is empty. Silence encircles everything—except, of course, for the faucet. Reproachfully it patters, *tsk tsk tsk*.

Towels around her head and torso, Batya scampers into the kitchen. She brews the Turkish coffee the way he

130

wants it, four cubes per cup. Then she goes to the broom closet. One stale pita remains; the fruit, too, has gone soft. She must get to the *shuq*, whether he likes it or not. Somehow he must trust her.

She plants the tray on Marco's chest and on his head, a kiss. His eyes open one at a time, irritated by what they see: Batya completely dressed and carrying a plastic basket. He sits up abruptly and nearly spills the coffee, tries to turn, but his bad leg prevents him, entangled in the sheets. Batya giggles.

Marco growls, "Bat-ya," breaking the syllables in his teeth. But it no longer works; she knows too much. Batya frowns—a mother's face, flashed at an errant child.

"We're out of food, and tomorrow's Saturday." Batya shrugs as if to say *what can be done?*

He repeats, "Batya," imploring.

"How could you even think that, Marco?" She tucks the sheet up to his neck. "You rest some more, and wash that leg. Tonight, I'll make you the best Sabbath meal you ever tasted."

Batya skips out to the salon. She retrieves the keys from the stand by the door and gingerly opens the locks. She minces out into the hall but suddenly halts. Scratching her chin with the tips of the keys, Batya deliberates. Might he get the wrong impression? Would he hate her and break away? No, she decides, Marco would understand. Batya turns the locks behind her, one, two, three—a precaution, she inwardly laughs, against burglars.

The morning's sweltering and the number four's

packed, but Batya scarcely notices. She's afloat on cool currents, sailing. She even finds a seat, gazing through the window and its metal safety bars. The bus rambles down streets strewn with dust and garbage, past dilapidated buildings with laundry dangling like tongues. But Batya sees none of this. The world suddenly is radiant for her, luminous. Twenty minutes pass like so many seconds. The bus belches and distends its doors, and Batya flies out into the *shuq*.

A covered market, the air inside is miasmic. Hawkers shout, shoppers clot the passages, but Batya ambles as if she were alone, roaming about the desert. Swinging her basket, she cuts a straight path through the crowd. Her fingers skim over the fruit. She buys quickly: potatoes, beans, a fresh chicken. Her basket fills, but it doesn't get any heavier. Its handles won't cut her palm.

Deeper she bores into the *shuq*. Beyond the food vendors and into the murky precincts of ragmen and tinkers, cobblers and smiths. Here, she selects several pairs of workmen's trousers and shirts, socks and underwear. She pays for two cartons of cigarettes—how much and which ones she has no idea. Somehow, these, too, fit into the basket, which now is close to bursting.

Her list completed, Batya heads for the bus. Approaching the stop, she sees, on the corner, an Escort. White with red plates, a blue light on its roof, it looks like any other police car. Yet this one *is* different. The decals on its windshield—soccer balls and paratroop wings—mark it as Rami Cohen's.

Perhaps he's gone off for a falafel or a chat with the boys and won't see her. But no such luck. Veering wide around the car, she nearly collides with him. Crisp in his summer uniform, Rami Cohen snaps to attention. He is stunned by running into her here on Friday, not her usual day, and with a basket so palpably stuffed. They both stutter, but Batya is the first to speak.

"Rami Cohen in the *shuq*? I don't believe it. Where's the hold-up?"

"I wish." His hands turn up and waver, a supplication to God. "Just some break-ins. Small fry, like always." His voice lowers, as if in shame. "I'm on patrol till next week."

"Well, it's not the end of the world. You used to like coming to the *shuq*. When you were in the army, and on the team . . ."

Rami Cohen turns away, addresses a pick-up truck with sheep. "Batya, that was seven years ago."

She'd reach up and pat his cheek, if her hands weren't full. She might even kiss him, still a handsome man with raisin-colored hair and finely-sculpted features, imposing in spite of his paunch. Batya says, "You have to have faith, like my mother always tells me. You must be patient."

"Patient! You're the one to talk . . ." He's facing her again, lording over and scolding her as if she were still that little girl. A finger wags in her face. "One break, that's all, just one."

"It'll come, I know it will."

"My ass . . ."

The basket drops. "Rami Cohen," she rebukes him.

133

Rami Cohen mutters some apology and bends to pick up the basket. Batya reaches it first, but not before he assesses the contents.

"Pants. Underwear. Cigarettes. Batya, you don't smoke."

Batya hugs the basket to her hip.

"You have someone," he states, almost an accusation. And then to himself: "You have . . . someone."

She wants to tell him that it's none of his business. He lost that right years ago. She wants to tell him that the fault is his, but just then the number four arrives. "*Shabbat shalom*," Batya huffs, and quickly moves toward the bus.

But Rami Cohen will not be left. Not like this. "I want to know who it is, Batya," he hollers after her. "I *demand* to know."

Batya turns back from the top of the steps, eyes narrowed, as the bus door sibilantly shuts.

The bus ride has grown longer, she swears; the twenty minutes to her building feels like fifty. It's not the heat or the weight of the basket, but anticipation, the thought that he'll be there when she returns. She'll rush into his arms and they'll enclose her, sweep her breathlessly to the bed. The two of them welded, shackled, for life—she can think of no sweeter sentence.

"No help today, Mr. Nafarstig," Batya shouts as she bounds up the staircase, "I can manage alone."

The keys jiggle in her hand. They seem to resist, reluctant to enter their holes. Moments pass before she can open the locks and push her way through the door. Batya expects to find him in the armchair, gazing out the window at the world he left behind. But the salon is empty, the kitchen, too. Batya heaves the basket onto the table and stands before the TV set, regarding her frightened reflection in the screen. She tries to pronounce his name, but tension grips her throat. She peeks into the bedroom. The bed is made and Marco's not in it. That leaves only the bathroom . . .

Batya enters and gasps. A pair of legs protrude from the cabinet beneath the sink. Next to them lies her knife—the murder weapon; she can almost see it, tagged and numbered. They've found him, his old underworld foes. Waited for her to leave and then pounced on him. If only she'd hadn't gone . . .

"*Sharmuta,* whore." Foul words never sounded so sweet. Marco wriggles out from under the cabinet. His face is smeared with grime, his chest with brownish liquid. "I can't fix this thing," he gripes.

"Oh, Marco," Batya cries. "Of course you can't."

She seizes his wrist and leaning backward, pulls him to his feet. Half-naked, Marco is dirty and confused. She leads him into the salon. The basket sits, a centerpiece, on the table. Proudly she shows him the pants and the shirts, his first pair of clean underwear in days. Marco says nothing, until she produces the cartons. Like a beggar offered loaves, he snatches them from her.

"It's even my brand . . ."

Batya pouts coquettishly. "You mean you're not angry?"

The cartons crisscross behind her neck as Marco

135

embraces her. They scratch her nape as he lifts her, as he did that first night, toward the ceiling. Only now she doesn't mind the pain; she's breathless, but only with desire. Batya laughs and bites the tattered ear. "You know what I want?" she whispers. "The tub."

The water's cold at first, then very hot, but they're too busy clutching to adjust it. Kneeling, she lathers his legs, his wound, lovingly, working her way up to his erection which she washes with great attention, but Batya cannot wait. She pivots on her knees and invites him to enter her from behind. The clap of thighs resounds about the porcelain. A quickening ovation that ends with cries, their juices mixed with spume.

Batya bakes a curried chicken with sautéed beans and fried potatoes. Every so often, she steals a glance into the salon, at Marco in his brand-new denims, in her armchair, smoking. She sets a Sabbath table, covered *Challah* and sweet red wine. Silver candlesticks that her mother had given her, hoping that someday she'd light them like this, in the presence of her own beloved.

It's nearly dusk when she at last invites him to the table. Batya in a white cotton dress waving her hands over the candles, covering her eyes while quietly she utters the prayer. She passes the cup to Marco, inviting him to bless the wine. He resists at first, shaking his head, but Batya's insistent. He chants off-key, blesses and breaks the bread. She listens to him eagerly and watches. The ridges of his jaw are burnished by the light, the keenness of his eyes is blunted. Could such a face look straight into another's and kill him? It's a question she has wanted to ask him ever since they first made love. The time, she feels, is right.

"Who did you murder?"

Marco pauses, inclines his head as if to ponder a flavor, then swallows. "Men. Two men, to be exact. Brothers." He washes his mouth with wine. "The Anjils, remember them?"

She does, vaguely. A front page story years ago, not long after she left home, with its grainy photo of what looked like oil-stained sacks. A gangland slaying, the latest in a grisly series. It was the topic of conversation that Sabbath: Rami Cohen going on and on about what a break it would be to catch the killer, and her mother turning up her nose and scowling, "Bless the Holy Name, two less."

How had she felt at the time? Ashamed, perhaps: Why was it always Moroccans, her people, who committed the crimes? But also tantalized, the thought of the underworld gunmen at large.

"Why?"

Marco fidgets with his food. "They had bad hearts," he tells her cynically, sarcastically, trying to change the subject.

"And yours?"

"Worse."

"I can't believe that." She reaches across the table for his hand. Marco takes it, but stares into his plate. He looks trapped, she thinks, caught between impulses.

"You couldn't," he mutters, "could you?"

*　　*　　*

Tonight they make love slowly. Languorous strokes, limbs knotted and woven lazily. Their bodies cleaving, sweated, until climax fastens them tight. And for hours they lie on their backs, Marco blowing clouds into the ceiling while Batya tells stories of her father, the former champion, and of her mother, who rose to rule her house. He admits to different tales—of break-ins and hit jobs, a politician bought and another eliminated. Once such talk might have revolted her, but now she's almost enticed.

"I think I'd make a good criminal."

"You?" Marco guffaws. "*Sharmuta.*"

"Don't underestimate me," Batya warns as her fingers encompass his balls. "And don't call me a whore again. Ever."

"You win, you win." He raises his hands in surrender. "It's just that I can't quite see you in prison."

"I might surprise you. I might do well."

"Don't be stupid." Now Marco turns his back, rolling over toward the window. "Prison is death."

"No. Death is living alone. In jail, at least, you had people."

"Reminding you how dead you were. The same faces, the same routine. Every day."

Batya nuzzles the scars on his back. "I was dead. Before I met you . . ."

"You wouldn't last a day in prison."

"Ah, but you'd be there to protect me." The nuzzle becomes a scrape, so sharp it makes him flinch. "Together," she murmurs, "we'd survive."

*   *   *

By local standards, Batya's parents live far away. Their neighborhood, once considered a suburb, now sits in the center of town. Over the years, the city has spread, like an oil slick, over the desert, reaching out toward the penitentiary. Given the urge, she could run to the jail in ten minutes, but to her parents' house it's an hour's walk at least. And walk she does, each Sabbath, in respect for their tradition.

She arrives drenched with sweat in the summer, in winter with rain, desperate to rest. But rest is the last thing she gets. As the unmarried daughter, that same tradition condemns her to the kitchen, alone with her mother.

"I tried calling you several times this week, Bati. Don't you answer your phone any more?"

"It's broken. A man's coming on Tuesday."

Batya ladles the main course out of a cauldron. Moroccan fare: eggplants, peppers, onions and beets, all stuffed. She takes shelter behind the noise from the dining room, which her mother's words can't breach.

"You've been acting different. You look different, too. Have you weighed yourself lately?"

Her mother knows something's afoot—no doubt Rami Cohen told her—but she's too artful to ask outright. She has to inch up to it, pouncing from behind. She and Marco have much in common, Batya decides, as she fills the family plates.

"Why won't you tell me, Bati?"

"Tell you what, Mother? What do you want me to tell?"

139

Her mother wipes her hands on the front of her apron. The apron that Batya has seen tighten with each passing year, her mother's dimensions expanding while her father's steadily shrink. Batya wonders if the same will happen to her—if she, too, will rise and widen, grow strong enough to head a house. And will Marco, ferocious Marco, become meager and tame? Removing a dirty bowl from the counter, Batya imagines him slouching over her table, staring at his tobacco-stained hands, sporting a shiny homburg.

"You know just what I'm talking about, Batya. *Ne me manquez de fou.* You have somebody."

In the dining room, raucous with in-laws and kids, Rami Cohen is going on with his talk of manhunts and shake-downs, the breaks that never come, barely nodding at her. She sits beside her father and kisses his bristly jowl. Tries to eat, but she hungers only for freedom. On her plate, the rice trades places with the pepper, an onion orbits the rim.

She waits until the coffee is poured, and then she makes her move. Batya slips out of the door, down the stairs and out onto the fiery pavement. There she breaks into a run, sprinting as she hasn't since she was a child, fleeing from the boys who taunted her. But today she is a woman and dashing to the man she loves. She's sure of that now. No longer a fantasy, but a real man with a tortured past but happy, now, with her.

She hurries through the deserted streets. The rising wind is to her back and before her the image of Marco—his face, his thighs, his smoky breath. A vision that obscures everything else, the garbage and the dust and the white Escort that has followed her from the beginning and only now draws alongside.

"Forget something in the oven?"

Batya keeps running. The car jolts ahead and screeches; the passenger door snaps open. Rami Cohen in mirror shades grips the wheel.

"Get in," he commands, as if to a suspect.

Batya ignores him. She feels tough, almost invulnerable, not even panting, in spite of the distance she's run.

"Batya, get in," Rami Cohen repeats, removing his glasses. The eyes beneath them are pleading.

She has no choice but to stop. Batya peers down the street. Less than a kilometer remains to her building; she could easily make it. But to flee now would only raise questions. Rather, she'll play it as Marco would, innocent and cool, indifferent. She climbs inside the car.

The air is redolent of pine—that, and the cologne he's affected. Four whole blocks they ride in silence. Rami Cohen scans the alleys and rooftops, forever acting the cop. Batya, lowering the sun visor, busies herself with her hair. But she can't help glancing at him sideways, and the sight she sees astounds her. Loosened skin around the mouth, about the temples tiny slivers of gray. No more the rookie with wings on his chest, a football spinning on his finger, Rami Cohen has aged.

"Batya . . . what I said in the *shuq* . . ."

"Forget it."

"I don't want to forget it."

"But you have to." Batya's expression is sympathetic; truly she feels sorry for him. "It's over, whatever it was. I'm not sure it ever began. You made decisions, just as I did, and we have to live with them." She examines herself in the mirror again. She looks composed, even detached, as the Escort nears her building. Deception comes easily to her, Batya decides.

"You have your life, Rami Cohen, and I have mine."

The park opposite the building is deserted. It's the hour when the old men sit talking in synagogue and children take their naps. Still, she hopes he has the sense to stay clear of the bathroom window. Of course he does—he's Marco. But what if he's taking a shower or a pee? And even if he goes unseen, who's to say he won't spy her coming out, of all things, a patrol car? Why hasn't she told him about Rami Cohen?

"Let me take you upstairs."

"No. I want to go alone."

"There's been break-ins around here. At least let me do my job."

How can she turn him down? Yet giving in would be madness—neither man must know about the other. She stands, pondering, while Rami Cohen comes around and opens her door. She's snared; now he'll certainly follow. *Scream something,* Batya tells herself, *Murder! Rape!* Somehow, she has to warn Marco.

She'll slip into the apartment, nimbly as she can, and slam the door behind her. But when, in the hall, she starts to fumble with her keys, Rami Cohen grabs them. He opens the locks and precedes her into the salon. There, his compassion vanishing, Rami Cohen is again the cop. He sniffs around the salon, pinches a crumb from the table and rolls it between his fingers. The kitchen, he confirms, is vacant—the bathroom and bedroom too. Heart drumming, Batya pursues him. The apartment is orderly, dusted, just as she would have left it. There's no evidence, no sound except that of the leaky faucet.

As Batya glares at him from the door, Rami Cohen slumps into the armchair. He picks at a stain on his uniform and bends to retie his shoes, anything to stall. But he has run out of excuses. Rami Cohen plants a hand on each of the chair arms, rises, then theatrically falls back. In the center of the left arm, bold in the worn upholstery, is a neat black hole: a cigarette burn.

"His, I suppose," Rami Cohen says.

"I don't know what you're talking about."

He inserts a finger into the hole, examining, as though it had been made by a bullet. "He comes here a lot . . ."

"Depends what you mean by a lot."

"And stays."

Batya marches across the salon. She stands above the policeman, feet planted, arms akimbo. "I think you'd better leave," she says.

The look he gives her is meant to be threatening, but it barely disguises his pain. Humbled, Rami Cohen rises. Shoulders hunched, hands in his pockets, he lumbers into the hall. Batya's last sight of him lingering on the staircase as the door closes, leaves her feeling sad. Poor Rami Cohen!

He'd never understand that he'd had his break and lost it, seven years ago, when his girlfriend first left home.

But Batya has no time for pity. She listens to the retreating footsteps on the stairs, then rushes to the bathroom and yanks the curtain aside. Then into the bedroom where, falling to her knees, she searches beneath the bed. Heartsick, she returns to the salon. Marco's gone. He doesn't love her, never did. Took the first opportunity and flew, winging to some hideaway up north. Now it's Batya's turn to sink into the armchair. She is going to cry, for the first time in years, really weep. But before the tears can come, she remembers something: the one place Rami Cohen didn't check, which only a prisoner would think of.

Batya walks into the kitchen. She clutches the pendant and holds her breath as she approaches the broom closet. Jiggles the knob until the door cantankerously swings free.

Another woman might have screamed, but the sight of him, knees tucked to his chest and the plastic basket over his head, makes her laugh. She laughs so loud, so uproariously, that Rami Cohen might hear it in his car below and think it was meant for him. Marco scowls. *You see,* his expression asks, *what I won't go through for you?*

Batya's still laughing much later, in bed. She keeps describing the look on his face behind the web of her basket. The look of a jackal trapped. Marco is not amused. He lies with arms crossed over his chest, chin down and brooding. He waits for her laugher to ebb, then lunges.

"So who's the cop?"

"You . . . saw?"

"Heard. The heart might be bad, but the ears are good. The nose, too. I can smell a cop from a hundred meters."

Batya buries her head in the pillow. "He's an old family friend."

"I think he's more than that."

"A friend. Or used to be. Now he's nothing."

"You can say that again." Now Marco begins to laugh, snidely. "The most obvious place and not once did he think to look."

This remark for some reason irks her. It's one thing for her to make fun of Rami Cohen, quite another for Marco.

"He was upset, he wasn't himself. I know what you're thinking Marco, but he's not . . ."

"Stupid? I told you, all cops are."

Marco leans his body onto hers, droning into her ear. "They're so stupid. They look all over the country, up north in the cities, as far away as possible, because they say to themselves—that's where a convict would run. The last place on earth they'd look is right in front of their noses."

Batya bites her pendant. She doesn't appreciate this conversation, doesn't like where it's leading.

"Don't think it was easy," Marco continues. "Seven years I planned, down to the smallest detail." He shifts himself away, staring at the window. "Seven years plotting how I would pay off the electrician to short-circuit the lights just when I wanted. How I'd get cocaine for the guard who'd be on duty that very night. Seven years with a pair of binoculars high up on the smokestack—that cost a pretty penny too—picking out my spot."

"You did this—" Batya doesn't want the answer, but still she asks—"by yourself?"

"Oh, there were others, too. Mostly hacks trying for a peep at some whore. But not me. I had serious business."

He swings out of bed and strides to the window. "This one. Two more—one in the TV room and one in the kitchen. Three windows, I counted them, and always the same figure looking out."

Batya's sitting up now. "Me?"

He winks at her skeptically, as if she hadn't guessed.

"A young woman all by herself—lonely, from the looks of her. The perfect arrangement. Perfect."

She starts to cry, sniffs hard but can't stop it. A setup, that's all it ever was, worked out step by step like a heist. For a moment she sees herself framed in his binoculars. Starry-eyed, a dupe. She could kill herself—she'd kill him if she had the knife. How could she have been so blind to think that this man, this murderer, could feel for a woman like her? How could she have been so—the word is unavoidable—stupid?

Batya sobs, so miserably that she hardly notices the arms that wrap around her. And when she does her first reaction is to strike at the face with its tobacco-reeking grin. Her fists hammer his cheeks, his crown. "Kill me, Marco! Kill me now!" she howls.

His fingers find her lips but she shrinks from them. "Listen to me, Batya," he begs. "Listen." How was he to know what kind of person she was, Marco tells her. How kind and good-hearted, beautiful and sexy? How could he have known that he would fall in love—there, the word, he used it.

"I only needed to scare you, Batya, a little bit. I never wanted to hurt you."

His embrace grows ardent, riveted by a kiss, unrelenting until finally she returns it. Tighter, harder, she hugs, her hands linked behind his back, fingernails anchored in his skin. Passionately, she pins him.

Batya scribbles a hasty note and lays it by his pillow, hoping he won't awaken. Shuffling to the door, she turns the locks quietly, flinching with each click. Batya steps into the hall and makes her way down the stairs. There's no sound from Nafarstig's, only the whining of cats. Haze lies heavy on the street outside, and around the number four, crowded with drowsy workers. She takes the bus one stop past the *shuq*, to a run-down government building. Ceiling fans and flickering neon, the nagging clack of keyboards. These are the sounds, the deadened light, of the Registry.

This is where Batya has worked for the last seven years, since leaving home, logging plots for new construction. At any hour of the day, lines of contractors and speculators form before the desks. Rough men in workboots and khaki, smoking and spitting, wait to submit their claims. The merchandise is always the same—the desert. Marked off and parceled out, sold at discount rates, the sands are pressed into pavement; buildings sprout from the dunes. So the city expands, year after year, dunam by dunam. Spreading out until, someday, the prison will grace its hub.

Batya takes her station behind one of the desks. Piles of paper clips and staples, rubber stamps and an inkpad. These are her tools, her weapons for fending off the claimants. She attaches their applications, approves an affidavit or two, and directs them to the next station, her eyes scarcely rising from the blotter. A tiny cog in the bureaucracy, insignificant if not absurd, Batya is nevertheless diligent, patient and always polite. Rarely has she ever been absent.

Work begins promptly at eight. The manager, Mr. Levy, emerges from his glassed-in office. A wiry man, dark, bald and stooped, he's hardly said a word to her in seven years. But neither has he ever scolded her—she's never given him reason. Until now. Away for three straight days without so much as a phone call; she's sure she's in for trouble. But if Mr. Levy sees Batya he doesn't acknowledge her. She might have been seriously ill or mourning a family death, but he doesn't ask, doesn't summon her. He merely steps back, opening the door to a flood of hungry men, then swiftly retreats to his office.

"Stamp this!" Documents snap in her face. "Now. I'm in a rush," one of the contractors demands.

Batya just looks at him. "Have you ever heard of the word 'please'?" she retorts. And, "Who are *you* ordering me around?"

The contractor—bovine, cigar-chewing—gapes at her. So do the other secretaries, for a moment, before whispering censoriously among themselves.

"Do you mind waiting your turn?" she chides another applicant, a Bedouin *sheikh,* unused to acerbic women. Then, to the lawyer in the linen suit: "Shame to get ink on that, laying your sleeves on my desk."

The whispering thickens, the claimants start protesting on line. By mid-morning, the commotion's loud enough to draw Mr. Levy from his office. Batya tenses behind her desk. She's prepared for the worst—or the best, for now she's itching for a fight. But Mr. Levy only blinks in the fluorescence, blandly shaking his head.

Batya's furious. Batya's scared, confused by the change that has occurred in her. Something inside of her, pent-up—a will, a passion—has been freed. That was Marco's doing. But now, that change is threatened. Will he stay with her, will he leave? Though he says he loves her, will his own love of freedom be greater? For all his promises, will Marco still stick to his plan?

The possibility haunts her throughout the day. At work's end, she bolts out of the Registry and barges onto the number four, through the throngs of weary passengers. Hoarding a seat, she grips the window bars and tries to sort her emotions—fearful and indignant, desperate and resolved. They envelop her like a sand devil, whirling. Somehow she must break out.

"What are you doing?" Batya demands—she doesn't ask— as she enters.

*   *   *

Marco kneels on the floor, next to the stand with the telephone, fixing its severed cord. The faucet may have eluded him, a man used to tampering, but not this, as he twists the last of the wires. "There!" he exclaims and raises the droning receiver, but Batya waves it away.

"Marco, we have to talk." She sits in the armchair, looking grave, and motions Marco to the table. "This can't go on," she says.

"But of course it can't!" Marco slaps his heart, ruptured, supposedly, by her doubts. "The plan, remember?"

She does, but she also remembers the binoculars. She sees herself caught in them, a lonely woman pining at the window.

"Do you think I'd get this far without figuring out the rest? What do think I am, stupid?" Marco rises from the table, carefully, as if at gunpoint. "I have the means, Batya," he reveals to her, "Jewelry and cash, stashed away, right here in the city." She turns her chin, only to have it returned by his finger.

"Do you hear me, Batya? The minute I dig it up we're gone."

"Gone?"

"Up north, out of the country—Cyprus. We could get new passports, change our identities. Leave it to me."

"And money, will there be enough for the two of us?"

"More than enough," Marco winks. "Enough to last forever."

* * *

That evening, he devotes himself to her breasts. Once merely swellings, in recent days they seem to have blossomed—bigger, rounder, firm. The change is not lost on him. He spends long periods fondling them, rolling their nipples between his lips. And while he works, Batya continues her questions: "Where do you think we could go from Cyprus? How about France—Marseilles, I have family there. *Mes parents parlent français, et les tiens?*"

Marco licks, he nibbles, a little too greedily for affection. Batya pats the back of his head. "And children. We could have our first right away. I'm not so young, you know, and we should get started." His tongue circles the base of each breast. "And you should get a decent job. Enough of this criminal stuff. You could be anything—I saw you with that phone. An electrician."

She presses down on his shoulders. His eyes entreat her, but Batya shoves him down the span of her belly and between her opening thighs. His face is hidden in her pubic hair; he's stalling for time. But Batya's impatient. She grabs his ears and pulls them forward. Marco can do nothing but lap.

"And where is this treasure?"

Marco gasps. "Not far."

"Where?" she sighs.

"Cemetery. Muslim . . . cemetery."

Fingers entwined in his hair, she tugs. "The one next to the *shuq*?"

His head, bobbing, motions faster.

"And this was also part of the plan?"

151

Marco doesn't answer. "Yes, Marco, yes?" Her legs are a vise around his neck, compressing it.

"Yes!" he confesses finally, and her cry seems to mimic him: "*Yes . . .*"

Only now she lets him return. Like a repentant child, he sidles up to her and enters her timidly. Unlike the other nights, it doesn't take long, no more than two or three thrusts and already he's soughing. He rears to extract himself, as usual, only this time her hands prevent him, roughly cupping his buttocks. So snared, Marco comes inside her.

There is no talk, no caresses. Marco snores, a prisoner's sleep, dreamless and sweaty. But Batya is fully awake. She lies on her back, watching as the search beam wanders her walls. Yellow light reflects on her belly, while inside it, a new life is stirring. All is silent: no barking dogs, no jeeps growling outside. Even the faucet is mute. Alone in the night, Batya smiles as Marco might have done during those long summer nights in his cell. She's becoming like him, even better. She, too, has her plans.

Tuesday morning, Batya showers; she brushes her teeth and steps into a floral skirt. Like any other day in the last seven years, she drinks her coffee at the table and browses through her magazine. Occasionally, she takes note of the window. The prison is stark; a breeze has stolen the haze. Batya returns to the magazine, to a statuesque model in pants.

"I like that," she pronounces, and dog-ears the page. She places the cup in the sink next to the knife. She turns to leave and practically hollers. Marco in his underwear is standing right behind her, disheveled, ruthlessly scratching his chest.

"Where are you going?"

"To work, like always."

"Again?"

"What do mean, again? I have a job, Marco."

Batya pushes past him and heads for the door. Marco follows. "About what you said last night. You're right, this can't go on. I'm beginning to feel like I'm in jail again, all day sealed up in here. I've got to get out."

Batya pockets the three keys lying next to the phone. "Well, you've got a plan, Marco. Follow it."

He scans the corners, as if for a way out. "Too dangerous right now. I need more time."

"Then fix the faucet," Batya sniggers. "I'll buy you some more cigarettes."

Marco blocks the doorway. Batya moves her head from side to side, pouting, as if to say 'aren't we too big for this?' He holds out for another moment, then backs down. Steps aside and mumbles, "What time do you think you'll be back?"

"Same hour as usual," she informs him from the hall. "Four o'clock."

But four o'clock is eight hours away. A long time to wait, counting the minutes, until she makes her move. Batya, behind her desk, is even more irascible with the applicants. Twice Mr. Levy is forced to come out of his office, though by now he knows the source of the trouble. He lowers at her before slinking behind the glass, but one of these times, Batya's sure, she'll be scolded or even fired. She doesn't care. Soon she'll be leaving, the Registry and the city as well, perhaps as soon as today.

Lunch breaks, the secretaries eat in a local cafeteria. Over french fries and humus, there's the usual small talk about men. Batya for the most part eats alone. So the others aren't any the wiser when she packs up the remains of her sandwich and throws it in the trash. She hurries through the rear door of the cafeteria, into an alley and down a parallel street where there's a stop for the number four.

At this hour the bus is almost empty. Up front, a pair of old men lean bitterly over their canes; children in the back trade punches. Batya takes a seat in the middle of the bus. She feels strangely composed for one whose life is about to change. All those years she has dreaded it, the very thought of change, but now she's making it happen. Batya rests her head on the window and gazes beyond its bars.

Up the stairs she hurdles, heedless of Mr. Nafarstig. Out in the hall, through her door, she can hear Marco talking. His voice is dreamy—the voice that has wooed her in bed— only the name it utters is different. Distinctly, she hears him say, "Dina." She turns the keys quickly—no more fumbling—and breaks in.

"You stupid bastard," Batya snarls as she swipes the receiver from his ear and slams it onto the phone. "And you call yourself a professional."

Marco's nonplussed, shrinking at the head of the table.

"I . . . didn't . . ."

Batya drops into the armchair. Her eyes taper into slits, imperiously viewing the prisoner.

"Who is she?"

Marco shrugs.

"Dina, right? Of course, Dina. And don't look so surprised. You call out her name every night."

"She's a friend."

"She's a whore."

He starts to rise in protest: "Batya!"

"She's a whore and you know it, Marco. Sit down."

Marco sits as Batya moves to the opposite end of the table. Her voice is urgent but hushed: "You don't need her anymore. I will find the treasure. You just tell me where to go."

All of it comes back to her—the terror and ardor, the passion and the lies. "I'll do it," she tells him. "And you'll let me."

The table turns into the cemetery; cigarettes mark its stones. Marco explains, step by step: third row from the southern gate, ninth plot behind a eucalyptus tree. "Here," he thumps the table, "this is where you dig."

Batya nods, almost imperceptibly. She could find it, she feels, blindfolded. She rises from the table and enters the kitchen. From the broom closet she exhumes the plastic basket and from the sink, her knife.

"Couldn't you wait a bit," Marco begs as she prepares to exit. "You could always go tomorrow."

"But Marco, just this morning you were saying what a rush you're in. And besides," Batya rattles her basket, "this is Tuesday, my afternoon shopping in the *shuq*."

She kisses him on the lips. An open-mouthed kiss, lustful but hard. She ends it abruptly and leaves without once looking back, without even locking her door.

The fastest route is the number four, but to avoid detection she boards the eight. This, too, skirts the *shuq*, but detours toward the central station. It's a bustling place, people rushing to their connections up north; nobody will notice her. Batya advances along the terminals, past the ticket booths and falafel stands. A garbage dump behind the toilets provides a stealthy exit. Swinging her basket, Batya leaves the station and crosses a street, to the gates of the Muslim cemetery.

Unattended, overgrown, it's the only open lot in the city, the only space which the Registry cannot harness—its residents, protected by law, are free. Batya picks through the weeds, silently counts the headstones and their rows. She takes out a kerchief and totally covers her head. To anybody watching she is just another mourner, the descendant of some forgotten *sheikh*. The eucalyptus is not hard to find, huddling over the grave.

Batya stands before the headstone. The inscription is magnificent, a maze of Arabic scrolls. She wished she could read it; wished she knew the identity of the one who had waited all these years, so patiently, for her. It would be nice to imagine him—or perhaps her—but there isn't time. Batya kneels and retrieves the knife from her basket.

She digs. Her wrist whisks hairs from her forehead and sweat from her upper lip. The heat in the cemetery is smothering; the dust is searing her lungs. But she dares not rest, stabbing, gouging, until the knife strikes something solid. Quickly, she clears away the dirt. The strongbox emerges, no heavier than a load of groceries, and like groceries, it fits inside her basket.

Batya rises and with her sneaker sweeps the soil back into the hole. She wipes her hands on her shirt, and adjusts her kerchief. Picking up the basket, its handle clamped in her palm, she sets off in the opposite direction. Out of the cemetery and through a congested intersection, she hurries, toward the bus stop. It's here, just outside the *shuq*, that her heart begins to flounce. She asks herself: "What if he won't be there?"

Batya rounds the corner. "Yes," she thinks, "yes." He's just where he said he'd be—*a week of patrols in the shuq*. No matter what Marco may say of him, he's reliable, that Rami Cohen.

Pausing on the opposite side of the street, she breaks the chain that holds her pendant. Back in jail, Marco must have it—that is her only condition. She clutches it firmly as she saunters across the street. The Escort has its motor running and Rami Cohen sits behind the wheel. As though he'd been waiting for seven long years, since the day that Batya left home.

*   *   *

She sits sideways in the armchair; her legs straddle its arms. It's early evening, time for the five o'clock news. But the TV's off and the chair's turned around, toward the window and its singular view. Through the haze of twilight she sees the gates and the towers, the wires and the guards. She scans the smokestack for peeping men and the desert for irregular patrols. Nothing; all is empty. Except for the sand devil. It whirls in the middle of no-man's land, like a slave writhing out of her bonds.

Her routine is now a memory. She won't be found riding the number four bus or shopping Tuesdays in the *shuq*. No more days at the Registry or nights alone with her dreams. Everything has changed, everything, apart from her name—the name her mother gave her, Batya, which Marco has made her keep.

158

She's a disgrace to her family, pregnant and unwed, a pariah. Yet she will manage. Mr. Nafarstig is always eager to run her errands, and as for money, as Marco said, there's more than enough for two. Good-hearted Rami Cohen offered to make everything right and marry her, but she wouldn't hear of it. He's a detective now, earning his shield with Marco's arrest, and he has his career to think of. Beside, he makes a better friend than a husband—Rami Cohen, an asset, with so many burglars about.

Undetected, time creeps by; dusk slips into night. In the pace of search beams, the pall of yellow lights, she closes her eyes and thinks of him. Envisions him lying on his bed, half-naked, with his skin all pitted and scarred. He smokes a cigarette and blows blue rings to the walls. Occasionally, he fingers the pendant. Marco is thinking of her, she imagines, as she now remembers him. Mates of soul and cell, they will stay like this for the rest of their lives, she at her window and he behind bars, with nothing but the desert between them.

Batya senses the walls around her, the grates on the windows, and the locks in the door. She feels the fetus interned in her womb. Ours is a world of bondage, she understands; moons chained to planets and planets to stars, circling the universe's yard. Brains in their cavities and hearts behind ribs. All people are prisoners, she knows, some of them to each other.

The Maestro of Yerucham

He writes through the final movement, as always. His shoulders jerk and his waist swivels; a baton turns circles around his head. Perched on an apple crate, a humpbacked, big-eared man, short and stocky, he convulses. It could be the heat or some nervous condition, or maybe it's just the symphony—Shostakovich's fifth, adapted for a twelve-piece band, with solos for xylophone and lute—which is enough to set anyone fidgeting. Yet he doesn't seem to mind. He just goes on thrashing as if he were conducting the Israel Philharmonic. Right up to the closing bar when he rises on his toes and freezes—surrenders, with his hands in the air, the baton thrust high like the ghost of his missing index finger. Then, all at once, he sags. Head slung and his arms dangling, the Maestro takes his bow.

Applause crackles through the stands. The ovation's as enthusiastic as ever, yet it only makes him cringe. The clapping reminds him of small arms fire, of the depth of his current indignity. To think: a man of his past, his caliber, conducting an ensemble of fools, and in what—a concert hall? A theater? No. A gymnasium. And the audience! Hooligans, all of them, babbling in their tongues, a rash of red and brown faces. The mere sight of them rankles him.

He's grateful when the rabble disperses; now he can make his get-away. He steps off the apple crate and retreats to the back of the gym. Dodges the ladies of the Culture Committee whose job it is to thank him, skirts Sarka and Leibowitz, the rival cellists, who want him to second their duel. He picks his way past wrestling mats, through the ropes and chains hanging like instruments of torture.

164

Liberation is a question of meters. Slipping into his cap and jacket, he scampers across the parquet floor and out through the emergency exit. Straight into a fanfare of heat, the sun like a cymbal, crashing. But anything's better than that gym. He sheathes his baton in his jacket pocket, and tries to straighten his back. A free man, Roman Tolchowsky enters Yerucham.

He limps along Tabenkin, the main street which runs from the train stop up through the center of town. Past the synagogue and the Union Hall, along rows of apartment blocks bent on reverting to sand. This is Yerucham. Built as an immigrant camp forty years before, the immigrants have stayed—Moroccans, Indians, Rumanians, Uzbekis— steeped in dirt, desert-bound. You can see them today, chattering in the coffee shops, pausing only to eye a stranger or the Arabs who sweep their streets. Forgotten by the outside world, they remain like relics, like memorials to the original, the biblical meaning—*He Shall Have Mercy*—of Yerucham.

Roman hobbles with his head cocked sideways as if to get a better view, but he looks at nothing. Not at the sky, invariably vacant, or the potholes in the street. Neither does he return the stares of the men in the coffee shops, the querulous looks that follow him, this limping man with a hump and the missing finger, in his cap and jacket in the sizzling sun. He ignores the salute of Gershonshvilli, Yerucham's one and only policeman, stationed in the center of Tabenkin Street, waiting for traffic.

Roman hasn't the patience for fools, not today. His ears are still ringing with the din of the gymnasium, still burning with frustration. Yet he knows he shouldn't grumble. Many of the new Russian émigrés would give their gold teeth to have what he has: a job and a roof to sleep under. Life here is certainly easier than it was in Siberia. Apart from lessons, and the occasional concert in the gym, he has more than enough time to do whatever he wants to—read through old scores, reminisce. Or rather he used to. This afternoon, time is what he has the least of.

How could he have got himself into such a muddle? He's at an age when most men think of taking it easy, basking in the afterglow of their past. But his thoughts are fixed on the evening's rehearsal and the audition just one week away.

Panting up Tabenkin Street, he's beset by the hump and by phantom pains from his finger. There's a searing pain in his chest. Yet he insists on berating himself—for being so spineless, for playing, once again, the fool.

Of course it was foolishness that had brought him here— what else could it have been? How else could he have fallen for that oldest of bureaucratic tricks?

It was almost a year ago, that day when he'd arrived at the airport, a lone drop in a murky stream of immigrants. Channeled into one of many improvised cubicles, he'd confronted her: the clerk from the Absorption Ministry. He should have sensed the deception instantly; her painted smile was a give-away. So was the starched white shirt, the plaited hair. She could have been any Soviet official. Only her Russian—stilted, too grammatical—seemed out of place, as was the map behind her head, of Israel.

"Name?"

Roman told her. He began to spell it out, but the clerk was already scribbling.

"Date of birth?"

The clerk received it, and frowned. She looked him over, this short lame man in his seventies, in his cap and jacket of an indifferent dark shade, and her frown said it all: indigent, another taxpayer's burden. She stared at the violin case he carried, intrigued by the curious rattle it made when he set it down, wondering just what—trinkets, pills— he was trying to smuggle into the country.

"Profession?" was her next question, only this time

she didn't wait for an answer. There was a joke circulating at the time: what do you call a Russian immigrant without a violin case? And the answer was: a pianist. "Musician," she sighed.

Roman shook his head. He was going to tell her about his career in lumberjacking, to inquire whether they had any forests in Israel and if they could use another axe. But he said none of this. Instead, he uttered a single word, inexplicably, without thinking. The very sound of it shocked him.

"Conductor."

His response seemed to entertain the clerk, for a moment. Biting her painted lips, smirking, she beamed, "You're the sixth we've had today." But then her expression turned rueful. "All of them unemployed." She flipped through a dog-eared manual. "Still . . . I think we may have something. A position in a small city just south of here. Perhaps you've heard of it? Yerucham."

He repeated the name—Ye ru cham—in three even syllables, which was consent enough for the clerk. Roman watched, tugging his ear, as she filled out the form. He'd been through this routine before, and knew when to keep his mouth shut. It didn't take long. The bare facts, the skeleton of his life, lay on the affidavit. The clerk slid the paper across the desk, and handed him a pen. For several seconds he just stared at the scrawl of Hebrew letters which he recalled learning as a child in the village. The clerk waited. She seemed impatient, afraid perhaps that he'd change his mind—people could do that here, he'd heard—

but Roman's was settled. He signed in Cyrillic on the dotted line, and courteously returned her pen.

Now it was the clerk's turn to be puzzled, if by nothing other than his complacency. But the painted smile soon resurfaced. The clerk lifted her head to offer congratulations, or so Roman thought, but all she said was "Next!"

Whom did she think she was fooling? Before leaving the office, Roman stole a glance at the map. His eyes scaled down the country's green interior, through the freckles of towns and villages, down, down, to the unblemished bronze below. There, in the vicinity of absolutely nothing, he found it. Five Hebrew letters spelled out the name: Yerucham. *A city just south of here*, he recalled her saying, and almost laughed out loud.

168   Then the journey. Like so many journeys in his past, it began in a train station, though this one was little more than a garage. Nor was the train much better: an old-fashioned rattler with wooden seats and grimy windows, stuffy beyond description inside. Its single car was cramped with workers—truckers and miners with their brutish wives and children who behaved like demons, poking fun at him, plotting to steal his case.

Bedeviled by winds, by flocks of camels and goats, the train lurched southward. In a daze he sat, disoriented by the time changes, by the strangeness of the faces and smells. Here was a wilderness as barren as Siberia's, with sand instead of snow. Yet, for all his discomfort, lulled by the dunes, he eventually fell asleep. His body pitched and jolted, bobbed over roiling dreams, until all of a sudden it stiffened. An ear-splitting screech ripped through the car as the train broke to a halt. Roman awoke to find himself alone, the workers and their families gone. This was the last stop, a conductor announced. He had no choice but to exit.

He staggered down to a concrete platform. Dust choked him; the heat was vicious. In his cap and jacket, clutching his case, he watched as the train slithered toward the horizon. Soon, there was only a thread of smoke, and a distant whistle, like laughter. Only then did he notice the sign. Gnarled with rust and punctuated by bullet holes, were those same portentous letters he'd first seen on the map. Welcome, they spelled, to Yerucham.

Halfway up Tabenkin Street, Roman stops to catch his breath. The climb is steep; it grows longer every day. The heat gets heavier, baking like a brick around him. He has walked great distances in his life but none, he thinks, as grueling. And yet it is barely a kilometer, the pathetic breadth of Yerucham, to his house at the top of the hill. He has his excuses, of course: his age, the hardships. The limp that joined him a great many years ago on the road to Minsk, and the finger he lost in the war. And now there's this hump—his newest malaise—rising on his back like a dune. But the worst is the pain in his chest: a swollen, burning sensation behind his ribs, as if his heart were seething in acid.

It was one of his earliest memories, that pain. By the age of four he was already suffering from it constantly. It kept him from playing with other boys, and confined him to his family's house in their village in Poland. His father, a luggage salesman—valises and trunks—was often on the road, and the boy was left alone with his mother. She was a large and warm-hearted woman who'd do anything in the world for him, her only child. She took him to doctors such as the village had, men of dubious credentials, all of them smelling of schnapps. Their diagnoses ran anywhere from angina to the grippe, their cures were inhalations, camphor or salts. But the pain only worsened. That is until one of these so-called physicians—Roman remembered his gravy-spattered vest—ventured a different theory. The problem was not physical at all, he surmised, but spiritual. The boy had something inside him, a need, that had to be sated— freed, as it were. He suggested a course of instruction, in leather-working, for example, or carpentry, or music.

170

She needed to hear no more. From the doctor's his mother hurried down to the market and there bargained for a secondhand fiddle. She surprised him with it that night. "Nu, Romileh?" she asked, after laying it in his arms. His mouth fell open. Warped and worm-eaten, the instrument nonetheless enchanted him. Haltingly, he drew the bow across the strings. They screeched like the ghosts of the cats they'd come from. But to him the sound was angelic; already it soothed the pain.

A teacher was found, Misha Beckenstein, a fixture at village festivities. Wiry, ferret-faced with the impish manner of one who fiddled at the foot of marriage beds, he chortled at the first notes Roman plucked. But the boy learned fast. He practiced late into each night, discordant twangs that were unbearable to everybody—the neighbors complained—but his mother. She encouraged him, some would say drove him, until the twangs became melodies and the melodies, finally, music.

Within a year, Roman had learned all that he could from Misha Beckenstein. He was passed on to Mordechai Krauss who, as everybody knew and none was ever allowed to forget, had once auditioned for the State Symphony.

Krauss—*Professor* Kraus, with his starched collars, his blunt, cold features hardened with pride—considered the boy a prodigy. In the room where the professor lived alone with his moldy honors, Roman worked through his drills. Scales and octaves, arpeggios which wafted up and down with the speed of harried servants. The lessons left him drained and blurry-eyed, so that by the time he plodded home he could hardly think of anything but bed. But there his mother waited with a cup of tea and one of her inscrutable proverbs, and begged him to perform. And he played, with raw fingers and a chafed chin he ran through the drills of the day.

Another year ended and, with it, the lessons with Krauss. The professor had no more to teach him; Roman had mastered the drills. He could play the most challenging compositions, could sight-read and improvise on themes. Already at the age of eight, he began exhibiting the convulsions that would someday be his trademark. The rotating hips and swaying shoulders, as if the music were his very lifeblood spurting out. By then his mother had realized that he required a teacher of unique capabilities, a mentor. Such a teacher could no longer be found in their village, nor in the surrounding ones. They would have to travel to Vilnius—Vilna, the Jews called it—the old provincial capital.

They made the trip by train—for him, the first of many. But of all the journeys he would later make, none would be more magical. From the village with its ramshackle barns, its mud and soot and chickens, he emerged into a world of white stone. Everything seemed to be made of it, from the shimmering sidewalks to the buildings as big as castles. Hand-in-hand with his mother, he paused to stare at the people. At the rabbis in their ermine-collared caftans, scholars of the great *Gaon*, debating loudly as they walked. Gentlemen with bowler hats and ladies in stoles paraded down boulevards, with their uniformed children in tow. How awkward he felt in his hand-me-down clothes, so stilted in his jacket and cap. But each time he dawdled, his hand was sharply tugged. "Hurry, Romileh," his mother urged him, "We can't be late for the Maestro."

He remembered his embarrassment as his mother accosted passers-by with a scrap of paper with the address scribbled on it, questioning them in her Yiddish. The rabbis gave conflicting directions and the gentlemen just shook their heads, and they wandered for what seemed like hours. Yet for Roman the streets only became more marvelous, the houses grander and whiter. But then, as if truly by miracle, it appeared—a building so stately he first mistook it for a church. Even the doorbell pealed. The vision was quickly shattered, though, by a housemaid, withered and gray, who opened the door and barked at them in German. Scowling, she tried to shoo them away, but his mother kept pressing her with that scrap of paper. The housemaid deigned to take it finally, if only to get rid of them, sneering as she read, then gruffly ordered them inside.

They were led into a parlor, and told to wait, to touch nothing. His mother appeared upset: If the maid was so rude what could she expect from the Maestro? But Roman was too awestruck to fret, amazed by the sights of the parlor. Crimson brocade on the curtains, crystal in the glinting chandelier. A carpet comprised of every geometric shape ever conjured, he thought, each with its own shade of red. Thick with time and dust, the air absorbed every sound— all except for the toll of a grandfather clock. It guarded them as they waited, a sentry beside a corridor that seemed to be leading nowhere.

"Romileh," his mother fought for his attention. But Roman was elsewhere, imagining the audition. He saw himself blazing through the scherzo, the andante and the cadenza, taking his bow while the Maestro rose, clapping, and exclaimed, "Genius!"

His mother shook him by the shoulder. "Romileh, du herst?"

Roman gaped at her. She suddenly seemed so out of place in the parlor, worn-out and coarse, with her musty village smell: a stranger. What was she doing here at all, he wondered? It was music, not his mother, that had brought him.

"You just play your best, Romileh, and try not to bobble." She hitched up his jacket, and stuffed the cap in his pocket.

Plump and curly-haired, with ears too big for his head, he was aware of his plain appearance. His shirt-sleeves and pants were too short. Only the fiddle felt right, balanced in his hand. He swung the case jauntily, like a small valise, and imagined himself embarking on a long journey. The image must have occurred to his mother as well, for all at once she clasped him, pressed his face into her breast, and started sowing his head with kisses. She rocked like a woman in mourning, but Roman didn't move. He was mesmerized by the thought of adventure, by the beat of the clock, low and measured, like the chug of a departing train.

The maid reentered. With a stamp of her heel, she instructed Roman to follow. He started to peel away from his mother, but then she, herself, stepped back. Her eyes were damp, her lips trembled. "Remember, Romileh," she choked, and he braced himself for what he knew was coming: a proverb, one of her many sayings whose meanings had always escaped him.

"The mind wanders far for fame and riches, but your heart"—she tapped her own fervidly—"that's where the love is. That's home."

He repeated it slowly to show her that he'd understood, but the words fell flat from his tongue. What did she want from him?—to share her sorrow?—but how could he, with his imagination all fired up? He backed away from her, out of the parlor and down the corridor and into the Maestro's world.

The housemaid's heels hammered like gavels; portraits of sour-looking men, previous maestros perhaps, judged him from the walls. The corridor stretched interminably, as if in some kind of dream, a nightmare in which he blundered in darkness forever. But then, suddenly, the way was blocked by an oaken door. The housemaid knocked and cleared her throat; she leered at him. Bumpkin, she was thinking, kike; the nerve of him wasting her time, never mind the Maestro's. But he would show her—her and everybody else. Someday they would brag of how they'd once met him. She knocked again, and this time received her reply: a voice so thunderous that the floor actually shook. "Enter," it roared, and the housemaid shoved him inside.

The room was dim. Music stands, like tombstones, tilted out of the shadows; a piano sat sepulchral on the floor. A spooky place, so unlike the parlor, and the anticipation he'd felt there quickly curdled into fear. His eyes darted from wall to wall, from ceiling to carpet, but saw nobody. He wanted to turn and bolt down the corridor, flying back to his mother, but he wouldn't give the maid that satisfaction.

Roman was on the brink of tears. But then, from somewhere, came the rustle of papers, followed by an arduous sigh. He squinted into the gloom, at the smoky pyramid of light suspended behind the piano. Finally he saw it: the imposing figure bent over a desk, pouring over scores.

"Name," the Maestro demanded, without looking up from his work.

He began, "Rom..." but was cut off by the door shutting hard behind him. He was terrified. The Maestro seemed mountainous, even when seated, in his high-collared frock coat, with his hoary crest of hair.

"Speak up, boy!" The Maestro twisted around and glowered. His face was ashen, angular and cold. A winterscape, except for the eyes. They burned an acetylene blue.

Roman mustered his courage. "Tolchowsky, sir," he stated, "Roman Tolchowsky."

The Maestro winced, as if the name's very sound were painful, then repeated it: "Roman Tolchowsky, I see. And how many years have you studied?"

Roman hugged the case to his breast, and began to stammer in Yiddish: "Ich chop ungahoiven tzo..."

"German," the Maestro snapped, then massaged the bridge of his nose. "If you please."

Roman fumbled for the words. "Funf auder sechs..."

"Enough," the Maestro scowled, "If you can't speak, one can hardly expect you to play."

The Maestro fished through the papers on his desk, pausing now and then to hold one up to the lamp. Like a butcher selecting his knife, he appeared to be seeking the keenest, the one that would do the job as neatly as possible. He nodded, finally, and arched his arm toward Roman. Long, pale fingers dealt him the score.

A Paganini caprice, more intricate than any he'd ever

attempted, labyrinthine. Roman opened his case and removed the fiddle, dutifully tuned its strings. He arranged the score on the stand—everything was ready, but all he could do was stare. The staffs seem to blend together; the notes were an inky blur. The Maestro looked on, increasingly irked, but still Roman waited. Any second the maid would be summoned to cast him out, he figured. He'd be returned to his mother, a failure, apprenticed to his father, selling trunks.

Then, finally, it flowed, a trickle at first—a warm, wet sensation behind his ribs. He imagined it coursing down his arms and hands, into the fiddle which began to rise, and then through the bow, quivering over the fingerboard. The opening chords sounded strange, distant, as they'd been struck by somebody else in another room. But those were his fingers urging the bow, skipping up and down as though the strings were too hot to settle on.

The audition had begun. His shoulders started to rock and his waist gyrated; his head cut figure-eights in the air. The music was unleashed. He was no longer aware of the room or even of the Maestro. Though the tempo was brisk, *molto allegro*, he nearly ran ahead of it. As if he sensed the chords before they appeared, understood them as the composer might at the very flash of creation. He was inside the piece now, possessing it just as he, too, was possessed.

He didn't want it to end. Dizzied by the scherzo, giddy, he toyed with the pitch. He teased the vibrato so mischievously it almost made him laugh. Yet, when the finale came, he rose on his tiptoes and stiffened. With a ruthless slice he cut the last chord, then limply slumped to the floor.

The room fell totally quiet, and for a moment Roman was filled with dread. Perhaps he'd gone too far. Down on one knee like a penitent child, he waited for his punishment. But all he heard was another sigh, and felt the Maestro looming over him.

"On your feet," the voice said, not peevish anymore, but still stern. Roman did as he was told, but continued gazing at the floor, at the Maestro's shoes. They were shaped like violins.

"These are the rules," the Maestro began, "and you will obey them." The shoes clicked smartly on his every point. "Begin every morning at eight. Morning rehearsal three hours, two in the afternoon, followed by drills, theory and style." He paused. The long, pale fingers pinched Roman's collar, the released it. "And you will dress properly here. Rags are not acceptable."

"And above all, you will be dignified, Roman Tolchowsky," the Maestro explained. From that moment on, he was to be part of a line that led to the Maestro's own teacher, Oppenheim, and from Oppenheim through Marcucio and Volyushin, and so on and so on, back, "all the way to Mendelssohn in Leipzig."

Roman was still nodding, still shivering, as he packed his bow and fiddle. And before he could shut the latches, he heard the Maestro grumble, "And for God's sake, get rid of that piece of junk."

*   *   *

He did, that very day. His mother pawned her own mother's jewelry and bought him a new violin, a real one. There would be others as well, as he passed his first five years in Vilnius, practicing furiously. Then, on his thirteenth birthday, he received the instrument that was to serve him the rest of his life. No ordinary violin, but itself a work of art, crafted by a Venetian master famous with the virtuosos of Europe. Immaterial, almost spectral, the way the instrument ascended to his chin and hovered there. Pegs and scroll of the supplest wood, a graceful waist and tailpiece, with f-shaped holes like portals to untold realms of sound. Even the case, sleek with a slate-colored buff, was classic.

This was no gift from his mother but from the Maestro himself, a sign that his star pupil had come of age. The transition seemed perfectly natural to Roman, as he rarely saw his mother any more, preferring to remain at the boarding house close to the studio, even on holidays. She continued sending him letters crammed with village news—horses bought, barnyards burnt to the ground—and sealed with the inevitable proverb, but her son's thoughts were elsewhere by now: on his approaching debut in the Hall of the State Symphony.

That night arrived, a sparkling winter's night with the snow flitting blue on the marquee. The theater was packed. They'd come from around the city, those same splendid people at whom Roman had once gawked. If only his mother, increasingly infirm, could have seen this! He barely had time to think about her, though, the excitement was too intense.

Inside, the audience hummed; the lights, dazzling, went dim. He heard the rustle of the curtain as it parted, the applause as he strode onto the stage. He bowed awkwardly, stiff in his collar, his cummerbund. But suddenly it didn't matter. Neither his clothes nor the orchestra nor the tap of the conductor's baton. Only the music, a Saint-Saens Concerto. Writhing, he wrung every drop of sweetness from the score, pure as nectar.

Roman still remembers that night to the smallest detail. The curtain-calls and the incessant howls of "bravo." He remembers the impresarios who rushed backstage to sign him up. Here was a protégé, the latest in a prestigious line that had begun over a century ago with Mendelssohn in Leipzig. The old Maestro proposed a toast to the dynasty, and Roman had his first taste of champagne—to laughter all around. The reception continued late into the night, long after he'd coiled between the arms of a sofa, fast asleep in his tails.

He can still hear the sounds of that night, recreate its colors, even here in the bareness of Yerucham. These were events that took place more than sixty years ago, impossibly far away, and yet their memory is still so sharp—piercing, like the pain that has rekindled in his chest.

Near the top of Tabenkin Street, he stops to catch his breath. Below him he can see the melange of dilapidated buildings, and below them, the train tracks stretching over the horizon, as silent as unbowed strings. Less than a year has passed since he stepped off that train, yet it seems like half his life. A life that has been miraculously renewed, just when he thought it was over. Who would have imagined that here, in a place as run-down and forgotten as the one he was born in, he would find what he'd always been looking for, what he had long accepted as lost?

Roman climbs again. With his hump thrust forward, his stiff leg revolving like a paddle, he hurries to be on time for the rehearsal. Two hours, that's all he has with her, and one meager week before the audition at the academy in Jerusalem. Yet even now he sees the slack on the jaws of the judges. He can hear their pencils smack as they lay them down and mutter, "This, gentlemen, is genius."

Roman's home is a converted warehouse on the city's edge, a combined studio and apartment that belonged to Yerucham's last conductor, a Bulgarian who was rumored to have lasted a month. Concrete floors, corrugated roof, even on the best of days it's barely more than a shack. Roman can feel the heat pulsing through the door as he fumbles with the lock, feel it through his shoes as he enters. He turns on the switch, and watches the fluorescent lights flicker. Here is a music stand and there a baby grand piano, "A Gift of Congregation Beth Shalom, Paramus, New Jersey." The metal shelves are stacked with scores, their margins diminished by mice; in the rear, the alcove with his bed, a hot plate and a small refrigerator. And tucked away in a dusty corner, a violin case. Coal-gray and deeply veined, its form vaguely sarcophagal, the latches on its side are rusted solid, sealed.

*   *   *

181

Roman removes his jacket, lays it on top of the piano beside the tuning fork, the resin bars and the metronome—the sundry tools of his trade. He drops onto the stool and waits.

She'll be late again tonight, he knows it. He can see her sauntering in well after sunset as if nothing in the world were the matter, or else acting contrite. Yasmin in a pink taffeta dress and patent leather pumps, her hair all done up in ribbons. So her father dresses her, like a doll. Except for the scabs on her knees, you'd never know she was human. And her eyes. Dark and petal-shaped, how those eyes glinted the first time she held a violin. That's when he first detected it—he'd have to be a fool not to. *This, gentlemen, is genius.* If only she'd take it as seriously as he had at her age. Why, Roman sighs, why can't she be on time?

To distract himself, Roman gazes through his only window, at the city dump sprawling on the hill outside. A rhapsody of junk—hubcaps, iron rods, an upside-down baby carriage with its wheels turning—it's a pretty depressing sight even at sunset. But at least the smell isn't bad; the desert stifles all odors. Evenings, a refreshing breeze rolls down the hill and through his open window, rifling through the music scores, unsettling his cap and jacket. The violin case rattles in its corner.

He smokes a cigarette, and watches the sun sink behind the dump. Soon it is dark outside, and still no sign of Yasmin. What if she doesn't come, he asks himself in horror. What if her father has finally put his foot down? Roman twirls the tufts of hair on his temples, he tugs at an ear. He winds and rewinds the metronome that rocks like a worried mother, clicking its tongue.

Then, at last, footsteps crunching on the gravel outside his door. A tense duet of voices, then more crunches leaving, and a quiet knock on the door. He doesn't answer it, though, doesn't move, but listens as the squeal of hinges gives way to a sheepish scrape on the floor. It's a sound he knows well, that mince. But this time he won't give in. He'll scold her for her tardiness—unforgivable in any circumstances, but especially now, before the audition. Resolved, Roman straightens his back as much as possible, sits upright. The scraping grows louder as the shadows part like curtains, revealing an eight-year-old girl.

She's acting contrite, just as he expected. Head down, shoulders hunched, knees thumping against her violin case, she inches across the floor. Roman wants to yell at her, to shake her by those stupid ribbons in her hair and tell her exactly what he thinks. But he doesn't. All at once his resentment melts; he hasn't a bone in his body. Is it the face—the thimble nose, the chin split by an enormous dimple, the pink plump lips and cheeks—less like a real face than a confection? Or is it the wonder that lies behind it? "Yasmin!" he exclaims with his hands in the air—"Yasmin!"—as much in delight as surrender.

"Please forgive me, Maestro. I forgot what time it was."

Her tone is as strident as a fife's, and nearly as hollow. Shamelessly coddled, she knows nothing of regret. But it's not the tone that interests him or her insincerity; it's her

183

kneecaps. They're freshly scabbed, he can see, though she tries to conceal them with her violin case.

"You've hurt yourself again. How many times do I have to tell you that you've got to be more careful. You've been given this gift, Yasmin, this blessing, but you've got to guard it every minute of your life. One slip, one broken bone, and it's gone. Believe me," Roman says, holding up his stump, "I know."

Head still lowered, Yasmin nods; she's positively oozing remorse. Yet he knows she's only humoring him; behind that pout there's a smile. She shows it to him, finally, the minute he motions toward the music stand saying, "We must not waste any more time."

Giggling, she drops to her knees and flips open her case, as if it were some kind of toy. She takes out the instrument—an imitation Amati, richly shellacked—and swabs its neck with a cloth. She tunes each string with a testy pluck, and resins the length of her bow. Simple actions, but for Roman they're a source of astonishment, tangible proof of miracles.

Yasmin rises with her chin on the button, her bow poised diagonally over the strings. She's ready. Roman hands her the score he's chosen for the audition, Schubert's Fantasy in C Major, a daunting piece, and as if to punish her, he starts with its most difficult passage, the adagio. But if Yasmin's intimidated, she doesn't show it. She enters precisely on cue and performs the arpeggios, executes the runs with fingers pumping piston-like up and down the strings. At such moments, Roman would have been whirling, but

her body is perfectly still, ramrod, so that the only movement is the music's. But what music! Roman can hardly
concentrate. He fights the urge to lean back on his stool,
to revel in that celestial sound.

This is what he discovered shortly after arriving here,
a rare gem among the slag of remedial students. Dazzling
but terribly rough, in need of constant refinement, each day
another facet. And see how his work has paid off. In less
than a year she's where a normal student would have been
in seven. Spiccato, pizzicato—listen to that lyricism, that
tonality! Her errors, the few he hears, sound deliberate, as
if she were flirting with the composer, skirting the limits
of his patience.

The music ceases, suddenly. Roman jumps from his
stool.

"What? Have you broken a string?"

"I finished," Yasmin says.

"Finished?"

"The adagio, Maestro. I played it."

Roman shakes his head. "Very well. Once again, then,
from the coda."

The coda: *D.C. al Fine*—the end brings him back to the
beginning. From Yerucham to the gilded concert halls of
Europe. By age seventeen he had played them all: Paris,
Vienna, Lucerne. He had played Bartók in Prague, and
Prokofiev for Toscanini at Salzburg, had signed a contract
with Deutsche Grammophon, and would have begun record-
ing there, were it not for the changes occurring in Berlin.

He traveled by rail, in first-class berths, alone with the case on his lap. His mother's letters followed, but he rarely had time to answer them. Hardly knew what date it was or where the train was headed. Yet wherever he arrived there was always a crowd to meet him: reporters and booking agents and women. Older women, not just girls, pursued him. It didn't seem to matter that he was short for his age and pudgy. They wanted him for his talent, or more precisely, for his fame. They'd wait for him outside the theater, even in the wings, with the hope of seducing him. And they succeeded. He grew accustomed to their adoration, affected a pencil-line mustache and a pince-nez—a dandy. And why shouldn't he have been? The reviews he received were invariably raving, his ovations, standing. His concerts sold out weeks in advance.

It was at one of these command performances that he learned of his mother's illness. His father had died several years before, on the road selling luggage, his body returned in a trunk. And now her turn had come. The situation was clear from the wire: *Return immediately. Stop. Mother's condition worsening.* But how could he return? Wherever he was must have been days away from the village; one just couldn't cancel recitals. He pocketed the telegram and walked onto the stage. The curtain went up and later went down, each time to thunderous applause, but later he couldn't recall having played at all, it was as if he'd slept through the entire performance. His only proof was in the morning papers, the critics who praised his Tchaikovsky Concerto as the finest rendition in memory.

D.C. al Fine. Just when he thought it had ended, it begins again, out of the blue. Yasmin: his discovery, his hope. See how she flourishes, the way she manipulates those chords. Not even the stuffiest of judges in Jerusalem could doubt it —genius. Roman abandons the piano and again leans back on his stool, lilts wistfully from side to side as if he, himself, were performing. Memories fade and with them, the pain. In over forty years, it's the first real peace he's known.

Heavy steps on the gravel. Roman gazes up from his piano with a look of dismay. Is it possible that two hours had passed already? The metronome nods grimly as the steps pound up to the door, then barge through. But Yasmin hears nothing. As indifferent to time as she is to his disappointment, she goes on playing as the shadows scatter behind her. Not until the man imposes himself between the stand and the piano does she take her eyes off the score. But then, seeing him, she instantly ceases. She lowers her head as the violin drops, like a toy that needs rewinding. "Abba," she simpers: *Daddy.*

Roman debates whether to stand or stay seated. The chief of the Union Hall, a synagogue president, her father is a highly respected man in Yerucham. He's used to being feared. Any given day he can be seen strolling the length of Tabenkin Street, patrolling the town with Gershonshvilli, that ape-like lug, as if it were his own little kingdom. The men in the coffee shops tip their hats, their turbans and berets; the Arabs bow over their brooms. They live in dread of him, and Roman's no exception. A stranger to the city, he can hardly afford to be insolent, especially with the audition only a week away. He rises to his feet, and for the first time removes his cap. "Good evening, Mr. Toledano," he says.

Toledano all but ignores him. "And to you," he mumbles, while leering about the room. An overweight man, massive in his baggy shirt and trousers, he exudes a mawkish smell: scented soap and Brilliantine. Yet for all the slovenliness, there's an attractiveness to his face, and it's clear where Yasmin's comes from—the dimples and the deeply cleft chin. Together with the skullcap, it's the perfect disguise for undoing his rivals at the Union Hall. But Roman can't be fooled. Toledano can be cunning, cruel even, especially when it comes to his daughter.

Toledano adjusts the ribbons in her hair—she seems to enjoy the preening—then sends her to pack her instrument. Only then does he approach the piano. With pudgy fingers, he thumps the lid. He picks up the metronome, the tuning fork, picks them up and puts them down, while Roman just stands there, speechless.

He begins tentatively—"Your daughter has made tremendous progress"—innocuously enough. Though his Hebrew is good for an immigrant's, he's aware of his Russian accent, and he keeps his sentences short. "You should be proud."

"I'm proud of her just as she is."

"Yes, of course, but . . . the audition . . ."

Toledano looks up, eyes narrowed. "We have to talk," he says, "you know that, Tolchowsky."

Roman is stunned. It's been some time since he's been threatened, since he heard the sound of his own name. Everyone in town, even Gershonshvilli, calls him Maestro. Not knowing what else to do, he opens his palm toward the stool, inviting Toledano to sit.

The father shakes his head. "We must be alone," he replies, and then with a glance at Yasmin: "It's late."

"Of course, I understand . . ."

"But we *will* talk, and soon. Depend on it."

Yasmin is ready. She smoothes down the front of her dress, gazing into the music stand as if it were a mirror. Oblivious again to Roman, Toledano admires her. Around town, his love for her is legendary. The youngest of six children, the last his dying wife bore him, Yasmin is his treasure, his only weakness. Though he never takes her anywhere, confining her to this little town, she's had the best the town could offer—clothes, toys, violin lessons— and is thoroughly spoiled. Parents, teachers, all complain of her arrogance, but never once to Toledano—never, certainly, to his face. Nobody dares to challenge him, and yet here is Roman, the newcomer, planning to do just that.

Toledano is positioned behind Yasmin, her shoulders cupped in his hands. How she relishes his attention, Roman observes. He watches as her father bends to whisper in her ear, and Yasmin nods and smiles. "Good night, Maestro," she chimes, "and thank you so much for the lesson."

"You're welcome," Roman responds, also as if instructed. But a sudden urge makes him add: "And tomorrow, let's try to be on time."

189

As if the situation weren't bad enough—Roman could kick himself. Toledano will not have his daughter reproached, and surely not by a stranger. He snarls before pivoting her and hastening her toward the door. Roman can only watch as she disappears into the shadows, vanishing with the flick of a ribbon. For a second, he imagines himself running after them and snatching her back. But he remains behind the piano, shifting from foot to foot as if to mimic the metronome. He pulls hard on his ear, punishing himself with the squeal of the door's hinges, followed by its slam.

He is alone, as much as any time in his life. His chest is burning—bursting, as if his very heart-strings were frayed. But he mustn't give up, not for another week. It might mean his job or even banishment, yet he's determined to take the risk. Until that day in Jerusalem, Roman swears, he can never surrender.

Roman sits on the side of his bed—little more than a cot, really—in the alcove. It's late and he's had a long day, but he knows he won't sleep. His thoughts keep racing around Toledano, the power he holds over his Yasmin. It seemed impossible to break, yet he had to try. But then again, what if he failed? All of his sacrifices, his wanderings, would have been for nothing. Huddled, Roman shivers. He's afraid of dying anonymously, like his parents, with no marker or testament to his life. Like the family he abandoned during the war. He needs someone to carry on his name as he's borne that of others, to continue Mendelssohn's line.

Futile thoughts! Roman banishes them and lifts himself from the bed. Encased in aluminum, the studio is sti-
fling. He must get out and get some air; he needs some
human comfort. He retrieves his cap and bolts through the
door, the neon guttering behind him.

Yerucham looks different in the dark. TV antennas
and telephone poles poke through the gloom, like the masts
of a scuttled ship. Street lamps buoy between spreading
slicks of moonlight. Roman steps carefully down Tabenkin;
its potholes are as hazardous as snares. Fortunately, the
street runs straight to the city center, past the synagogue
and the Union Hall—Toledano's haunts—and the rows of
dissolving buildings.

Roman counts the corners; on the fourth he takes a
left. He wades down an alleyway shin-high with garbage,
with cats scurrying underneath. Housing blocs, seemingly
deserted, close in from either side. He enters the third of
these and feels around for the light button, finds and pushes
it, but the bulb is dead. Roman reaches out for the railing
and fumbles for the steps. Blindly, he labors up the five
steep flights to Lubova's apartment.

This is where he comes, several times a week, as his
energy permits. As desire and loneliness drive him. If nothing else, Luba is superior company. Always ready to listen
to him, even when she's drunk; to laugh, especially at his
expense. He doesn't mind, not often anyway, just as long
as he can rest his head on those voluminous breasts and
sink into her arms. The mere thought of it is enough to
lift his mood, to strip away the tension. Ascending through

the darkness, he can almost forget his deformities. Forget everything, as if he were no longer a man at all, but a strand of free-floating music.

The stairwell resounds with Moroccan ballads and the shouts of some family quarrel. The air, rank with piss and cabbage, is scarcely breathable. But the image of Luba draws him upward, reeling him in until he flops, twitching, onto her landing.

He raps twice on her door, then waits as always with his hands in his pockets and the cap pulled down to his brows. Roman hates this part—Luba's game—and wishes that for once he'd be let in without begging.

But she has to tease him, torturing him to the point of surrender. The bitch, Roman grouses; he should have his head examined indulging her the way he does. Yet he returns as often as he can, as if she were one of those rapturous women he knew in his youth, who seduced him in the wings of theaters. Lubova Yakobovitch: the antebellum debutante, ex-partisan fighter and Politburo friend, once pursued by commissars and now left like him, alone in the desert. Luba, the temptress of Yerucham.

Roman knocks again—her last chance, he tells himself—and turns back to the stairs. Tonight he hasn't the patience for her wiles. He hesitates, though, before the thought of returning down that pitch-black stairwell, the long retreat up Tabenkin. But he will not be made a fool of, not by Lubova. Bad leg first, like a bather testing the waters, Roman fishes for the steps, misses and falls to his knees. And that's how she finds him, prostrated. The rectangle of light explodes into a blinding beam, and in its glow, a stocky silhouette: Lubova.

"Why Romashka," she pouts, "since when must you beg?"

Roman pulls himself to his feet. He shunts his cap and tugs on an ear.

"May you fester in Hell," he says, lovingly, as he brushes past her.

He enters her apartment, her museum of restless clutter. Antique dolls and strangely shaped bottles, brushes and nail polish vials. Ostrich plumes in a plastic vase and in plastic bowls, artificial flowers afloat. Clutter and disrepair: feathers bleeding from her sofa and the paint from every wall. Water drips in the kitchen sink onto stacks of unwashed dishes.

"Ah, but *daragoy*," Luba laughs, "Darling, I already am!"

Roman staggers to her card table and sinks into one of its chairs. His head lies listlessly between his hands. Luba says nothing but places a bottle and a glass and plate of sardines before him. He touches none of it yet, but spies her through the gap of his missing finger as she shuffles across the floor.

She wears pink terry cloth slippers and a matching bathrobe beneath which her body looks squat. A bulbous nose and full-blown lips, hair teased high and copper-coated—it's hard to imagine her once a great beauty. But there's the glimmer in her eyes, a devilishness, which Roman finds hard to resist. Under the strata of makeup and the caps on her teeth, there's something alluring about her, sexy. Amazing, when Roman remembers all she's been through—the war, the camps, the death of everyone she ever loved or cared about. He marvels at the gnarled yet still feminine hand protruding from her sleeve, at the numbers on her wrist, as she fills his glass with vodka.

"Drink," Luba commands him, "it'll make you strong."

Roman swigs then grimaces. A homemade brew, it tastes alarmingly like diesel fuel, but he holds out his glass for more. Luba pours lustfully—she likes her men soused— as she bites off the head of a sardine. She chews as she speaks, loudly crunching bones.

"So how's the cupcake?"

Roman leers over the rim of his glass. "Stop talking about her like that," he snaps, "she's an artist."

"Artist, my rump," Luba huffs. She nods at the crumpled sofa. "There," she says, "that's where you make the music."

"Hooligan, you wouldn't know music from a fart." He bolts the second glass. "I once brought happiness to thousands."

Luba leans back triumphantly, waving the fishtail at Roman. "And I didn't?"

They bicker, but at least it's in Russian, a relief after a day of breaking his teeth on Hebrew. Intricate, passionate, Russian comes more naturally to him now, after forty years of using it, German less so. His mother tongue, he prefers to think, is music.

Roman's ready for another bout—perhaps they'll argue about finances, always good for a row—but he sees that her mind has drifted. Her eyes, too, gazing beyond his cap, across the room to a shelf above the sofa. Not a real shelf, but a plywood plank which, though splintered and warped, serves an exalted purpose. This is her altar. Here, too, there is clutter, but not like all the rest. Pipes and lighters, pocketknives and charms. These are the relics of her former lovers; her shrine to the passionate days when heroes died uttering her name. Silver flask, bronze medal—Order of Lenin, Second Class—the binoculars of the marshal who saved her from the purges before he, himself, was shot.

"Do you see that over there?" Luba points a lacquered finger. "Second from the left, the compass."

Roman lifts his head wearily. He pretends to look.

"That—I'll show it to you sometime, it glows in the dark—that belonged to Alexander Davidovich, commander of the Riga partisans. A poet, he was quite well known before the war, my Sasha. And a tiger, you should have seen him. Moving through the woods with barely a sound, closing in for the kill . . ."

Roman rolls his eyes. This, too, is part of her routine. He supposes it's meant to make him jealous, slicing him down to size before building him up again, in bed. Only with him it doesn't work, never has; it only brings him sadness. Sadness for Alexander Davidovitch, half a century and more in his grave, but most of all for her, a woman who, behind her games and her little keepsakes, has led a devastating life.

"And what kills!" she goes on. "Talk about art, this was genius. The way he conducted our band, like an orchestra! Swinging his bayonet like a baton and the music he made—so sweet, those shots, the screams—you should've heard it, Romashka!"

Luba could be quite a poet herself, with two or three vodkas under her belt. Roman did his best to look attentive, even riveted, if it made her happy. A man who survived on memories, he'd be the last to deny her hers.

But just then Luba grows silent. Her stare distant and her cheeks flushed; the flesh on her neck starts quivering. Grinning lasciviously, she is stretched across the table—it's liable to collapse, Roman fears. She whispers: "Do you know what it feels like to fuck a man who's splattered with enemy blood?"

Roman recoils from her. "Lubova Yakobovitch, you're drunk!" He withdraws into his jacket, crosses his arms over his chest. He expects to hear her whimper, maybe even burst out in sobs—a dreadful scene, he'll have to apologize and take back everything he said. But the sound that comes out of her totally unnerves him: laughter! Unbridled, scandalous, Luba rocking back and forth in a folding chair that creaks hysterically, as if it, too, were sharing the joke. With a brutal movement, she snatches his hands and tugs him forward, plants a clammy kiss on his mouth. "*Poshli yitbotsha,*" she hisses, "Take me. Now."

Roman is shocked and disgusted—at her, first, but also at himself. It seems he's gotten aroused. "But I'm not covered with blood . . ."

"*Dabeel*,"—idiot, she twitters as she hauls him toward the sofa. "Of course you are."

Luba yanks off his jacket and tosses away his cap, unhitches his trousers with the skill of a scrub nurse. Except for the hump and the missing finger, his body is well preserved, solid from his years of work in the sawmills. He still has his teeth, his tufts of curly gray hair. Only his ears have grown even larger with time, as old ears tend to do, though he likes to say it's a result of their yearning for music, like flowers craning toward the sun.

Luba kneels beside him, and quickly unties her sash. The bathrobe slides apart, releasing her breasts, prodigious and veined, her belly with its ruddy thicket. Beneath the cheap perfume, the swill of cigarettes and booze, she has a powerful smell, a woman's smell, and that, alone, can usually excite him. But suddenly he finds himself distracted. His eyes pace the walls, across the magazine cutouts—Swiss chalets, tropical shores—that hide the cracks, and up to the shelf above him. Luba bestrides his waist and grinds her hips, recites her best obscenities, but his desire refuses to revive. He grunts, she groans and swears, then falls to the sofa beside him.

"Poor Maestro, you've lost your baton," she frowns. With her long, polished nails she tickles the rim of his penis, pinches its crumpled skin. "Was it all that talk of Sasha?"

"Yes," Roman lies. He hopes she'll leave it at that. But not Luba. She slaps him, hard, on the stomach.

"Bullshit. You can't fool me, Roman Tolchowsky. It's that girl you've been playing with, that cupcake."

Roman rolls onto his side, away from her. "Oh, please . . ."

"I can understand a little perversion, gone in for it myself at times, but of all girls, Roman. You know who her father is."

"*Dabeel*," he quips, "You don't know what you're saying. It's the audition, one week to go and I don't know if she's ready. Worse—I don't even know if he'll let her."

"But of course he won't. How could he, with a decrepit old cripple like you?"

Roman moans into a cushion. The pain in his chest is pounding, hammering with every breath.

"Now, now, Romashka . . ." Luba mews. She rubs his shoulders and massages his hump. "You mustn't hurt yourself like this. The two of us, haven't we been through enough?"

"I haven't much time, Lubova."

She places a hand under his armpit and pulls him gently around, licks his neck and his ear. "Then darling," she whispers, "why waste it?"

He limps through the snow that gropes at his ankles. Snow as hot and as sharp as sand, it lashes his face and neck. He limps through the drifts, hugging the case to his chest as if somehow it could give off heat. But the winter is engulfing; it surrounds him on all sides, walls of wasteland narrowing as he wanders.

There, at the top of a dune, she greets him. Clapping her hands and jumping up and down while the hem of her pinafore bobs. He is startled by the sight. Imagine finding her after so many years still young and vibrant. And alive! Yes, she is: her hair has never been redder, the eyes more electrically green. There's an aura of warmth around her . . .

"Vati! Vati!" she sings, "Play!"

He feels his head moving from side to side. The snow, the cold, are bad enough, but playing would be too much. The pain gnaws fiercely inside him.

"Please, Vati. I've come so far . . ."

He holds up his index finger, the one shorn off at the joint.

"Don't be silly, Vati. You can play just as well without it."

She leaves him no choice, no chance of escape. He lays the case on the hard-packed ground, and struggles to lift its latches. But she cannot wait. She dances, whirling around in breathtaking arcs, her arms cracking like whips. He claws at the rust, but still the latches won't budge. Faster and faster she spins, churning up clouds of snow and sand until he can no longer see her at all. Play, he must play, before it's too late. He paws and scrapes until at last, one, two, the latches spring. The lid yawns open.

But the dance has consumed her. Layers of lace, of color and flesh, fly off into the wind. Through the mist of snowy sand he sees, turning, her skeleton. He delves into the case and pulls out the bow but it, too, is only a bone.

"Play! Vati, play!" she sings, and her voice rings on in the wilderness.

*   *   *

Tearing at his hair, panting, Roman shudders awake. He's confused in the dark. Is he in Vilnius, fifty years back, or here, tonight, in Yerucham?

Luba provides the answer. An undulating lump under a sheet beside him, she snores. She's been dreaming as well, and now and then murmurs a word that Roman recognizes—'*dacha*'—'firing pin.' He wonders what time it is, and scans the shelf for a clock. But all he can see is the compass that's gaping like some luminous clam.

The air in the room is sweltering. He removes Luba's arm from his stomach, and covers its numbers with the sheet. Swinging his bad leg over the sofa, Roman scrounges around for his clothes. He dresses quickly, quietly, so as not to disturb her, retrieves his cap and makes for the door.

200   It must be near dawn, though the sky is still dark. The moon hunkers over the shipwreck of the city, as if in search of survivors. Still reeling from his dream at Luba's, Roman escapes up Tabenkin. The Union Hall and the synagogue, the ruined buildings all fall away and soon he is on the gravel path to his studio. But he doesn't go in; the mere thought of sleep is abhorrent. Instead, he continues upward to the city dump, through the iron rods and the hubcaps, around the baby carriage, until eventually he reaches the summit. There, at the edge of a vast crater, stands the Liberators' Memorial.

The Liberators' Memorial: testament to Those Who Gave Their Lives To Free The Desert—as if a desert ever needs to be freed. Though Roman knows little of the battles it commemorates, he approaches the structure with reverence, removing his cap. He has spent many nights here, fleeing both his sleeplessness and his dreams, waiting for sunrise and dreading another day in Yerucham.

He enters a dome of cast-iron arches, like an orchestra shell, and indeed the acoustics inside are superb, ideal for concerts. And yet there is a dreariness about the site. There's nothing but sand inside, and a sense of captivity. How odd, he observes, that a place dedicated to liberation should look so much like a jail. Roman steps over empty bottles and cigarette packs—the memorial is a favorite among Yerucham's youth, for parties and midnight trysts. They couldn't care less about the past.

Finding an unlittered corner, Roman sinks to his knees. He gazes at the stars through the arches, at the moon, like a whole note set between bars. He dares not look down. Directly beneath him yawns the crater. Surrounded by jagged cliffs, desolate at the bottom, it's all that remains of a once-fierce volcano, itself a kind of memorial. Today, where lava once boiled, are mines for extracting minerals— phosphates, bromines—and a freight train to haul them north. Down there is a factory and work for any man who wants it, an hour's trek down a serpentine trail that begins just below the memorial. Roman has never taken it, though; he wouldn't think of it. He has a problem with heights, a man who's lived much of his life on tundras, and with little sense of direction, he's afraid of getting lost.

The desert grows cold at night. He tugs up his collar and clutches his jacket's lapels. The inner pocket still holds

201

his baton; its tip pricks the skin on his chest. How easy it would be to jab it all the way through—a favorite fantasy of his—spearing his heart so that the acid would finally drain out. Imagine it: freedom from pain, from nightmares. But then he remembers Yasmin, miraculous Yasmin, and the audition only one week away. Again, he sees the astonishment in the judge's faces. He sees Toledano, and the image of Jerusalem just as quickly unwinds. He's back to where he started from—*D.C. al Fine*—sleepless and cold.

He must make that audition. Yasmin must have her chance. But how? Roman rocks back and forth on his haunches, pondering. He recalls facing a similar dilemma years ago, and how the solution materialized one night out of nowhere. But he's an old man now, lame and humped, without the panache of his youth. He thinks and shivers, shields his eyes from the sand. Strong winds surge through the memorial. They whistle through the arches with a ghostly sound—some say the crater is haunted—that is echoed by another, far away: the sound of the northbound freight.

There had to be an answer.

He was still a young man, but already his career had peaked. True, the invitations still poured in and his seasons were booked, but the theaters were becoming more and more provincial, the audiences smaller, less enthralled. A prodigy is one thing, a grown-up musician another, or so his producers explained. Europe was full of virtuosos, almost as common as thieves.

Their words did little to improve his finances. Times were difficult, especially for one who lived on the road. Standards had to be met, but so did his bills—for transportation, tailors, lodging. The debts kept mounting as his reputation shrank, and being a Jew didn't help matters, politics being what they were. Budapest, Bucharest had cancelled on him; Berlin was out of the question. His situation was becoming critical. It was suggested that he take up residence in some large city, open a school, but the thought of teaching rich, bratty children offended him. Something had to be done, but what—Roman wracked his brain—what?

The answer materialized on the night of his annual concert in Vilnius, one of the few cities where he was still considered a star. Peering from the wings before the curtain, he caught sight of a young woman in the audience. A woman of contrasts—pale skin and jet-black hair, a child's tear-shaped face, and eyes dark with maturity. There was a haughtiness about her, the way she raised her nose and tucked in her chin, as if the theater itself were beneath her. Next to her sat an older, portly man, with ruddy mutton-chops and a cane: a figure from the previous century. *Was she his mistress?* Roman wondered. He decided to forget about her, and tried, yet the woman's image followed him as he walked out on stage, haunting him throughout the concert.

What torture it was getting through that performance, the encore and his bows. The curtain had barely closed when he broke into a run. He thrust his violin at the nearest stagehand, and dashed through the porter's exit.

A haze of fast-melting snow hung outside the theater. He pushed through the crowd, hindered by puddles and requests for his autograph, straining for any sign of her. Long minutes passed before he could break free and search the open streets. But by then she was gone. He'd missed his chance and would never see her again, he felt certain.

To save the fare, he made his way home on foot, following the trolley tracks through the better part of town. The slush-muffled streets were deserted and silent. But then, around a corner, he spotted a flurry of shadows. Roman sprinted, skidded on the slippery pavement. Two silhouettes came into view, the one broad, the other narrow—the old man and that intriguing slender woman. But by then they had seen him as well, rushing at them like a madman. The old man turned with his cane in the air, ready to strike, while the woman clutched at his sleeve. Roman was terror-struck. The police would be called; he'd be arrested and his career, what remained of it, ruined.

Matters might have progressed that way, too, if not for the fortuitous presence of a lamppost. By its glow, suddenly, Roman was recognized. The cane was lowered and the old man bowed. "Sir," he declared, "it is an honor."

Roman bent clumsily—he was totally winded—and mumbled that the honor was his. The old man introduced himself as Marius Wolf. Roman knew the name, had seen it posted on building sites around the city. Marius Wolf, the lumber magnate, owner of entire forests, of an expanding chain of mills. A very wealthy man indeed, certainly rich enough to keep a woman as young and beautiful as this. The woman, though, said nothing. She continued to cleave to the old man's side as if unconvinced of Roman's identity. He couldn't help staring at her. Tall and attenuated with scarcely a hint of contours, her long neck angled skyward. And when she looked back at him, so defiant, he wanted to melt with the snow.

The old man sensed his predicament. "So rude of me," he apologized and nudged the woman forward. Roman braced himself "Permit me to introduce Bernice," Marius beamed, "my daughter."

Marius invited Roman to his house. The place was sumptuous, far more so than the Maestro's had been, and preserved just as Marius' wife had left it, five years earlier, at her death. Its prize feature was a library, lined with books and busts of the immortal composers, large enough for the concerts that Marius held there—chamber music mostly, for music was his deepest passion. Sipping his brandy, puffing a cigar, Roman listened as his host went on about the virtuosos he'd known, the talents he'd sponsored. Life's greatest gift, he called it, the ability to make music; if only he'd been blessed with it. How he'd hoped his daughter would be. Bernice, his other obsession, had been lavished with first-class lessons—piano, harp—but while she gained some proficiency, she had never showed that spark.

Bernice sat through all this without uttering a sound, as if her father's litany were all too familiar. Severe in her high-backed chair, in a black serge gown which accentuated her thinness and pallor, she resembled nothing so much as a treble clef. At least that's how Roman saw her, the key to a harmonious future. But what would she, this affluent beauty, want with a has-been like him? He barely had a *zloty* to his name, and his wardrobe was beginning to show it. Frayed cuffs, that telltale shine on his suit—Bernice obviously noticed. He could tell by the way she looked at him, down the length of her illustrious nose. If genius hadn't impressed her, how could his lack of means?

Roman left the house after midnight, but not without an invitation for dinner the next evening. He'd made a show of declining at first, but Marius insisted, and so he came that night, and the night after that as well. They sat for hours discussing concertos, dissecting them theme by theme as played on Marius' immense Victrola. Bernice kept to her chair. Eyes unyielding, hands folded over her lap, speaking only when she rose to say goodnight. Marius watched Roman's expression as she left the room, hoping to detect in it some sign of disappointment. He already had it planned. Roman's genius was worth more to him than a dozen sawmills, than myriad trees, and he wanted it. He wanted his two loves wed, be a father to both daughter *and* musician.

No fool, Roman sensed his opportunity, though the ease of it surprised him. A casual proposition that he made to Marius one week later, after listening to Mahler's Third, settled everything. The fact that Bernice was never consulted appeared to hamper neither of them. She loved her father utterly, and would do whatever he bid. Roman and Marius merely shook hands—an old world affair—and so the matter was closed.

The wedding, a great society event, would have been remembered long after that had it not been for the war. Hundreds of guests, the cream of the city, gathered. An abundance of the finest food, the best wines, all served on tables effulgent with silver. And there was music, of course, a full orchestra that performed polkas and waltzes and even some jazz, playing uninterruptedly until the ceremony began. Roman pronounced the vows. Then, stomping mightily, he broke the glass, and as the guests applauded, he raised Bernice's veil. The face behind it was just as delicate, just as white—another veil, but one that could not be lifted. He kissed her with a flourish, and gave her a sip a wine.

Later, near dawn, Marius Wolf proposed a toast—not to the happy couple or even to his departed wife, but to music.

"To music," he said, embracing the guests with his glass, "the home which unites us, no matter where we come from or where we go. Our common heart." He drank, and summoned Roman to play.

The groom raised his arms in refusal only to find them laden with his violin case. The guests kept applauding until Roman gave in. Flipping the latches, he lifted the lid as reverently as he had that veil, and the instrument emerged to a round of sighs. Roman placed the bow across the strings, he breathed deeply, and played. The cadenza from Mendelssohn's Concerto: dulcet, impassioned, he swooned with it. Like a man entranced, he wheeled and trembled; his fingers ravished the strings. Music filled the hall, just as Marius had wanted. It rang in the crystal and rippled the wedding canopy. Several of the women wept. Roman spun through the final bars and then went rigid, holding the trilled harmonic. Then, opening his eyes, he saw her. Alone in the back of the room, under decorations already wilting, stood his wife with an expression he'd never seen on her before—wistful, fatigued perhaps, but unmistakably adoring.

That look had gone, later, when they reached their marriage bed. Bernice let Roman undress her. She lay motionless as he fiddled with her clasps. Her body, shorn of its gown, looked blanched, almost skeletal. She was even thinner than he'd imagined, a Modigliani body, with ribs and hip bones protruding. Yet he found her irresistible. He turned her on her back and spread her hair on the pillow, and for a long time just stared. The small, floury breasts with their cinnamon nipples, her stomach flat and sloping toward the furry gap between her thighs. His fingers plied her neck and shoulders, the secret places he'd learned about in theater wings. But Bernice didn't stir. She stretched out before him, magnificent and mute.

He made love to her, a short, technical operation which left him feeling cheated. He would try again many times in their first weeks of marriage, but always with the same frustration. Yet, slowly, he reconciled himself to her lack of ardor. This was the price he had to pay for the luxury of performing, for life in the house of Wolf. An investment, perhaps, but with one unexpected dividend: within a year, the birth of a baby girl.

*   *   *

The scrape of his shoes on the gravel reminds him of the sound that Luba makes, chewing bones. Drunk with exhaustion, he has trouble with the lock. It takes much fumbling before he finally opens the door. But then, instead of the usual creaking noise, he hears a chord—a discord, rather: A, C Minor, E, struck on the piano inside. Anxiously, Roman pulls on his ear and considers the possibilities: the wind? A cat alighting on the keyboard? A bandit, perhaps, or one of those ghosts who supposedly haunt the crater? But he doesn't believe in ghosts, and there's nothing worth stealing inside—or so he thinks at first. Then he remembers the case.

Roman darts, leg flapping, into the darkness. He reaches out for the switch, wincing as other chords jar—B flat, D minor—and the fluorescence pulses. He can sense a presence, though at first sees nothing, not in the alcove nor behind the metal shelves. It's not until he comes to the piano that he finds him, a man dressed in white, or what had once been white, rags. He's barefoot and gaunt, with a shaven head that's bent to the keyboard, as if to impart a secret.

Roman stammers: "What are you . . . how did you . . . ?"

"I hate to tell you this," the visitor says, and tries another chord, "but this thing's really out of tune."

"The door was locked."

A sullied thumb points at the window. "Though I don't blame you for keeping it open. Splendid breeze tonight."

Roman is losing his temper. Frazzled body and soul, he hasn't got time for this lunatic. "I want you away from my piano and out of my home, now, before I call the police."

"The police," the visitor gasps, and makes a monkey face—a clear reference to Gershonshvilli. "Oh, my," he says, and then in the same breath: "got anything to munch around here? I'm famished."

Roman leans on the music stand, and tries to clear his thoughts: Why is this happening to him, now, when he least needs it? Why did he go to Luba's house, and what in God's holy name is he doing in Yerucham? But he knows there'll be no answers, and giving up, Roman groans: "Elipaz."

"You have a memory."

"More than one, alas."

"Forget 'em," Elipaz says, "We can mull things over later, you and me, over dinner."

Roman retreats to the alcove. He'll feed the bum, get rid of him, then try to get some sleep. He opens his refrigerator, grateful for the untainted air inside. The desert that stifles all smells seems to have made an exception with Elipaz. Garlic and motor oil, campfires and sweat—a noxious pall seems to hover over him; it clings to his rags, and to the grimy satchel he carries around with him everywhere.

Foraging, Roman finds some sweet rolls and an aged wedge of cheese. He gathers these up and turns to catch Elipaz behind him, toying with the violin case.

"What've you got in here?," Elipaz asks, shaking the case to his ear. "Sea shells? Dice?"

Roman snatches it away from him. "Don't ever touch that, ever!" he hollers, and restores the case to its corner.

"Know how you feel," Elipaz says while following Roman out of the alcove. "I'm real sensitive about my satchel, too, and there's nothing in there but water."

Roman sets two plates on the piano lid, and around them arranges the food. Bug-eyed, Elipaz looks on. Large, stained teeth strain his lipless mouth. A man of uncertain age and sanity, he'd once before entered Roman's home—the door was open—and it had nearly cost him his life. Roman was freshly arrived from Siberia, a lawless land, and had a method for dealing with bandits. He drew out his baton and charged. It was only Elipaz's satchel that saved him, absorbing the initial thrust, and then his kindred look—hunted, haunted—of a survivor.

"You call that a meal?"

Roman slices the rolls and cuts the mold from the cheese. "A feast where I come from," he says.

"Pity. All the way over here I could only think of . . ." Elipaz stuffs a roll in his mouth. "Mutton."

"I thought you were a vegetarian."

Swearing off meat was last year's vow, Elipaz explains. "Now it's mayonnaise."

"You truly are a holy man."

"Not holy, repentant."

"Must've been some sin, then. What was it?"

Elipaz scratches a scalp that is utterly shorn of hair,

cloudy gray in color, like a burnt-out light bulb. "Can't say I recall," he confesses, "but I'm sure it was something serious." He flattens the cheese on the second roll and fits them both in his mouth. "I mean, the way I look at it, we all commit at least one really big one at some time in our lives. I'm just playing it safe."

Roman nods sympathetically. "Smart move," he says, "but how?"

"How what?"

"How does one repent?"

Elipaz swallows his sandwich; it slides in a lump down his throat. "'fraid I don't know that either," he gulps. "But this much I do know: when it happens, there'll be no mistake about it. The minute you atone, you get to go home."

212

"And if we have no home?"

"You will, once you've atoned."

These words said, Elipaz steps away from the piano, takes his satchel, and turns not toward the door, as his host longs for him to do, but to the alcove. "I really could go for some shut-eye," Elipaz mutters, and before Roman can stop him, he's collapsed on the bed and snoring.

There's no use trying to wake him; the sheets are already soiled. Propped on his stool, Roman lays his head on the piano. If only he can get an hour or two of sleep, real sleep, undisturbed. He starts to doze and his body, slumping, presses the keyboard. Another chord sounds, this one shrill. It reverberates around the room, from the shelves to his bed and the violin case, and then winds through his dreams, becoming first a scream and then a young girl's laughter.

Roman was hardly himself. He pitched and swayed as usual, and his fingering was characteristically clean, but he just wasn't concentrating. He couldn't. He kept losing the cadence, the flow. The timbre seemed to flee from him, like a child who taunted him and ran.

The child: it was all her fault. Merely by sitting there with her pinafore hitched from sliding off the chair, with her mouth puckered and her knees splayed, waiting for the moment when their eyes would meet so that she could stick out a tongue brightly blackened by licorice. It was all a game to her, distracting him. What did she care if her father looked like a fool?

Fortunately, his father-in-law didn't notice. Heavily blanketed in his wheelchair, Marius was happy just to be out of bed and in his own library again, listening to music. He beamed and applauded, as did the other guests at what had become a Sunday afternoon tradition—the library concerts, the only performances that Roman now gave.

Bernice was there as well, pinioned between a Mozart bust and the bookshelves, and she saw it all. She relished it, seeing her husband flustered like that, and the power the little girl held over him, her pluck. She had no doubt that Roman would be furious at her later, but still she did nothing to intervene. She remained half-hidden where she was, and clapped politely when the concert was over.

Trays of canapés were brought in, and champagne—

unthinkable luxuries at the time. The city of Vilnius had passed from Polish to Lithuanian rule, and even basic supplies had grown scarce. The guests wasted no time in gorging themselves. It occurred to Roman that this was why they had really come, for the food, rather than for his playing. Especially after this performance, who could honestly say that he deserved the maestro's title anymore? Replacing his violin in the case, he gazed through a rain-spangled window while the little girl, crouched behind Beethoven, tried but failed to snare his attention.

Under their umbrellas, laughing, the guests finally departed. Marius was wheeled back to bed. Only Roman and Bernice remained in the library, seated at opposite ends with their daughter in-between.

"You ought to be ashamed of yourself," Roman was saying, "I ought to punish you and good." The girl kept rolling her eyes. "Do you hear me, Elena?"

Elena leaned forward on her chair, elbows poised on her knees. "Do you always have to shout so much, Vati?" she asked, almost sincerely. "I swear, your voice is as big as your ears."

Bernice made a choking sound, and turned quickly back to the books. Roman frowned at her. "There you go. You heard that, and yet you just ignore it. I ask you, is that any way for a girl to talk to her father?"

"How *should* a girl talk?" Elena interrupted.

"Not like that, I'm sure." Roman folded his arms. He stomped his foot. "Nor should she be making silly faces when her father is in the middle of a concert."

Elena arched her brows empathetically. She was not a pretty girl, at least not in the conventional sense, freckled with a nose sufficiently curved to give her a brash, slightly predatory air. But her hair and her eyes were striking—the hair wild and cranberry red and the eyes a green so stark it was almost garish. She had none of her mother's grace, nor her father's aptitude for music. She seemed to belong to neither of them, and yet here she was, their daughter, and all they had between them.

"I'm sorry, Vati, really I am." Elena made a half-hearted effort to keep from giggling, and failed. "You just look so funny squirming . . ."

"Enough of this!" Roman bellowed to no one in particular, and then to Bernice. "I won't stand for it anymore."

This brought her from beside the bookshelves to behind her daughter's chair. "Elena, I think it's time you went to your room."

"And stay there," Roman added.

The girl rose slowly, demurely as if she were about to bow. But instead she stood, head flung back so that her fiery hair licked the back of her thighs, her freckled nose thrust high. "Maestro," she proclaimed, "I believe you are a genius." Then, with a whisk of her pinafore, she about-faced and strode out of the room.

Roman rocked on his heels, flustered. He'd grown fatter over the years, and swaying, he looked to Bernice like a buoy in choppy seas. She turned toward the books again, this time with a hand across her mouth.

"You're laughing at me, too" Roman snorted. "You're as bad as she is, indulging her like that."

"At least I don't ignore her."

"It wouldn't hurt now and then—the girl's thoroughly spoiled."

"No thanks to you, that's for certain. With your society friends and your . . ." She was still speaking to the books. "Distractions."

"I don't want to discuss this," he said. Now it was his turn to look away, to the window and her reflection framed in its panes. As stout as he'd become, so she'd grown thinner—her once-elegant clothes hung from her bones— and as pale as the library's busts. Yet she still retained her beauty, Roman thought, she wore it like a habit. Her stark, elusive beauty.

"Society was your idea, nor mine," he continued. "Yours and your father's. And as for my distractions, as you call them, I'd have thought you'd be grateful."

Bernice dropped into the chair where Elena had sat, with a heaviness that belied her weight. She appeared about to cry. But then she straightened her head, abruptly, and folded her hands on her lap. "You've changed," she said.

"Well at least one of us has."

"All day long you sit and complain how hard it is not to perform, how much you miss being on the road. And yet, when an invitation finally comes along, the first thing you do is turn it down."

"Invitation? From where for example?"

"From Moscow—it's the second you've rejected. It's not polite, to say nothing of intelligent."

Roman's hands plumbed his pockets. "I will not play for Reds."

"For students, then, but you turn them away, too. What about that heir you were always talking about, your precious dynasty?"

"There's time enough for that." He left the window and moved behind her, bending to hiss in her ear. "All the time in the world."

Bernice retorted: "Then make some for your daughter."

This remark, at last, got to him. He'd never had any interest in children, and especially not in this child, Elena. She was no musician, no heir to the line that passed through him backward to Liepzig. On the contrary, in time he'd come to blame her for the eclipse of his own career. Her early illnesses had confounded his schedule, just as her pranks now chipped at his pride. *She* was the cause, not the waning of his talents or the economic crisis in Europe, not the closing of so many borders to Jews. It was an irrational thought—that at least he knew—but he couldn't help dwelling on it.

Roman threw his hands up. "What do you want me to do?"

"You could take her for a trip—it needn't be a long one. A picnic."

"A picnic, yes, and then what?"

"Then you may look back at it fondly someday."

217

Bernice paused, almost indulging a smile, "as the happiest day of your life."

Roman hugs himself against the cold. A layer of fog now covers the crater—it looks thick enough to step on—as dawn seeps into the sky. Inside the Liberators' Memorial where he sits, the wind's still swirling, still whistling with a twitter that reminds him of laughter.

Bernice was right, and it was one thing he would never forgive her for. Imagine how differently his life would have turned out for him had it not been for that day? Had he not experienced that moment of vast, unqualified happiness, he would never have known its loss. He might have given up wandering after the war, settled down, fathered more children—who knows? He could have thrown his old violin case away, once and for all, or better yet, sold it, and got on with things.

He would never have heard of Yerucham.

The day was intensely sunny, so bright its memory could still make Roman wince. Sparkles turned on the slow-moving waters of the Neris, boats slid effortlessly by. Along the banks, the high grass waved in the cross-breezes, back and forth, keeping time.

Sweating in a woolen suit too thick for the weather, Roman plodded. In one hand he carried a picnic basket, duly packed by Bernice, and in the other, his violin case. A blanket was slung over his arm. Elena carried nothing. Several paces ahead of him she skipped, barefoot and carrying her pumps, dress fluttering. She picked flowers and sang songs that were, to Roman's ear, void of either sense or melody. Elena danced, and her father panted behind her.

But then, suddenly, she stopped—in mid-air almost, on her tip-toes. "Here!" she shouted. She dropped to her knees, and smoothed the grass in front of her. "Here, Vati. God made this spot, one million trillion years ago, just for us."

Roman could see the grass was wet, and tried to lay out a blanket—tried but the breeze kept rolling it back at him. With a groan, he finally threw up his hands, and sank to the ground. Elena busied herself unpacking. Neatly she laid out the preserves and the biscuits, soda bottles and a roasted chicken. She folded a napkin and placed it on Roman's lap. "There, you're my perfect picnic Vati," she declared.

Though conversation would have been proper at this point, he couldn't think of anything to say. But Elena didn't care. She spread jam on the biscuits and poured them both something to drink, humming all the while. Roman accepted whatever she gave him, chewing dutifully as his eyes followed the river winding through the fields, away toward a smoke-spewing factory. He watched Elena as she gobbled up a drumstick, then tossed the bone in the water.

"You know what I think, Vati?" she asked. She smacked her hands together. "Guess!"

Roman hadn't a clue. He peered at her, at her wide face, pale except for the freckles and the ferrous green of her eyes, her hair seemingly aflame. The sheer luster of her struck him suddenly, and the thought that this ten-year-old child—she *was* ten, wasn't she?—was his daughter.

She gave his ear a tug. "I think your ears are gigantic. Are all musicians' ears like that, so they hear better?"

Roman didn't answer her. Though meant to be playful, the tug had stung and annoyed him. "You shouldn't do that," he complained, vigorously massaging the lobe.

Elena giggled, "I'm doing you a favor, don't you see? The bigger they are the better you'll play. Just wait, soon they'll be the size of an elephant's, then you won't have to stay at home so much. You can go back on the road."

"The road? Where do you get these things?"

"From Mommy. From *you*. When the two of you were talking in the library."

Roman blushed. Clearly she'd heard everything.

"And about those distractions—did I say the word right?—I think Mommy *would* be grateful. She really does care, you know. I mean about your music. More than anything."

"Please, Elena . . ." Roman groped for a seasoned response, but ended up being dismissive. "You don't know what you're talking about."

But Elena wasn't put off. "And why won't you play for those people in Moscow?" She tousled her hair and winked at him. "What's wrong with Reds?"

"I won't go, and that's that."

"It's all my fault." She stretched a hand toward his face. Roman leaned away, fearing another tug, but she only touched his cheek. "You're staying because of me."

That was enough for Roman. He said, "If you've finished eating, I think we should be heading back."

"Now? But why?" She clicked her tongue at him reproachfully. "Silly Vati, we *do* have time—I heard you say that, too—all the time in the world."

With this, Elena sprung from the grass, and swooped up the violin case. "Play for me now. Please. For *me?*"

Again, he was at a loss for words. It'd been Bernice's idea, taking the violin, not his, and he'd felt foolish carrying it. But there was Elena opening the latches, removing the instrument and its bow. Roman looked this way and that. No one was watching; they were alone. What choice had she left him?

Smetana's *Maldou* was the piece he chose—or rather it chose him. Brave serenade, it seemed to bound off the strings and skim the surface of the water. Soon, he, too, was sailing, thrust between conflicting currents, twisted this way and that. And Elena twisted with him. Though he couldn't see her, she imitated his every movement, his gyrations, his jerks, building up to the finale when his body went rigid and straight. Then, all of a sudden and without warning, she pounced on him, and so hard he almost fell flat on his back.

"Oh, Vati, that was magnificent!"

Roman clutched his instrument. "Elena," he gasped.

"Promise me you'll play for me always," she cried. She hadn't let go of him yet. "Promise you'll take me with you wherever you go, even if Mommy says no." A note of

221

conspiracy crept into her voice. "I read a story once, about a father who ran away with his daughter, far away where no one could harm them. It'd be like that, like you kidnapped me."

He wanted to tell her that he wasn't going anywhere, to stop talking nonsense. But he couldn't get the words out, not with her arms tight around his neck, and after a while, he gave up trying. He placed his hands on her head, crowned it with his violin and bow. They stood there, entwined, for an entire minute or more. A whistle sounded at the factory; its stack belched fire and smoke. "I promise," he said. "Now I really do think we should start home."

At sunset, they retraced their steps along the Neris. The river moved swiftly now, like a conveyor belt whirring toward the factory. But Roman took his time. He wanted the trip to last, hoping that somewhere along the way he'd find the right words, the ones that he knew she'd been waiting to hear. If only he'd gone on playing—in his own fashion he could have said everything. You mustn't be so impatient, he counseled himself, there'd be other conversations, other picnics. For now, he settled for lobbing the empty basket onto the water, and freeing his hand for hers.

The next year saw Soviet tanks in the streets of the city, and all the street signs changed to Russian. The country was occupied, the result of a pact between the USSR and Nazi Germany, and Red flags flew over Vilnius. People were shot, people they knew disappeared and for no reason other than the jobs they'd held or a chance remark they had made. Within a year the world they'd known had vanished. Red army troops were billeted throughout the house, leaving them only the library. There they lived with scant furnishings, among the busts and the bookshelves—subsisted—he and Bernice and Elena, all except for Marius who'd been blessed with a timelier death.

"You *will* go," Bernice insisted. "It's your only hope."

Roman stood with his hands at his sides, in a posture of rapt attention. It was the same attitude he adopted almost daily now, during the forced lectures on capitalist crimes, on the glories of the workers' dictatorship. He appeared to listen while, inside his head, music played. Rondos, fugues, bagatelles—he envisioned the scores, mentally executed the fingerings. Now he was working on a Haydn saraband, a singularly brooding piece, while Bernice lectured him as well.

"Your last hope," she was repeating. "They know about the two rejections. There are rumors about your arrest. God only knows why they invited you again, but to turn it down now would be suicide."

Roman sighed; he hadn't the energy. The last year had drained him—the deprivations, the threats. He'd lost much weight, acquired a wan, deflated look.

"What do you want from me?" he asked finally. "To exhibit myself like some fool?"

"So that's your problem—looking like a fool," Bernice fumed. She'd also grown thinner—she, who had a lot less to lose—and paler, too. Yet, despite their travails, she'd lost none of her presence, nothing of her former poise.

She still looked down at Roman. "That's just what you'll be if you stay here. And a dead fool at that."

Roman felt like cowering. He abandoned his show of attention, dipped hands deep into his pockets, rummaging for an excuse. Just then he heard it: music. Not within his head but from the far end of the library, from behind the sheets they'd slung between the busts. Within her makeshift bedroom, Elena was singing.

"She'll want to come, you know. I promised her."

Bernice frowned. "Then you really are a fool, Roman Tolchowsky. Even if the Russians invited her—and they didn't—she'd only be a burden to you." Her voice fell below a whisper. "It'll be the death of both of you."

Roman's hands flew from his pockets and into the air over his head.

"Death! What am I, some kind of fugitive? From what, exactly, am I running?"

"Shut up," Bernice scolded him. "You know as well as I do. Everybody in this city has, for days." Brittle fingers dug into his sleeve. "There isn't much time. You've been given this chance, take it."

Were they actually having this conversation, Roman wondered? Was he really understanding her right? He gestured toward the partition. "And what about her?"

"She'll agree, she's smart enough." Bernice paused and sighed. "*And* she loves you."

Elena's music was, as usual, atonal, but it sounded like an aria to Roman. Warily he approached the partition, unsure of what he was going to say. "Knock, knock," he called into the sheet, and was told in sing-song to enter.

Elena lay on her stomach with her ankles crossed above her back, chin wedged between her palms. She had an absorbed look on her face, as any child might, gazing into a book or a photo album, only she had neither, only the faded patterns on her bed.

"That's quite a song, haven't I heard it before?"

"Of course not, silly, I just made it up," Elena giggled. "For you."

Roman sat on the edge of the bed. He wanted to take her head in his hands as on that day along the Neris, and he might have, too, had he been a different man. He might have told her finally what she wanted to hear—how their picnic had changed everything for him, made him see things and feel in ways he'd never imagined, and how that day had sustained him through the arduous times that followed. But instead he said nothing, just hunkered there with his arms in his lap, studying the tips of his shoes.

225

"What's wrong, Vati? You shouldn't look so sad." She wriggled across the bed, closer to him, and reached to tug his ear. "This one's getting bigger already. You'll see, two weeks and you're a genius."

Roman shrugged; he didn't push her away. "Elena . . . There's this trip . . ."

"We're going, yes!" She swung around onto her knees and started bouncing. "To China? South America? Oh, I really want to see Bolivia!"

His mouth opened, but not a sound came out of it. He couldn't go through with it, he knew, this disappointing her after everything she'd endured because of him—his pride, his indulgences. He might have left it at that, too, left her to her daydreaming, but just then Bernice appeared. She stood at the foot of the bed with that grave and unyielding look on her face, the one Roman could never oppose, and their daughter at once understood.

"You promised," she sobbed.

Roman started stammering: "I know . . . I know I did. That was then . . . things were better. Now . . ."

"It's your fault," Elena bawled, and pointed a finger at Bernice. All of sudden she wasn't crying anymore; she was furious. "You made him do it! We were just fine without you!" She put her face up to her father's. "Remember that part about running away? You were going to kidnap me, like in the story . . ."

Without thinking, Roman put his fingers to her lips. He clutched her shoulders and brought her to his chest. "I'm so sorry," he muttered.

He was expecting her to go on crying, had already resigned himself to it, but then something happened. Something between Elena with her cheek on his neck, and Bernice standing behind him: a look exchanged, a language. Next thing he knew there was Elena pulling away from him, stroking *his* face, while hers bore a look of caring.

"It's all right, Vati. I know that you have to go alone. I knew it all along, really."

Roman was dumbfounded, moved and confused at

once. "I'll come back for you," he managed to croak. "That I *do* promise."

Now it was her fingers on his lips. "You don't have to," she said, "I know you will."

Fragments. Of all the episodes of his life that he remembers in intricate detail, of all the journeys he took, that one, to Moscow, he's all but forgotten.

There was the Vilnius station, the same one he'd arrived at with his mother—what was it, fifteen, twenty years before?—only this time it was bustling with soldiers. The tones were dull, black and white almost, but set against them was the shock of Elena's red hair, the intense green of her eyes: two colors that would keep on flashing in his mind, alternating on and off, like rail signals. And there was Bernice as well. Hers was the last face he saw as the train pulled out, and on it the adoring expression he hadn't seen in many years, since their wedding night.

And more fragments: factory workers blinking through acrid fumes, feigning to hear him as he rose and stiffened, slumped and bowed to the applause of hydraulic machinery; the two thugs in black leather coats, his guides, who never left him alone; three or four concerts a day, bad food and unspeakable accommodation. Slivers of Moscow—churches, a kiosk—and inklings of that old burning sensation deep inside his chest.

He fought to stay awake throughout the trip home, afraid of missing some connection, but exhaustion eventually caught up with him. It was just outside of Minsk.

Roman fell asleep, and he dreamt of gliding rivers. But then he was startled by a horrific whistle—from the train or a factory, at first he wasn't sure which—followed by a woman's screams. Around him was chaos: passengers scrambling on the floor, luggage raining. The soldier who'd been sitting next to him—pasty blonde, pitted face—fumbled for his rifle; others were already firing from the windows. Roman flinched; he'd never heard a shot in his life. Nor did he recognize the shriek of the Luftwaffe divebomber, a Stuka, as it dove to strafe the train.

Windows shattered and walls burst apart, glass and metal spewed, and all Roman could think of was to keep his hands behind him as he fell. Screams and shots and a terrific blast raved around his ears. The train, no longer moving, listed to its side. But the plane came in for one more pass, and afterward there was no more screaming, only moans and cries for help.

Roman was drenched in blood. He hoisted himself back to his seat and examined himself—his arms, each of his fingers individually. It was only then, when assured that all of his appendages were intact, that he looked around him. Bodies lay in the aisle and slumped over their seats. On the seat next to him, the pasty blonde soldier still had his rifle raised, but the top of his head was gone. The wounded who could groped toward the exit. Roman followed them. Skidding on the slippery floor, clutching his violin case, he managed to get free of the train, but only to find himself caught up in another procession.

Refugees, thousands of them, lumbering. Men and

women with bundles on their backs, ragged children dragging dolls, soldiers—all had the same dazed look on their
faces. Behind them, the city of Minsk was a churning pall
of smoke.

He tried accosting some of the stragglers, asking if
they'd come from the Vilnius, whether they knew or had
heard any news of the Tolchowsky family. He cursed himself for not having brought even a single photograph, to
show them his wife and daughter. But, seemingly sleepwalk-
ing, few of the refugees bothered answering him, and those
who did merely shook their heads. Vilnius had fallen to the
enemy already, and terrible things had happened. To the Jews
especially, hauled away on freight trains to someplace deep in
the forest. They'd dug their own graves and were shot.

Roman was torn. He stood ankle-deep in the mud
and deliberated: Which way he should he go? With the
other survivors, back to Moscow, or keep trying to get
home? But what if he had no home anymore? What if the
Germans caught him first? He hugged the violin case,
rocked back and forth, while the stream past him by.

But then the Stuka returned. With a shrieking decres-
cendo, it swooped over the refugees who scattered and abandoned everything—animals, baggage, children. Roman had
no intention of moving, but his legs had thoughts of their
own. They sent him plummeting headlong into a drainage
ditch where he remained with his face buried in the sludge,
with his body shielding the case, and his hands folded
beneath it. The bomber howled overhead. He shut his eyes
and fought to conjure pleasant images—of Elena joining

him after all on his tour to Moscow, strolling with him through the station and the crowd that parted deferentially, for the Maestro and his daughter. He heard the steam building, the conductor calling "all aboard"—the picture was so stark, so stunning. From somewhere behind him someone shouted "All clear!"

Roman picked himself up from the mud, and clawed his way out of the ditch. Adrift on the road were bundles and bodies, bawling children and overturned carts. Through the refuse, he staggered. He limped on a leg that had gone weak and stiff, though he couldn't recall having injured it. Something had broken, though, inside: a grievous wound to his soul. The refugees churned past him, faster now, and he could no longer resist their pull. He let himself be carried, deep into the Russian interior.

He escaped, but the war pursued him, snapping at his heels. As a child, Roman remembered hearing of the great steppe fires, wind-driven blazes that could outstrip the swiftest runner. So it was with the war. Try though he did to get away from it, the fighting followed him; pummeled the ground throughout the day; it slashed the night sky with its razors. He hid where he could, in haystacks and culverts, and went through the pockets of the dead. Despite the new lameness in his leg, with nothing more than the violin case to burden him, he managed to keep up a decent pace. But it wasn't fast enough.

The outbreak of the great battle caught Roman in, of all places, a pigsty. He'd just climbed over a fence when the first barrage went off, and by the time he'd curled under one of the troughs, squirming through the muck, the entire night was ablaze. Shells crashed all around him, scattering earth and hunks of pig. The sty was in a crossfire: he couldn't stay. But neither could he run anymore, exhausted and lame. He had to surrender, but to whom? To the Germans who'd kill him as a Jew, or to the Russians, later to be shot as a spy?

A mortar round exploded close by—close enough to have blown his head off if not for the trough. Now was the moment; there wouldn't be another. Roman scampered through the mud, tried to stand but was flattened by another blast. He lunged, got to his feet, and scooping up the violin case, hobbled toward some woods.

Guns flickered between the trees. He could hear bullets sizzling around his ears, whacking the ground near his feet, but he kept moving. Kept waving his one free hand and shouting in the best Russian he could remember: *Nyez smotri!*—don't shoot. A string of tracers sailed above his head, so low it singed his hair. And then he felt it: a screaming harmonic of pain. His body for an instant lifted upward, then just as suddenly, collapsed. On his knees, holding one bloody hand in the other, Roman waited for the shot that would finish him off; he prayed for it.

But that shot never came. Instead, there was an officer sticking his head out from behind one of the trunks, and signaling him with his pistol. "*Bistre! Bistre!*" the officer urged him—hurry—in Russian.

*   *   *

The bullet had sheared off an index finger, just above the joint. The medic, a surly Asian woman with a Tommy gun, bandaged it as quickly as she could. The army was falling back. No one bothered to ask him questions, who he was or where he came from; there wasn't time. The Germans were closing in on Moscow.

Roman joined the retreat, one of the countless casualties limping in the army's tracks. He felt nothing, neither hunger nor fatigue nor the stiffness in his leg, only the pain in his chest. It had come back, that same burning sensation that had tormented him as a child, before he'd started to play. As if the music that had once flowed through that finger, faucet-like, was blocked and festering inside. He'd forgotten how maddening that pain could be, searing and piercing at once, and wondered how he'd ever survived it.

And yet he survived it now as well. He kept walking—for what purpose he'd couldn't say—cradling his case like the many mothers he saw still clutching their infants, refusing to believe they were dead.

Death was all around him, ubiquitous as the mud. Bombs burst, planes strafed, but one didn't need the enemy to die in this war. There were thieves as well, and deserters, desperate people who'd cut your throat for your shoes. But nobody bothered Roman. It took him a while to figure it out: the matted hair, the suit reduced to rags, and of course, the violin case—the perfect touch. He was an idiot, a fool, not worth anybody's time, much less their ammunition. He completed the picture, affecting a crazed expression, allowed himself to drool.

And a fool could travel just about anywhere, he discovered. Through burning villages and shattered cities, he wandered, farther than any musician, and with no audiences whatsoever required. Yet he had them. "Play us a tune, fiddler," the soldiers taunted him, "*Katyusha*—no, *Vacharni Zvon*."

Children pelted him with stones. But Roman just brayed at them, showed them a bit of foam. He hobbled on, through mud that turned to ice and then to mud again, indifferent to the cold as he was to the rain or to the motorcycle that nearly ran him down outside Kirov one day at the very height of spring. The cyclist, a huge, drunken Cossack, swerved and came speeding at Roman again. But instead of killing him, he snatched him in a bear hug and kissed him full on the lips. "*Tovarish*," the big man bellowed. "It's over!"

Dancing and drunkenness in the streets—all Russia was celebrating, but Roman took no part in it. He merely turned around, and limped back the way he'd come. The trek took weeks or months, he wouldn't know how long. But then one early autumn morning he found himself nearby Vilnius, in a forest, beside a patch of grass.

"Here! Here! This is where they did it," his companion clucked at him like a chicken. He hopped like a chicken, too.

Roman stared at him as he might into a mirror, seeing himself for the first time in years. His companion was a fool, a real one, with small eyes pinched absurdly together and a fat wagging tongue; his clothes were a patchwork of uniforms. They'd met on the road from Minsk, and greeted one another like brothers. But when it came to sharing his sausage, Roman demanded a price: "Tell me, in Vilnius, what did they do with the Jews?"

"Why should I care," the fool slobbered, and then lurched for the sausage, but Roman held it aloft. Fools did not care, true, but they heard things, they saw.

"The forest," his companion cried, and then nabbing the sausage from Roman's hand, stuffed it full in his mouth. "Made 'em . . . strip . . . the pit . . ."

So he learned everything, following the fool who acted it all out for him—the praying men, the women who pleaded for their children—as he rambled down the road, across a field and then into the forest. Finally, they reached the patch of grass, sparse as though only recently planted, overly symmetrical—man-made. Tongue wagging, the fool chattered, mimicking the sound of gunfire.

Roman stepped onto the patch. Its surface was smooth, as level as any stage he'd ever trodden, yet the earth seemed to shift beneath him, not quite settled yet. And there was a strange crunching noise. He knelt for a closer look and filled his fists with dirt, letting it sift through his fingers. What remained were nuggets and slivers of bone.

The fool watched all this from the edge of the forest, flapping and squawking, perplexed. The man he'd brought there had laid this dusty case he carried on the grass and opened it up. He seemed to be filling it with something, after he'd buried something else—just what, the fool couldn't see, only that the man was crying. Weeping with great rills of tears. But this was too crazy, even for the fool. He fell backward, tripping over roots and the tatters of his own clothes, until his head collided with a bough. He laughed, the fool, and skedaddled back into the forest.

Roman emerged dusting his knees and elbows, wiping his face with a sleeve. There was important work ahead. His performance had been brilliant, impeccable until now, but there was still the closing movement. He'd finish it as only a maestro could, standing stiffly, aware of his worth, then take his final bow.

The village buzzed with reconstruction: sawing, hammering. People were busy rebuilding their lives—too busy to pay attention to another filthy transient. They ignored Roman's inquiries, so it took him a while to find what he was looking for, and even then he would have missed if it hadn't been for the banners. Great red banners with the usual symbols— five-pointed stars, hammers and sickles—draped outside a tackle shop.

Roman didn't bother to knock, but tramped inside— smack into a dangling harness. Instantly, the shop rang with a young woman's laughter, a sound he hadn't heard in years. Squinting into the semi-darkness, he located its source. Seated behind a desk was a beautiful woman: blue- eyed with broad Tartar cheeks, blonde hair tied in a bun, her beauty offset by her drab officer's tunic. She laughed through the cigarette between her teeth, while a tall, grim- faced sergeant stood at attention next to her.

"I came . . ." Roman declared, "to surrender."

This only made her laugh louder. "Surrender?" she spat, "to whom and what for?"

Roman stuck out his chest. "To you, for crimes committed against the state."

"A collaborator?" the sergeant inquired.

Roman shook his head. "My name is Tolchowsky, and before the war I was a musician, the Maestro of Vilnius." He saw the sergeant glance at the officer, but her eyes were fixed him, this stranger and his even stranger confession. "In my bourgeois pride I turned down two invitations, not one but two, to play before the workers of the Soviet Socialist Republic. And now, having seen the courage of the triumphant Red Army, I am ready to accept my punishment."

The officer stubbed out her cigarette. She planted her hands flat on the desk, and furrowed her golden brows. "What you've described is indeed a serious crime, Comrade Tolchowsky. From this moment, consider yourself under arrest."

The sergeant locked him in a shed behind the shop. There, between the scythes, he squatted throughout the night, listening to the snap of reins and the peals of the officer's laughter. Sleep must have overtaken him, though, as he awoke to sunlight piercing the shed. Another hour passed before the sergeant's boots came thudding.

He led Roman back to the officer, still seated as she had been the day before, behind her desk. She looked just as beautiful, with only a wisp of her hair displaced. But her demeanor was very correct.

"Comrade Tolchowsky," the officer began, "I have found you guilty of high treason, and by my authority as commander of this district, I sentence you to death by firing squad." She sighed, "But lacking the aforesaid squad, I hereby remand you to," and pronounced a name Roman had never heard before, "for the carrying out of sentence."

Roman didn't react. This was what he'd expected, had fervidly hoped for. He merely picked up his violin case, and followed the sergeant out of the headquarters, taking care this time to avoid the dangling harness and ignore the laughter that broke out behind him.

They walked to a small platform where a train was already waiting. There was only one car, stripped of seats and crammed with wooden crates, with stacks of paintings still in their frames, and bolts of fine-looking cloth. Guarding this were two old and bedraggled soldiers with whom the sergeant exchanged some words.

"This train leaves in half an hour," the sergeant then informed Roman. His expression was still grim—the stamp of war, Roman surmised, much like the officer's laughter. The sergeant went on: "These men will guard you throughout much of the trip, but I wouldn't try escaping if I were you, Comrade. Your death can also be slow."

For three days and four nights, the train plodded eastward. The guards shared their food with Roman, but otherwise ignored him, keeping to their own side of the car. He sat listening to the crates' tinkling—there were wine bottles inside—like a thousand tiny bells, and studying a painting of a man and woman in a rowboat—brightly colorful, but out of focus. Outside, though, the picture was vivid enough: barren fields, torched cities. Roman slept for long stretches, through entire days it seemed, and on the morning of the fourth he awakened to find himself alone. The guards, the booty, everything was gone. Only the train kept chugging, plowing through a trackless expanse of snow.

Only then Roman realized that he was no longer under arrest. There would be no firing squad, no grand finale. He understood the officer's laughter. When the train halted at his destination—its name no longer mattered—he disembarked into a temperature lower than any he'd ever felt. His teeth, loosened by a thousand miles of track, were too sore to chatter; his clothes wouldn't have warmed him in spring. He clutched the violin case to his chest as if somehow it could warm him, and gazed into the infinite white.

Elipaz is still curled on the bed, wrapped in Roman's sheets, farting and snoring at intervals. It's morning, and though desperate to lie down himself, Roman hasn't the heart to wake him. Instead, he resumes his place on the piano stool, and tries to recall some sequence.

In all he'd spent over forty years in Siberia, yet very few details remain. He remembers a succession of mills. He would work at one for a few seasons, until the forest was completely felled, then hop on a freight train for the next. He never had trouble finding work—a missing finger, or even a hand, was nothing unusual in that line—becoming as proficient at sawing as he'd once been with a bow. And there were women as well. Big-boned, callused Siberian women starved by the dearth of men after the war, who took him in, clothed and fed him, and made love to him during the long artic nights. The outdoor work restored his robustness, made him burly, barrel-chested. It hardened him against the past.

Many women, many lumberyards: forty years of wandering north and east, in every direction, though he never knew which, and never cared. The longest tour of his life. But mostly he remembers the snow. Each day brought a new coat of it, shifting, burying, defying change.

Until the day that news came of tumultuous events in Moscow—the regime was collapsing, the gates of immigration prised open. As a Jew, one merely had to fill out a form, board a plane, and fly away to Israel. A warm country, lots of sun, no snow to speak of. Why not, he figured, if for nothing other than a change of scenery?

And so he left, Roman Tolchowsky, a crusty old man with nothing but his cap and his jacket and a violin case. And here he sits now in a converted warehouse on the fringe of the desert and watches some unwashed vagrant snoring away in his bed. He sits and tries to remember, tries to forget, but somehow manages neither. Wherever it wanders, his mind inexorably returns to that single thought, of the audition.

The gym is as hot as the crater, and the music's like the wind, howling. It's another insufferable rehearsal, and Roman, atop his apple crate, wants nothing more than to get the hell out. But there's no escape today. He's stuck with the likes of Sarka and Leibowitz, hunkering behind their cellos with their bows at each other's throats; with an obese trombonist named Smirkin, and Geraldine, a prune-faced born-again from Kansas, who arrived with an oboe in one hand, a Bible in the other, to save lost souls in Yerucham.

Roman fights to control the temper that all the musicians dread. Word is, the Maestro has a violent streak, that he's capable of unpredictable acts of fury, such as the one that cost him his finger—purportedly in a knife fight before the war. There are all sorts of rumors about Roman. They circulate the gym and make the rounds of the coffee shops, but he simply ignores them, much as he does everything here.

But can he ignore this, this cacophony? Smirkin blowing peddle-notes at Geraldine who appears to be on the verge of tears, and a percussionist named Buzaglo, an ex-con, bashing away at his snare? He can't go on any longer. Frustration surges through him like venom. It turns his legs, his arms, rigid, propels his baton through the air. One by one the musicians stop playing and just gape at him. He looks like a rocket about to take off. But instead of a blast, there's only a whimper. "Recess," Roman sighs, as his body at once goes limp.

Arguments, cat-calls, a pick-up basketball game—woodwinds against the strings—and the noise has become outrageous. But it gives Roman his cover. He doesn't head for the back wall this time, but shambles directly for the exit.

He nearly makes it, too. Just short of the door, though, he finds his way blocked by a substantial figure, a massive silhouette framed within the sun. It takes him a second to pick out the features: the fleshy face, the dimples, and finally, the skullcap. He should have known instantly. Toledano.

"What's the hurry." More of threat than a question. Rumors or no rumors about the Maestro, Toledano's afraid of no one.

"I was going out for a breath of air."

"Pity," Toledano says. "This time of day, not much air in Yerucham."

"Stupid of me, really. You're right, of course." In stepping backward, he skids on the parquet; Roman appears to bow.

"Don't sell yourself short," Toledano quips. "Now quit toadying, and follow me."

The shadow pivots and plunges into the late afternoon sun, and Roman, after a slight hesitation, follows. What choice does he have? It would only take one order, one gesture even, and Toledano would have his job. Yasmin, the audition—all of it would be lost.

Overweight though he is, Toledano moves like an athlete, like a hunter, chasing up Tabenkin Street. There are the usual tipped hats from the men in the coffee shops; dim-witted Gershonshvilli, the traffic cop, salutes. But Roman's too busy to notice. He's battling to keep pace, with sweat streaming down his face and his chest on fire, keeping his eyes on the skullcap as it catapults up the hill.

Where could he possibly be going, Roman asks himself? To the synagogue? It didn't seem logical—more likely to the Union Hall, there to give the conductor his notice. Yet they pass the center of town and keep ascending, up the hill, seemingly toward Roman's home. But Toledano suddenly veers off onto a path. Strange, but Roman can't remember it being there, and stranger still the sounds he begins to hear while following it: shouts and screams. It's not until he catches up with Toledano, and wipes the sweat from his eyes, that Roman sees who's making them.

Children. They dangle from swings and jostle inside a wooden stockade: a playground. And holding court in the center of it is Yasmin. She hollers at some of her classmates, punches others, her ribbons and skirt whipping. Nobody fights back, though, nor are there any adults around to intervene—not that they'd dare if they were. So preoccupied bullying, she doesn't notice her father and her teacher watching her. Is this the same child who tiptoes into his studio apologizing, Roman wonders? Is this his dynasty's heir?

"Well, what do you think?"

Roman is confused. What is Toledano asking him? "Charming," he ventures.

"Charming," Toledano repeats. "Not the word I'd have used. Priceless is more like it. Precious. Do you understand what I'm saying, Tolchowsky?"

He does, but he's not going to admit it so fast, not even to himself.

Toledano explains: "I'm talking about treasure. Treasure that a man like me will do anything to protect. Anything."

"What do you want of me?" Roman mutters finally.

"You seem surprised by what I'm telling you—you shouldn't be, a man as worldly as you. Or maybe it's wrong what people say, that you were once some kind of genius. Maybe you're just what you look like."

Roman winces sharply, hoping Toledano notices. He hopes that Toledano's only aim is to make him feel worthless, to treat him as he does the rest of the town. But Toledano is right; Roman is worldly. He knows what's coming next.

"There'll be no more lessons," Toledano states. "No mention of any audition up north. I told Yasmin you were sick and in any case too old to make the trip. She took it pretty well, I'm happy to say, in fact she was downright thrilled—relieved, if you know what I mean. So I wouldn't look so sad."

Toledano clasps the hump on Roman's shoulder; his grip steadily tightens.

"I believe I've made my point. Gershonshvilli will be keeping an eye on you, so don't try anything stupid. He's not quite as gentle as me."

Roman nods and says nothing. Toledano releases him. He smiles—it's Yasmin's smile, too—stands back, and admires the scene in front of him. "Charming, that *is* the word, yes," he says.

*   *   *

His cap and jacket are drenched with sweat, and his torso is crimped with pain, yet he finds the strength to climb the stairs, and to rap with the force of an axe-blow. He's frantic to sit and rest and gather his thoughts with the one person willing to listen to him. But that person is up to her old games again. He can hear her breathing on the other side of the door even as he pummels it.

"Please, Lubova Yakobovitch, I'm begging you." He slams the door with both fists. Other doors open above and below him, by neighbors lured by the prospects of a fight.

"Luba, I know you can hear me so for once listen to what I have to say." Defeated, he lays his cheek against the wood. "Something terrible has happened. Toledano came to see me and threatened to kill me if I ever saw Yasmin again. Luba, I think I'm in trouble . . ."

An interval of silence follows, broken only by the echoes of gossip on the stairs. Roman feels very old suddenly, and tired. His body slides down the length of the door, and comes to rest on the landing. It's then, of course, that Luba finally opens up, abruptly, and nearly sends him sprawling.

Arms akimbo, she looks down at him and chides, "Already you're bowing," before helping Roman to his feet. She brushes the dust from his jacket and leads him to the table where the glass is already filled and waiting. In a single chug, he tosses the vodka down his throat, swallows, gags, and demands another.

Luba, pouring, wears her old lascivious grin. She's wearing her bathrobe as well, like a fighter entering the ring; it's all he ever sees her in. He has no idea how she passes her days—not cleaning, that much is clear. Newly acquired bric-a-brac—tiny wooden camels, souvenir spoons—joins the clutter; dishes still mount in the sink. Only the special shelf is ever dusted, and its relics meticulously arranged.

"Drink, drink," Luba advises him. "But don't say I didn't warn you."

She massages his shoulders, and lays her chin on his cap. "What did you expect, Romashka? Even the most heartless man has a soft spot, the one thing that means more to him than anything, money or power. And there you come and threaten to take it away."

Roman reaches for the bottle. "I want to stay here. I need to sleep."

"Playing matinees now are we?"

"There was someone sleeping in my bed, a man. A guest. I don't know if he's still there, but I don't want to go back."

"First cupcakes and now men," Luba clicks her tongue. "You always surprise me, Roman Tolchowsky."

Later, when he's good and drunk, she guides him to the sofa and helps him get undressed. Luba disrobes as well, in a single movement, and squeezes onto the cushions beside him. She tries to arouse him, stroking and licking, grunting obscenities in his ears—fruitlessly. Roman's thoughts are elsewhere again, along with his desire. She lifts his lifeless member—"Will this bone not rise?" she says.

"Quiet now. Let's get some rest."

Sighing, Luba agrees, but then she, alone, dozes. Roman is wide awake, his brain still churning, for an hour or more. His eyes again wander to the shelf. There is the flask, the medal and the binoculars, the pipes and pocketknives and charms. And the compass. The compass that belonged to the dead partisan leader Alexander Davidovich—Sasha: blood-smeared lover, famed conductor of death.

Roman glances at Luba, fast asleep with her mouth agape, at her hoard of golden fillings. Beneath the makeup, her skin has a greenish tint and the numbers on her wrist are blue. He feels a rush of compassion for her, but it is short-lived. A moment later he is sliding out from under her arm, dressing silently, and stealing across the floor. He flips the cap onto his head, and taps the front of his jacket, over the pocket where his baton now clicks against something small, something dark and metallic.

From his lookout in the Liberators' Memorial, Roman keeps watch. The compass he has stolen is opened in his lap, and though he's never used one before, he's seen how soldiers do it. Quite easy, really: insert a finger stub through the ring on the bottom, and level an eye to the glass; line up the needle with the slot in the lid, and there you have it, your azimuth. He experiments several times, honing in on the stars which are at their brightest now, just before dawn.

When exactly it occurred to him, while he was gazing at Elipaz snoring or lying next to Luba, he wasn't sure.

His first reaction was to laugh, literally, out loud. Beyond foolishness, this was sheer insanity. But when he tried to move on to other thoughts, the notion wouldn't leave him. It kept turning in his mind, over and over, slowly taking form. "Could it be done?" he asked himself a dozen times, and always the same answer came back: "Impossible." Except for the last time. "Well . . . maybe," he admitted, and from that moment he was determined, working on his plan.

The basic problem was transport. One couldn't just stand out in the middle of Tabenkin Street and thumb a ride, even if there were any traffic, or catch the passenger train—somebody was bound to see. The problem seemed insurmountable. Then he remembered the crater. He remembered the trail leading down to the mines, to the factory. Yet how would he ever find it, at night, with his hopeless sense of direction?. He pictured himself wandering desperately in the dark, unable to find his way either back or forward, trapped.

He waits; it will only be minutes now. His eyes follow the compass as it turns, caught in a magnetic stream. His chest is throbbing and the air is biting cold, but he hardly minds with all his excitement. Then, all at once, it is dawn. The silent interlude between movements of darkness and light. Soon the crater will become a cauldron, the memorial an oven in which a man could rapidly bake. Roman squints, he strains his ears to hear. Where is it? Why hasn't it come as it has every other time, at sunrise?

It's not going to happen, he realizes; his entire scheme

is a sham. Disgusted with himself, furious, he decides to discard the compass. He rises on his toes, arms in the air to throw—and he nearly does. But just then Roman trips on something—a beer bottle—and stumbles. He pitches onto his gimpy leg and buckles toward the edge of the crater. Careening, falling almost, before catching hold of one of the arches.

Roman gasps. By a miracle he's saved himself, and the compass too, dangling at the end of his stub. He's relieved but also embarrassed, humiliated by what people would have said about him, *Just imagine, the snooty Maestro, a suicide.* He can almost hear their laughter, but realizes that it's only the wind. No, not the wind: a whistle! Far down in the crater, beyond the serpentine trail, twist slender filaments of smoke.

248

He lifts the compass and, blowing the dust from its glass, aims it where the smoke has begun to unravel. Where the freight train has come to a halt.

The Maestro is ill, or so says the sign on the gymnasium exit and the rumors that are circling the city. Confined to his studio, quarantined, no one is to go near him; all his lessons are canceled. In the coffee shops, the consensus is that the geezer has just about had it. And just as well, they say, he never did fit in, with his terrible temper and his airs of having been some kind of genius. But nothing ever changes in Yerucham. Soon there'll be another conductor, another stranger in a cap and jacket, ignoring them all as he limps down the length of Tabenkin.

The city has written him off, but not Toledano. In his office in the Union Hall, in the seat reserved for him in the synagogue, he broods, wondering what the Maestro is up to. He may be old but he's still strong; foolish perhaps, but sly. He's given orders to Gershonshvilli to keep a close watch on the Tolchowsky's warehouse day and night, and to report on any unusual movements. And as for Yasmin, she's to stay in the school or in the playground and go nowhere else but home. Above all, she must keep away from the Maestro, even if he comes to her. The illness, her father has warned her, is highly contagious.

Roman knows none of this, of course. He spends his days locked in his home, pouring over mouse-nibbled scores. Occasionally, he'll make his way to the window to stare at the city dump, observing how the refuse will sparkle or blaze, depending on the angle of the sun. He marvels at the wheels of that overturned carriage, spinning, slowly spinning, even when there's no sign of wind.

249

His days are peaceful, but the nights less so. Not only do dreams plague him, there is also Elipaz. The tramp keeps coming back, tapping at the door, scratching at the window. Roman can smell him, he swears, through the concrete. He makes his bed in the gravel and snores, or delivers sermons at all hours of the night, knowing that Roman must listen: "Now where was I . . . oh, yes, Moses. Talk about a guy who had nothing to repent for. Got the Children of Israel out of Egypt, gave up a kingdom and a perfectly good shepherding job, too, and then roamed around the desert for half a lifetime lugging the bones of Joseph and yet, when it comes to entering the Land, guess what happens? God won't let him in! The bones get buried but Moses just disappears. Strange, isn't it?"

Lying on his bed, Roman jams his cap over his ears and covers the cap with his jacket, anything to muffle the sound. Fortunately, Elipaz is gone by morning, and when night falls again, Roman can return to his scores and to rehearsing his coming performance.

So he passes the next three days, and survives the nights, and on the fourth dawn he rises, prepared. Despite little sleep, he feels invigorated, capable of walking through snow or sand for vast distances. And if there's a burning in his chest, it's the burning of an engine's furnace, driving him. He cleans the compass, polishes the glass until he can see his face in it, drawn but determined. He slips it into his jacket pocket, next to the baton, and then turns back to the alcove, to the corner and his violin case.

He lifts it gently, reverently, though its weight is insignificant. With his finger stump he traces the wrinkles in its leather and the feminine outlines of its form, hugs it and hears its rattle. Clutching the case, taking some bread and cheese, he moves to the piano stool and enjoys a parting meal.

But a knock on the door interrupts him. An agitated knock he's never heard before, too feeble for Toledano's but firmer than Yasmin's, and not Elipaz's either, not erratic. He wonders if it's Gershonshvilli, come to check if he's alive, but the imbecile would probably just bash down the door. The knock intensifies, accompanied now by words he has often used himself: "Let me in . . . please . . . I know you're there. Do you want me to beg?"

And the voice is all too familiar. Luba. What the hell is she doing here? Roman jumps from the stool and rushes to the door but then, with his hand on the lock, he hesitates.

"*Tebye Nemat*," Luba barks—*your mother's cunt*— taking a different tack. "I won't take no for an answer. You *will* open this door!"

He tries to picture her, flushed and lurid, dressed in nothing but a bathrobe. He's never seen her outside her apartment.

Luba's beseeching again: "Romashka . . . *Daragoy*, darling. If you want me to beg, I'll beg. I'll get down on my knees if it'll make you happy."

He feels for her, still needs her, but his hand remains frozen on the lock.

"Very well, you old shit, don't let me in," she cries, "but you listen to this: she's no damn good. You know who I'm talking about—your little cupcake, Toledano's jewel. Technically, maybe, she can play, but there's no soul in it, no spirit, there can't be! Don't ask me how I know it, I just do, and so does everybody else in Yerucham. Everybody except for the famous Maestro, Roman Tolchowsky, that fucking deluded fool."

With this, Luba stomps away, still cursing, pulverizing the gravel. Only Roman stays close by the door. He's ingesting what Luba had to say—what she'd always wanted to say to him, he sensed. Could it be true? The memory of Yasmin in the playground, screeching and hitting other children, troubled him. But there were other, more stirring memories—of Yasmin standing still, eyes closed, while notes like angels flew from her strings. Memories of music purer and more sublime than any he's heard since the war.

No, she's jealous, Luba, he concludes. And now that he knows that, he's glad that he hadn't opened the door for her. Once inside, she might have gone to work on him, tearing away his clothes and his confidence. Just as well she stormed away, it has only completed his disguise: a man too ill to even receive his lover. The Maestro must be dying.

It's late in the afternoon when he steps out of his home. He is leaving in much the way he came, in his cap and jacket and carrying a violin case. He has taken care to shut the lights, and left the door unlocked.

252

He dallies for a second, spying around for any sign of Toledano or Gershonshvilli, or Luba, who might be waiting in ambush. But the hillside is deserted, empty except for the dump, and the warehouse itself, of course, and the satchel he finds lying on the gravel. He bends to pick it up, Elipaz's satchel, which reeks as much as he does. Roman pinches it between thumb and stump and holds it away from him.

Yet, curious, he has to look inside. What he finds is water—Elipaz wasn't kidding about that—three large bottles, filled to the brim and plugged with rubber stoppers. Why had he left it here, Roman wonders. For him? Fact was he hadn't really thought about water, never had to in Siberia; snow, unlike sand, could be sucked. Telling himself that Elipaz couldn't be any worse off without it, ignoring the stench, Roman shoulders the satchel. He marches, then, to a syncopated beat, to the slosh of water and the rattle made by his case.

He starts down Tabenkin Street, but well short of the city center, turns onto the path that Toledano had shown him. What luck: before long he hears shouts and shrieks. The playground's teeming with kids. Presently, he sees them gathered in a tense circle, hollering and jumping up and down. He doesn't have to guess who's in the center of it all. Skirt dirtied and ribbons undone, it's Yasmin. She's throttling one of her playmates, a boy twice her size who takes his punishment stoically, not even fighting back.

Her hand is clenched, ready to punch—the boy crimps up in preparation—when she sees him. Instantly, her fist unfurls, and her expression melts, softens from almost murderous to coy. "My Maestro!" she exclaims to the crowd around her, "Look, he's come to see me!"

She skips toward him, smoothing her skirt, hiding the scabs on her knees. Her arms are outstretched, and for a moment he thinks she wants a hug, and he's more than pleased to give her one. But then, just out of his reach, she freezes.

"But Maestro, everybody says you're sick."

Roman guffaws, "Sick? Do I *look* sick to you?"

Yasmin seems confused; she shuts one eye and inspects him. "Well . . . no. But my father told me . . ."

"I know what your father told you," Roman says. He doesn't, really, but he can guess—more than that, he's

253

counted on it. "I also know why. It's because he loves you very much, and didn't want to spoil your surprise."

Yasmin claps her hands together, and cheers. "A surprise? For me?" A natural performer, she knows that everyone is watching.

"The best, one that will make you the most famous little girl in the world."

"Yes! Yes! Yes!" Her patent leather pumps rise and fall three times rapidly. But Yasmin's eyes are already narrowing, her neck craning right and left around Roman. "I want to see it," she demands, "Now."

Roman gives a short, quick laugh, and just as quickly grows serious. "I'll show it to you, I promise. But you have to come with me."

Now Yasmin's gone serious as well. She shrugs her shoulder and tilts an ear, and for a second seems to hesitate. Roman watches anxiously as Yasmin glances at the children behind her, wriggles her nose and wipes it with the back of her wrist. Then, *con affetto*, she grins and giggles, "What are we waiting for?"

He leads her on the path back to Tabenkin, and from there up to the crest of the hill. Dust turns to tarmac, to gravel and then to broken glass and garbage as he guides her through the dump. All along, Yasmin plies him with questions: Is it something to play with or something to eat? Is that cola she hears swishing inside the sack, and what kind of violin has he got, making such a silly rattle? He answers her each time with the same gentle, "Hush," his stub pressed to his lips. Gently, he nudges her when she pauses to spin the wheels of the baby carriage. Not until there're safe inside the arches of the Liberators' Memorial does Roman finally speak.

"Look there, way, way out, what do you see?"

Yasmin squints hard, flaring her nostrils. "Nothing. The crater."

"The crater, yes, and everything. Out there, outside of this tiny place where you were born, there is another world, a great and magical world full of the best things to wear and eat and hear—things that will all be yours simply because of who and what you are. What you have inside you."

"You mean I can have . . . *anything?*"

"More than you ever dreamed of."

Roman takes her hand—it's the very first time, he realizes. The skin is taut and clammy, but her grip is firm, determined, as befitting her father's daughter. Holding that hand, he threads through the arches to the lip of the crater, to the point where the trail begins. But Yasmin hesitates again, looking down. "It's getting night," she says. "Can't we do this tomorrow?"

He resists the urge to tug her. Time is growing short. The alarm has probably been sounded already and Toledano's men are out, combing the streets, the gymnasium, ransacking the warehouse. It won't take long before their search leads them here, to the memorial.

Squeezing her hand, Roman pulls her behind him, along the trail to the crater. She follows, but he can feel her resistance, her fear, and all the way down he talks: "Tomorrow you'll audition for the academy in Jerusalem. The judges will hear you, and you'll make their pencils drop, their mouths too, and they'll start muttering something that nobody else can hear. But we know what it is, don't we, Yasmin. Don't we?"

The trail down to the crater is much steeper than Roman anticipated, treacherous. The rains of the previous winter have cut crevices deeper than Tabenkin's potholes, and left the bedrock slippery with dust. Holding the case with one arm, he has only one hand free to help Yasmin, and on this she leans all of her weight. Progress is slow, planting his leg in the crevices while his other leg taps ahead. An hour passes and they're only halfway down the trail. Gazing back, he can still see the Liberators' Memorial, its shadow, riding the rim of his hump.

Yasmin whines, "Don't we take a bus to Jerusalem? How much longer?"

"Not far at all," he assures her. "Soon you can rest, maybe get a little sleep, and when you awake, we'll be there already."

"You've seen it before?"

"Yes," he lies. He has never been to Jerusalem in his life, not even to the academy; had only read about the audition in a flier. "Many, many times."

"What's it like, tell me. I've heard so many stories . . ."

"Imagine a city made entirely of marble," he begins, straining for breath and imagination. "The streets, the sidewalks, even the lampposts, everything as white as snow. And what buildings! Each one is like a castle, big enough to fit all of Yerucham."

He babbles on, aware that his story is meant as much for her as for him, to ease his nerves. He's counting on this head start, on getting to Jerusalem before Toledano puts two and two together and finally alerts the police. They'll be waiting to arrest him at the academy, he figures, but by then he can appeal to the judges. "At least hear her," he'll cry, and then how could they not? They'll hear her and they'll gasp and insist that she stay, long after he's been taken into custody. But Yasmin will always be his, just as he was his maestro's, and his maestro was Oppenheim's. As they all belonged to Mendelssohn in Leipzig.

"The people are splendid as well," Roman exclaims. "Just wait till you see them: men in suits and tall black hats walking arm-in-arm with their ladies all dressed in silk, and behind them their children—nothing like your playmates, oh no, these children wear uniforms of velvet, with tiny caps on their heads, like your father's, only finer."

So they make it down the trail. Just in time, too, for the night has fallen. Shadows lengthen and merge, steadily filling the crater. But the surface underfoot is level now, solid, and Roman can step up his pace. Yasmin, too, seems more sure of herself, pacified by his tales. She lets go of his hand and shambles along beside him.

He strides, and for the first time in weeks, feels the tension slough from his mind. Toledano, Gershonvilli, that ludicrous orchestra—all of them are behind him now, as if they never existed. As though his entire past had been swept beneath this limitless tarpaulin of dust. In the darkness before the moonrise, he feels free again, unbridled, floating.

The sensation ends, suddenly, with Yasmin's cry. He looks around him panicking; the girl is nowhere in sight. Whirling, Roman hobbles quickly in the direction he came from—what he thinks is the direction, though he can't be entirely sure. His thoughts stampede: she's hurt, she's lost and frightened. Hardly begun and already his plan is failing.

He finds her seated cross-legged in the dust, rubbing her knees and weeping. Breathless, he can barely ask her what happened. But he doesn't have to. She holds up one of her pumps, and shows him how the strap has broken.

"Can you walk?" he asks. She bites her lower lip and nods. "Remove your other shoe, then, and take my hand. We'll go very slowly," Roman says, and tries to smile, "imagine we're on a picnic."

But Yasmin won't take his hand. Instead, she clings to his sleeve, trembling. What to do now? Roman wraps his jacket around her, hugs her and helps her to her feet. With the girl leaning on his arm, he starts walking again, the two of them limping, each on a different leg. Barefoot, though, the ground is less than smooth. Stones cut into her soles, and soon Yasmin is bawling. Like a wounded animal she howls, wildly enough to be heard in Yerucham. He's grateful for the wind shrilly rising, and for the superstitions about the crater's ghosts. The sounds she makes are like nothing human.

It is midnight by the time they reach the base of the

crater. The air is still and very chilly; the dust on the ground is deep. Here the trail ends, splaying into half a dozen paths. While deciding which one to take, Roman reaches into his satchel, extracts one of the water bottles and gives it to Yasmin to drink. She hasn't howled for a long time now, nor even whimpered, but trudged along in silence, latched onto his arm. But now she takes the bottle and sits, slurps voraciously and all but empties its contents. Then, belching, she drops to her side and promptly falls asleep.

It's just as well, he thinks; he has work to do. He has to figure out which of the paths head in the right direction. He leans down to his jacket which is still wrapped around Yasmin, reaches into the inner pocket only to be pricked by his baton. Sucking on his finger, he delves in again with the other hand, but still comes up with nothing. The compass has disappeared.

Roman stomps the dust. He utters curses worthy of Luba and fights the urge to wake her. To scold her for being so careless. It takes a while before his temper abates, before he can clear his mind.

Closing his eyes, he imagines himself in the memorial again, looking down at the crater below. He pictures the train and the point where he'd marked it on the compass. Then, eyes opening, he links that point with a star. It's only a guess, he knows, but what else can he do? It's late and they have to start walking.

Returning to Yasmin, he pets her cheek and tickles her neck. Yet even that touch is abrasive. She awakens with a plaintive "Ow!" teeth bared, ready to pick a fight. Yet moments later she is weeping again, no longer loudly but sniveling. He loops his free arm around her, and whispers in her ear: "Listen to me, Yasmin, I know you're tired and your feet hurt, but it's very late and if we don't hurry that wonderful surprise I told you about, that world, will disappear, just like that."

Yasmin says nothing. She doesn't nod, but only glares at him coldly. The sudden strangeness of her behavior continues when they walk. She no longer needs his arm, no longer hobbles but capers. He has a hard time keeping up with her, sloshing and rattling behind. Roman's concerned, but at least they're making up for lost time; at least they still have a chance. If only he could be sure of the direction. But the star is moving as well—fleeing from them, it seems, ducking now behind a cloud and emerging again, camouflaged by constellations.

He puffs on, determined to stay his course, to keep Yasmin within his sight. The terrain, seemingly flat from a distance, up close reveals its ruggedness. Gullies and crags, dunes and mesas, block his way, force him into ever-widening detours. And Yasmin is pulling ahead. He wants to shout at her but he hasn't the air—the fire in his chest has consumed it. He slumps down again, despondent. Yasmin has utterly vanished.

He wanders on, perhaps in circles, doubling back on himself. He doesn't know or care about anything now except finding her. The moon at last rises, generously shedding its light, but the result is only more frustration. What appears to be a little girl dancing in place, is only a stunted acacia. Footprints in the dust are the mottled shadows of clouds. Then, hurrying toward what looks like fluttering pieces of cloth—a skirt? her ribbons?—he tumbles over the bank of a wadi.

He lands, hard, on his hands and knees, and moments pass before he can stand again and breathe. Collecting his cap, slapping the dust from it, he retrieves the violin case as well, which appears to have survived unbroken. But the satchel is soaking wet. One of the water bottles has burst, leaving him only one more. Parched as he is, he will not touch it, though, not even a sip. He has to save it for Yasmin.

Blindly he follows the wadi, swept by its phantom current. It narrows and deepens, becomes a ravine with pools that Roman has to edge around, his face pressed to the scarp. He wonders why he bothers, what's driving him now that the chances of finding her are slim? He feels his way around boulders, over bluffs and sand bars until the wadi gradually widens, fanning out onto a loessy plateau.

The ground is level and he can march again, but light has appeared on the horizon. The thinnest streak of light, as if the lid of night had been cracked. Dawn. That's it, Roman thinks, it'll be daybreak soon. The child will die in a few hours unless he returns with help. And that is just what he intends to do, turn himself into Toledano—it doesn't matter anymore, as long as the search parties are sent out, jeeps and helicopters, the whole army, whatever it takes to find Yasmin.

He turns to find the way back—*if* he can find it—and catches sight of something in the distance. A structure of some kind, rectangular and oblong: a building. Without knowing why, Roman runs toward it. The structure is not as far away as it at first appeared, and it's not a building at all, but a carriage—a carriage on wheels: a boxcar! Train tracks have got to be near.

But what good are tracks now without Yasmin? He pauses at the boxcar, if for no other reason than to catch his breath, and leaning inside, eases the satchel and his violin case onto the floor. He hears the slosh and the rattle and then another sound, unidentifiable at first, a halting, sniffling sound. Curled in a corner, still wrapped in his jacket, Yasmin sleeps.

He manages to hoist himself into the car, to crawl to the corner without disturbing her. There he sits, savoring her warmth and her breath; he can hardly believe it, Yasmin, alive! And so, too, is his plan. In a short while the freight will arrive to pick up its load of minerals, and that's when they'll catch it, hopping it just as he once hopped trains in Siberia. They'll ride it north as far as it goes, and from there flag a cab to Jerusalem.

With the satchel for a pillow, holding his violin case close, he rests. His leg, his hump, are aching, and his chest roils with pain. But he cannot sleep—he will not—and risk missing the train. He will stay alert, and when the time comes, carry her to the tracks; hold her the whole journey if he has to, until she wakes in the city of judges.

*   *   *

Something has gone terribly wrong. He is not supposed to be here, not supposed to be sleeping, much less dreaming. And yet he is dreaming and there is no escape . . .

A silver-haired officer looks him over, from the crippled leg to the hump and back down to the missing finger, and jerks his chin to the left. "Wait," Roman pleads, "I can be of use to you." He feels himself frozen in the officer's glare, in eyes like alpine ponds. "My name is Roman Tolchowsky, the renowned virtuoso, perhaps you've heard of me?"

The officer is impatient; the depot is teeming with new arrivals, with guards and barking dogs herding them into line. Only Roman refuses to move. He holds his ground and his violin case. The officer rises on the toes of his boots with his swagger stick in the air, about to strike, but then, in mid-motion, he stops.

"Tolchowsky, you say? Yes, I do remember. Berlin, 1932, the Brahms Concerto. I was merely a child, but, how could I forget . . ."

"Neither could I!" Roman exclaims. "Such a magnificent theater, and the orchestra . . ." He kisses his fingertips.

"Ah, but the curtain's closed," the officer sighs, again pointing to the left. "So sorry . . ."

"Please . . . I've heard you have an orchestra here as well. Did you know that I'm also a conductor?"

The officer rubs his chin. "A conductor you say? You may be in luck, after all. A position has just opened up."

*   *   *

He's begun his new career, elevated on a platform which also doubles as a gallows. True, his tails and cummerbund have been replaced by rags and wooden clogs, but otherwise he's in his element. Some of Europe's finest musicians are here, gathered beneath his baton. Awed by his reputation, too weak to resist, they speed up the tempo whenever he instructs them, accompanying the march of the doomed.

The procession's endless, streams of prisoners from around the continent converging in this one great flow. Beside them strut the guards with their whips and dogs, spurring them toward a factory with smokestacks spitting flame. Roman sees none of this, though; he barely hears the screams. His ears are numb with music: Brahm's Violin Concerto—ineffable, an excursion to beauty's bounds. But the performance is constantly interrupted; no sooner has one soloist begun, than he is dragged away and another brought in his place. The supply is quickly exhausted.

The officer watches all this, delighted, his swagger stick tapping to the tune. "Maestro," he smiles, and points his stick at the case. "S'il vous plait."

Roman's paralyzed. How can he tell him that he hasn't played in years—can't because of his missing finger? He lingers over the case. The orchestra is waiting, the guards, too. He positions his thumbs under the latches—who knows if they'll even open?

"Vati! Vati!"

The voice, that name . . . his head shoots up, his eyes rush through the prisoners.

"Play for me, Vati! For *me*!"

He searches, he scans, but finds only old people, strangers.

"Last chance, Maestro," says the officer.

Then he finally sees her. A blur of cranberry-red hair turning away from him, being turned by a thin, black-clad figure who's guiding her along, hurrying her so as not to disturb his playing.

He positions his thumbs under the latches. He's got it into his mind that, somehow, if only he can play, the entire procession will halt. But nothing happens when he presses.

"Play, Vati, play! Before it's too late!"

The case rattles, it shrieks, but the latches cannot be opened.

His mouth is opened to scream, but all that comes out is a whistle.

For a moment he has no idea where he is—still in the camp, perhaps. He looks around: on the floor lies the satchel, the violin case, the little girl wrapped in his jacket. Wands of dusty light dice the darkness, heat seeps through the slats. He's back in the boxcar. The sun has risen and the whistle he hears is the freight train's, pulling out.

Roman scampers, he paws across the floor and plunges out into the desert, lands at a run, hollering and waving his hands. Too late. The train has already taken the first bend, around a butte, and is steadily building up speed. There is no way of catching it. He stands with his hands in the air, surrendering. So close he'd come, so miraculously, and now everything—the audition, his legacy—is lost.

He'd kill himself if he had a knife or a rope, or let the desert do it—it wouldn't take long in this heat. But there is Yasmin. He has the girl to think of, to get her back safely to Yerucham.

He shuffles back to the boxcar. Inside, she is still sleeping but not soundly. Her expression is furrowed—her playground snarl—and the flush has drained from her cheeks. Sweat beads on her forehead that, when he touches it, feels alarmingly feverish.

"Yasmin," he shakes her gently. "Yasmin. It's time we were heading home."

She raises her head from the floor, grinds dirty fists in her eyes. "Home? But you said Jerusalem . . . the audition." Captiously she yawns. "You promised."

She's caught him off guard. He'd thought she'd be thrilled to go home. "I did, yes. But . . ."

"Liar," she spits.

What can he say? Nothing that could assuage her certainly. Her anger will be the least of his punishments.

He's prepared to carry her if necessary, but it isn't. With a startling leap she bounds from the car, on feet as limber as if they'd just swung out of bed. Roman gathers up the satchel and his violin case, and rushes in pursuit.

His intention is to lead her toward the factory. He can see it, not far away, shrouded in its own cloud of smoke. Yasmin has other ideas, though. She's heading back toward the trail—it's visible, now, in the daylight—and the climb to the Liberators' Memorial. But the distance appears immense, two kilometers at least across the plateau and around the wadi, and the sun's already blistering. The sand feels molten through his shoes. Only Yasmin isn't affected. Delirious, she seems to feel nothing, scurrying on bare feet, a trail of ribbons behind her.

He follows her as fast as he can. His feels strangely light-headed, rubber-kneed and queasy. He needs to drink urgently, he knows, but what little water remains must be saved for her. Already she veers off into a hummock of sand, and just sits there lolling.

"I feel . . . dizzy," she mutters.

"Do you think you'll throw up?"

"No . . . not yet."

"Good. You must drink—just a little, though. We have to make it last."

He uncorks the last bottle, and lifts it to her lips. Her first sips are tentative, painful, but quickly become ravenous. He wrenches the bottle away from her, but not before it's almost emptied.

"What did I just tell you?" he screams at her. "Bad girl!" and slaps her wrist.

Roman's stunned. He can't believe he just hit her; he's never hit a child, never hit anyone in his life. But Yasmin doesn't cry—on the contrary, she sneers, "You're not my father!"

He must carry her now. She's too weak, and the sand is too hot for her to walk on her own, even leaning on him. Clinging to his back, with her arms slung through the satchel, she lays her head on his hump. She doesn't weigh much, and parched and tired though he is, Roman keeps walking. He has no other choice. To stop, to stumble and not get up again would only mean death for them both. Where are the jeeps and the helicopters, he wonders? Was his plan so ingenious, so cunning, that not even Toledano had figured it out?

It's high noon by the time they touch the base of the trail. Roman winces into the sky, at the arches of the Liberators' Memorial. The ascent seems impossibly steep. He might make it on his own, with the violin case perhaps, but with the girl on his back, it's unlikely. Yet he begins. Gasping, grunting on legs that now seem equally lame, the pain in his chest insufferable. Any second, he imagines, and his heart will burst into flames. He tries to think of something else, something pleasant, but all he can conjure is the dream he dreamt in the boxcar. He tries to end it differently this time—this time he runs, Elena in his arms, beneath a fury of whizzing bullets. Away from the camp and into the woods, they escape, to the safety of Russian soldiers.

The vision is comforting, nourishing, until it is shattered by a strange rattling sound—not from the case, he realizes, but from deep down in Yasmin's throat. There isn't much time. He must reach the top where there's shade. He must concentrate now, not on his pain or his dream, but on getting there.

And he does. How exactly he's not sure, but at last finds himself teetering at the top of the trail, in front of the Liberators' Memorial. Before he can enter, though, he sees a large crowd making its way past the warehouse, scattering through the debris of the city dump, before consolidating just below the crest. At the front of the crowd, Toledano marches, and behind him plods Gershonshvilli with a gun.

Under the arches, Roman stumbles. He will wait for them here, with Yasmin. He finds a corner and lowers his violin case, and lets the girl slide slowly from his back. He lays her down and with the last drops of water, moistens her withered lips. She will live, he knows; she has to, and he will be arrested at once.

But no one approaches the memorial. Roman looks up and spies Toledano, lingering by the city dump. Lingering and pacing while behind him the people gather. A muddle of berets and turbans, caftans and robes—half the population of Yerucham, it seems, has assembled to witness the end, the Maestro's grand finale.

He's confused, his head is spinning, and the world around it spins too. It's not until he hears the bullhorn that Roman at last understands.

"You can't get out of there, Tolchowsky. Let her go, now."

Can this be true? Toledano, the man who fears nothing, seems to be afraid of the Maestro. Those rumors about his unpredictably, his violent streak—Toledano's not taking any chances. He sees how the old man cowers above his daughter, appearing to protect her but actually shielding himself, so close that Gershonshvilli can't get off a shot.

Toledano is still pacing, stomping, his baggy clothes slackened with sweat. The people savor his predicament; some start to heckle and cheer. Roman enjoys it, too; half-drunk with fever, he can't help himself. A smile cracks his lips, and then, from his throat comes a sound he hasn't heard in some time, years maybe. Tossing his head back, Roman Tolchowsky laughs, and the people, hearing him, start laughing too—even Gershonshvilli, further diverting his aim.

Toledano can't stand it anymore. He breaks away from the crowd and storms up the crest, indignantly. He'll kill me right here, Roman thinks. But then, just as abruptly as he started, Toledano halts, just paces short of the memorial.

"Listen to me, Tolchowsky," he shouts, but then checks himself and speaks carefully. "Maestro . . ." The big

man glances behind him, confirming that the crowd can't hear him, adjusts his skullcap and hitches his baggy pants. "Maestro. I know we haven't agreed on things . . . I know you hate my guts. But *Yasmin* . . ."

Toledano pauses; he seems to be choking on dust. "She's my daughter. Maybe you don't like hearing that, but think what that means—my *daughter*? For God's sake, Tolchowsky . . ."

He almost feels sorry for Toledano, who no longer looks so big to him, merely fat, quavering and sweating profusely. But then he glances at Yasmin. She's fast asleep, supine with her arms at her sides. There are no new bruises on her hands or knees, he notes with relief, and the color has returned to her cheeks.

Roman wipes a strand of hair from her face, and when he next looks up, Toledano is gone. He's turned and quickstepped back to where the crowd's still snickering at him. He gestures broadly at Gershonshvilli, who shoulders his rifle. Apish jaw protruding, his narrow forehead furled, the policeman takes aim, but he can't get a bead on his target. The old man is still too close to the girl.

Astonishing, thinks Roman. So this is why there are no jeeps or helicopters, no soldiers or squadrons of police. Toledano needs to show that he, alone, is in control—a man with an image to preserve. He won't be anybody's fool, least of all the Maestro's.

And so they wait. Either Roman will collapse finally or Gershonshvilli will get his shot. Or he simply can lift Yasmin up and deliver her to her father—the only logical thing to do, he senses, in spite of his thickening delirium. Deliver her, but not yet. He needs a few moments more with her, just looking.

He gazes at the sleeping child, but not for long before another commotion ruffles the crowd. It parts, and a thin, bald-headed man emerges. A man in once-white rags, barefoot, comes gliding across the sand toward the memorial. He tips the brim of an imaginary cap, and calls out, "Top of the morning to you, Maestro!"

Roman blinks hard in disbelief. "It's the afternoon . . ."

"Whatever," Elipaz replies, gazing up at the sky and scratching his pate. "I was never too good telling time."

"I *am*, and I think there's not much left. What's on your mind, Elipaz?"

Elipaz shrugs. The question confounds him, and why shouldn't it, Roman reckons, a man whose brain has been fried by the desert. Toledano must be pretty desperate to let such an imbecile come forward.

He spits in the sand, mixes it into a paste with his toe. "You look like shit," says Elipaz.

"Looked in a mirror lately?" Roman shakes his head in frustration. It's easier dealing with Toledano. "How am I supposed to look, idiot?"

"Try saintly," comes the answer. "Resplendent."

Now it's Roman's turn to shrug, as if brushing off a fly.

But Elipaz won't be shooed. "Don't you see, you made it," he explains. "You led the children of Israel— okay, okay, a child—across the wilderness and came into the Land. You're a regular Moses."

"Moses *didn't* make it, remember? You said so yourself."

"A minor detail," Elipaz snorts. "He stood up on the mountain and saw his people as one. He buried the bones of Joseph."

"You and your bones."

"It must've been quite a relief, after carting them around all those years."

"Yeah and then what?"

"Then? Why he was gathered up to heaven, just like that, *poof.* Not a bad ending, really, for a wanderer."

That's it. Elipaz grows silent. Between the arches he stands, framed, like some poorly-painted icon. If there was a meaning to his message, Roman is too befuddled to fathom it, too nauseous to bother. And what little awareness he has left is just then distracted by the rustle of sand behind him. Yasmin appears to be stirring.

He kneels down beside her, gently raises her head. Her eyelids are fluttering, and her lips.

"Don't try to speak. I've brought you back home, you're safe," he whispers, and though she says nothing, the crowd responds with laughter. They're making fun of him as well, the hooligans. Or is it Elipaz up to his old antics? Yet, when he next looks up, the crazy man is gone, and in his place is a sight even crazier still. Waddling up to the crest on stunted legs, in her terry cloth bathrobe and slippers, is none other than Lubova Yakobovitch—Luba, he can scarcely believe it, outdoors.

She arrives huffing and cursing under her breath, comes closer than either Toledano or Elipaz had dared before, and knocks on one of the arches.

"Door's open," he says wanly, "I'm not in the mood for games."

Luba frowns. "You think I've come for games?" She crosses her arms across her robe—Roman wonders if she's naked, as usual, beneath it—and ignores cat-calls from the crowd. "I've come to save you, you prick."

He squints at her knobby shins, the coppery corona of her hair. "Save me . . . For what?"

"For life."

"You call this life?" he chortles. "Yerucham?"

"Yerucham, Moscow, Paris. It doesn't matter—yes, life. You have any idea what I've paid for it?"

"I've seen your shelf . . ."

"Just the down-payment, Romashka. This," she says, smiling, rolling up one of her sleeves, "is the balance."

She's won, of course, as she knew she would, showing him those digits. Roman groans, "Give me another minute. I'll bring the girl. I promise."

Arms folded again, Luba raises a brow: a gesture of triumph or distrust. She leaves him then, waddling down the hill, but then turns back, her makeup muddy with tears. "Don't you dare let me die here alone," she hisses.

I won't, Roman thinks, but his throat is too parched to pronounce it. He stumbles after her, lunges first for the arch where a second ago Luba stood, but he gets no further.

"I'm ready," says a voice behind him. Yasmin's voice. She's on her feet, swaying slightly, and her eyes are wide— too wide—open. Her cheeks are unnaturally flushed. "I'd like to see my father."

Roman leans back against the arch. Furiously, he tugs his ear, pinches his mind back to consciousness. "Your father, yes . . ."

He goes to her, smoothes her tangled hair and reties what remains of her ribbons. Yasmin says nothing.

"Your father, yes," he repeats, "We'll go in a moment. But first, there's something I want you to have."

Yasmin looks on blankly, silently, as her teacher falls to his knees before the violin case, straining to open the latches. Rust-encrusted, they resist him at first, the case rattling in protest. But then, one, two, the latches flip up. The hinges crack and the lid rises.

If there is any smell—of a thousand theaters, of a wedding feast or the high grass along the Neris—the desert stifles it. But Roman is not disappointed. On the contrary, he's enthralled, transfixed as he reaches into the case and solemnly removes its contents.

"Maestro, it's beautiful." These words, from Yasmin, are proof enough that she *is* awake, alive and still his pupil.

"Yes, it is. And I've kept it all these years for you. Please . . ."

Her fingers extend to the body and then quickly retract, as if the wood itself were scalding.

"Don't be afraid . . ."

She hesitates a moment, unsure, unfocused—should she run to her father? But then, abruptly, she snatches the instrument, and hugs it, doll-like, to her breast. Roman beams. At least this, he thinks, at least this. He retrieves his cap and jacket from the dust, shakes them off and dons them. He's ready now, but Yasmin seems preoccupied, no longer in a rush to leave, too busy plucking and tuning. Seeing this, he rushes to hand her the bow. She draws it across the strings, merely a touch at first, tentative, followed by a keenly sliced chord.

The crowd murmurs at the shock of music, gasps and sighs together. Toledano pulls his hair. He can see the old man now hovering over his daughter, a long, sharp implement in his hand.

"Concerto in E Minor," Roman whispers to her, "allegro and andante, you know it."

She does. Mendelssohn's masterpiece, with beauty wrung from every note, driven to the borders of sanity. She performs without hesitation, from memory, flawlessly. Eyes shut, shoulders riveted. The idea sounds as fresh as the instant it was created. The concerto could be playing itself.

Yasmin plays and Roman's body spirals wildly, revolves around the radius of his hips. The memorial itself seems to whirl. Between its arches, he glimpses the crowd now silent and bunched in confusion, in awe. The red and brown faces have merged in a russet blur, yet here and there are features he can still discern—Elipaz and Luba. Sarka and Liebowitz are holding hands while Smirkin and Geraldine embrace. And others as well: Misha Beckenstein's ferret-face and starchy Mordechai Krauss, and his old Maestro from Vilnius, towering and hoary. Perhaps Oppenheim is here as well, and Marcucio and Volyushin.

Allegretto non troppo—Yasmin enters the finale. Already he can feel his torso stiffen, and his weight shift forward to his toes. His arms, his neck, stretch upward; the baton begins its ascent. Upward he feels himself floating, to the very top of the memorial, astride the arches and looking down at the people who are no longer people but a soft blue band of light.

The music is both punishing and ravishing, and yet

it restores him. Cures him: no more pain or deformities. A whole man, he stands rigidly, on tiptoes, as Yasmin slashes the final chords. The baton soars, it hovers over her head. And then, all at once, he sags. With only the faintest grunt, he crumples onto the sand, first onto his knees, and then rolling onto his side, curled, convulsing. No other sound— not of music, nor wind. Only the report of the gunshot, reverberating like a round of applause.

A slight wind lilts through the Liberators' Memorial. The people have long retreated down Tabenkin Street, each man to his home. It is night, or almost night: the furthest claims of dusk. But in the ghost of light, three figures can still be discerned. Shadowy figures; scavengers. Furtively they step forward, into the arches' lee.

The first, vaguely feminine in shape, ungainly, bends to retrieve something from the dust. An object thin and pallid: a baton. The figure clutches it like the holiest of relics and secrets it into her robes. Then, checking to see that no one is following her, she flees.

The second figure, as thin as the first one was plump, also stoops to the ground. He, too, finds what he wants. But instead of stealing it away, the figure buries it. With his hands he digs a hole and places the violin case inside it, refills it and smoothes it over with sand. Then the figure utters a prayer.

One figure remains. The smallest, the slightest— barely a smudge in the darkness—dim but for the flames of her hair. The figure does not seek, does not take or bury, but merely stands waiting as she has always waited, without complaint. Keeping watch throughout the night and holding fast to a promise.

About the author

Michael Bornstein

Michael Bornstein lives in Jerusalem with his wife and three children. He served as an officer in the Israel Defense Forces, and as advisor to the Israel delegation to the UN and to the government of the late Prime Minister Yitzhak Rabin. An historian with degrees from Princeton and Columbia, he has written extensively on the Middle East. He is also the author of several works of fiction and screenplays.

The fonts used in this book are from the Garamond and Frutiger families.